"I don't want to be a problem," Rose said. "The jerk back there, his name is Grift. He's a mean one. I told you, if they don't want me here—"

"Screw them. I want you." He glanced at her. "Here, I want you here."

Rose laughed, slow and soft.

Ryan knew he'd lied to her and himself. He wanted her. He'd met her two hours ago and he wanted her in his bed and in his life.

The white doublewide trailer that served as the construction office stood a hundred yards from the gate. When he parked, he unsnapped his seat belt, leaned over, caught her chin in his fingers and kissed her. Not with passion, but in sudden surrender to an overpowering desire to taste that soft mouth.

He released her, leaned back, then couldn't meet her eyes. Great! Now what did he do? "God, I'm sorry. I didn't mean to . . ."

"That's okay." Rose's voice sounded a bit shaky. "Moving a little too fast. That's all."

"Too fast." Ryan grinned with relief. "Ah . . . could you give me a timetable or something? So I won't get ahead of you again."

She smiled, her eyes bright with amusement. "Well, Mr. Vernon, let's start with a couple of beers and conversation. Get to know each other. Then, we talk about a date. How's that?"

Ryan couldn't believe it. He'd just negotiated a possible relationship. Mr. Vernon. She'd reminded him that he had come into her world a stranger.

"Sounds good to me."

Static Resistance and Rose

Lee Roland

Highland Press Publishing
Florida

Static Resistance and Rose

Copyright ©2009 – Lee Roland
Cover ©2009 – Cheryl Alldredge

Printed and bound in the United States of America. All rights reserved. No part of this book may be reproduced or transmitted in any form or by any means, electronic or mechanical, including photocopying, recording, or by an information storage and retrieval system— except by a reviewer who may quote brief passages in a review to be printed in a magazine, newspaper, or on the Web—without permission in writing from the publisher.

*For information, please contact
Highland Press Publishing,
PO Box 2292, High Springs, FL 32655.
www.highlandpress.org*

All characters in this book have no existence outside the imagination of the author and have no relation whatsoever to anyone bearing the same name or names, save actual historical figures. They are not even distantly inspired by any individual known or unknown to the author, and all incidents are pure invention.

ISBN: 978-0-9800356-7-4

HIGHLAND PRESS PUBLISHING

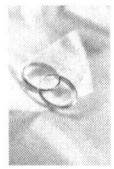

Circles of Gold

Dedication

For my husband who doesn't understand my obsession with words on paper, but loves and encourages me anyway.

My agent, Caren Johnson, who has faith in me.

Publisher Leanne Burroughs of Highland Press Publishing who is giving me a chance to prove I can do it.

Inkplotters past and present who have, over the years, praised, shredded and laughed at my prose. You've celebrated my success and shared my disappointment when the rejections arrived. I love you all and couldn't have done it without you.

My frontline reader-editors, the 'we work for food' ladies.

My friend Joe, who taught me not to use prepositional phrases. We all still miss you big guy.

Cheryl Norman, Assistant Editor

Polly McCrillis, Associate Editor

Venetta Bell, Associate Editor

Chapter 1

On a clear January morning in Jacksonville, Florida, 480 volts of electricity surged through Rose Norris's body and stopped her heart like a jumper hitting the sidewalk. The jolt that shocked her back to life sent a thick spike of agony slamming into her chest and screaming down her nerves. She jerked and twisted, but something held her tight.

"Try to relax," a female voice said. "We're almost at the hospital."

A cool hand brushed across her forehead, but she couldn't see the speaker. Her eyes felt like hot glass marbles rolling in her head. They allowed light to pass, but defied her efforts to focus.

Hospital? A siren wailed in the distance, faint and hollow. The agony eased to bearable pain, but that allowed another sensation to slide in—terror. Was she going to die?

When the siren ceased, they lifted and rolled her body, stripped off her clothes, and asked her questions she couldn't answer. Parched as the pages of an old newspaper, her tongue refused to form words. She lay under brilliant lights for uncertain hours while people flowed around her like an out of focus movie. After a while, the intensity of activity and the questions ceased. Mercifully, they slid her into a dimmer, softer, quieter place.

Jimmy hovered over her. At least it appeared to be Jimmy. She drew a deep breath, narrowed her eyes, and demanded that they function.

Success! Small tubing lay across her face, tickling her nose, and the faint whisper of oxygen came in her ears.

"Rose?" A strand of silver hair fell across Jimmy's rugged

face, a face twisted with concern. "Are you okay?"

Rose tried to say no and ask what happened, but the words crawled out in a pathetic, indecipherable wheeze.

"Sorry." Jimmy squeezed her hand. "You don't try to talk, baby."

Jimmy Beecher was a wonderful man, a good friend, and she loved him dearly in spite of the difficulty he often caused. She'd been an electrician for ten years, and a Master Electrician for five. She could hold her own on a jobsite full of testosterone-laden men—but not with Jimmy the Foreman treating her like a fragile, favorite daughter in serious need of protection. Right now, though, that protection seemed to be a good thing.

A petite, Asian-looking woman in a white coat came into view. "Good afternoon, Ms. Norris. I'm Doctor Liang." She laid a tiny hand on Rose's shoulder and stated the obvious. "By God's grace, you seem to have survived."

"Happened?" Rose managed a rough, frayed whisper.

"Electricity. Stopped your heart." Dr. Laing cocked her head to one side and smiled. "You only have minor burns. You're incredibly lucky. You must have barely touched that wire. I've seen . . . well, never mind."

Dr. Liang studied the readouts from a machine by the bed. "We're going to run a few tests, get you in a room where you can rest, and keep you overnight. If your extraordinary luck holds, you should be able to escape from this place in the morning." She smiled as she left, apparently receiving some personal satisfaction from her pronouncement.

Rose had recovered her voice, though she still sounded hoarse. "Accident? Jimmy, that panel wasn't hot. You know me. I checked it before I touched it. Oh, God, get me water."

"Sure, baby, you rest." He hurried away.

Rose lifted her trembling hands and studied them. A taped down IV stuck out from the back of her left hand, and a thin tube attached it to a plastic bag hanging from a steel pole. A slim crimson line cut across her right palm. She touched it with her finger. *Ouch.* Her chest ached. Hell, her whole body ached. She felt lethargic and at the same time uneasy.

Jimmy returned. He drew a bottle of water out of his

pocket. "It's cold. Got it out of a machine down the hall. Faster than begging them to bring it."

Rose struggled. "Help me sit up, Jimmy. I hate this." Lying down, helpless, terrified her. She dug her elbows into the mattress, determined to rise.

"Rose, honey, maybe you shouldn't."

She kept struggling and he gave in. He slipped his arm under her shoulders and lifted her. The pale pink hospital gown she wore gapped open in the back and slipped off. Close to panic, she clutched it against her breasts.

"God, I'm naked."

Jimmy gently tugged at the gown and tied the strings across her back, limiting exposure of bare skin. He opened the water bottle, held it, and allowed her minuscule sips.

Hospital noises drifted around her, and the air carried the faint odor of mandatory antiseptic. White curtained walls separated her from the other unfortunate residents. She had to be at Carrolton General, closest to the Solana Hotel construction site.

Jimmy averted his gaze. Now he seemed more restless than concerned. "I don't know what happened, honey. I came in and you were lying on the floor. You weren't breathing, your heart stopped. I did CPR. Paramedics got there fast and hit you with those paddle things." Misery creased his face, making him look eighty rather than sixty-four. They shared the same birthday, January 14th, but thirty-six years apart. He always told her he'd been born thirty-six years too soon, and she would tell him she'd been born thirty-six years too late.

"They lost you again in the ambulance, but you hung on." Jimmy's voice wavered. He draped an arm around her shoulders and drew her close. She leaned against him, her cheek on his smooth flannel shirt. Her fingers gripped his arm and dug in as if she could draw his strength into her. "You're tough, baby."

"Not so tough, Jimmy. I'm scared now."

"Don't you worry, honey." He smoothed her hair and kissed her forehead. "This is my fault. Jimmy's going to fix things."

Sitting up and holding onto him helped. Disorientation,

that feeling of wrongness, eased and the world seemed more normal.

A slim young man in blue scrubs tossed the curtain back and bounced into the room. He waved a clipboard. "Okay. Norris, Michelle Roseanne. Caucasian female, age twenty-eight, brown hair, green eyes." He grinned at her and sounded far too perky. "I'm Bobby, and I'm going to take you in for a head to toe scan. Isn't that excellent?"

"No, it is not excellent, Bobby." Rose straightened her spine and squared her shoulders. "But you're probably going to do it anyway."

Ah, that felt better. More in control.

Bobby grinned and tossed the clipboard onto her bed. "Look here, darling, you stood in a bucket of water, stuck your finger in a light socket and blew a fuse. Not my fault. What do you expect?"

"I expect to be treated with respect. Just like anyone who dies and comes back."

"Sorry, love. We're into different miracles these days. Accidental electrocution is passé. Hey! You get run over by a dump truck, then come back to life. Now *that* will get our attention."

Rose had to laugh, but it made her ache. "I'll try that next time."

* * * *

At ten thirty on Tuesday morning, Rose stood beside her hospital bed wearing nothing but her panties and shirt.

A man opened the door and walked into the room.

"Oops!" he said. "I . . ." He stared at her.

Rose stared back. At five-ten, she was taller than most women, but he had a good six or seven inches on her, most of it solid muscle and bone. Sandy blond hair, sexy coffee colored eyes, he wore jeans, a denim shirt, and had a tan that said he stayed outside a lot. He appeared about thirty-five, but the sun sometimes aged a man's skin.

"It's okay." Rose grinned at him. "The critical parts are covered. You can see more skin than this on the beach."

He nodded, as if to thank her for rescuing him from an embarrassing situation.

"Sorry," he said as he backed out.

Rose laughed softly under her breath. She'd never see him again, but she enjoyed his reaction. She slid on her jeans and sat in a chair beside the bed to get into her socks and boots. Her bra had gone missing in action somewhere in the ER, along with the buttons on her shirt. The nurses provided temporary closure via a couple of safety pins. Jimmy had left her two hours ago with a promise to return and liberate her. He'd raged at the hospital staff for a long time about sending her home so soon, but she knew workers comp insurance would pay only so much, and her private insurance wouldn't touch it since the injury happened on the job.

How had it happened? Lucky? Yes. Electricians didn't often get a second chance. Early morning, alone in a ground floor mechanical room, finishing one of the main panels, she'd removed her gloves to search her toolbox for a pair of pliers. She had no memory of the actual hit.

Power for construction on the site came courtesy of several powerful 910 kilowatt Detroit Diesel generators outside the building, generators that were never hooked to the panels. It would be months before electricity would go to the one she wired. The panel wasn't hot when she checked it, an automatic safeguard ingrained through years of training. The only possible explanation brought edgy discomfort. Could someone have wired it to the generator? Not everyone on the site liked her. Only one person hated her enough to harm her, and she seriously doubted he had sufficient brain cells to plan a moderately complex electrical murder.

Physically, Rose didn't feel bad. Time eased her discomfort, except for her mouth. It tasted dry and metallic, like she'd been chewing on copper pennies.

Tired of waiting and eager to be away from the place, she headed out to find Jimmy or call a cab. To her surprise, the attractive man who'd walked in on her without warning earlier, waited outside the room.

"Hi," he said. "I'm looking for an electrician named Norris.

I'm told that's you. I didn't want to intrude again."

Rose tried to keep her voice level, uncertain of how to respond to him. "I'm Rose Norris. Who are you?"

"Ryan Vernon." He smiled. A nice smile. Friendly, warm, and genuine.

"Vernon, as in Vernon Construction?" Astonishment filled her. "The name printed on my paycheck."

"The same. I've been running the job down in Miami. Haven't been around here much. I'd just arrived when Jimmy called. He asked me to pick you up and take you back to the site." He gave her that smile again. Disarming described it. Compelling, too. It forced her to smile back like a little girl given sweet chocolate candy when she expected a nice, healthy red apple.

Rose had worked for Vernon Construction for a year. Jimmy hired her while wiring a large office complex in Atlanta, and later persuaded her to come to Jacksonville for the current hotel project. The only Vernon she'd ever met was Carl, the Jacksonville job manager.

Rose went with Ryan, and by the time they left the hospital, morning had inched closer to noon and the brilliant Florida sun gently warmed the air. Cool mornings, beautiful days—that drew her to winter in Florida as much as Jimmy's plea for her to take the job.

Ryan escorted her out to a shiny black four-door pickup truck that made her own work truck look like a mini. Boxes and men's clothes covered the back seat.

Ah, luxury. She ran her fingers over the seat, feeling the luscious smoothness of fine, silver-colored leather. It had a new car smell. Her utilitarian work truck, a six-year-old Ford, had worn cloth seats and a rubber floor mat, not thick carpet. She fastened her seatbelt and leaned back to enjoy the ride.

"Can you tell me what happened?" Ryan asked as he fastened his own belt and started the engine.

"Don't remember," Rose said. "I woke up in the ambulance. Jimmy said he'd check on it when he went back."

"Well, I'm going to look into it, too," Ryan assured her. "I'm not much of an electrician. Would you show me?"

"Sure."

He had a gregarious manner about him, amicable and approachable. Too soon to tell, but at first impression he seemed strong, yet fair, the kind of manager who would bring out the best in his employees.

The truck rolled out of the hospital entry road, and he turned east on Beach Boulevard. Rose watched her driver out of the corner of her eye. A big man, Ryan Vernon, lean, not bulky, he came across as impressive rather than intimidating. The tight jeans revealed well-muscled legs, and his long fingered hands wore hard-earned calluses. He had the rugged body of a working man, not the owner of a multi-million dollar construction company.

No wedding band. That didn't mean anything, though. A dangerous combination, gold or silver metal rings and construction work. Rings and watches mixed with electricity equaled serious risk of injury. A ring on her hand yesterday might have cost her a finger—or the entire hand.

"I guess you're related to Carl," Rose said to him. "Don't see him much. He isn't one to hang around the construction area."

Ryan's mouth pinched. "Carl is my brother. And no, you won't find him where there's actual work occurring. Someone might ask him to do something. Have you heard of any more accidents on the site? Vandalism?"

When he asked the question, the metallic taste lingering in her mouth turned bitter. She'd misjudged him. The boss wasn't concerned about her welfare. He only wanted her to give him job site gossip. "No, I haven't seen anything." She couldn't keep cool edge out of her voice. "I mind my own business."

"So do I. And my business is Vernon Construction." He reached over and brushed his fingers over the hand she'd laid on the seat beside her. It startled her, that brief touch. Intimate, yet innocent, he'd raised their chance meeting to a higher level.

"Sorry," he said. "I didn't mean . . ."

"I's okay," Rose said, surprised that she found herself easing his discomfort again. "I know there's trouble at the site. I don't know what's wrong. Jimmy wouldn't say anything, and I didn't ask. He's a friend, and I figure he'll tell me what he wants me to know."

"A friend? Not . . ."

"No. Not a boyfriend. A beer-drinking, pool-playing buddy."

"Oh." He leaned back and relaxed, as if he'd received good news. That made her smile.

Ryan drove south onto A1A and Jacksonville Beach. Rose liked this beach. It offered low-key leisure time compared to the glitz and luxury of Fort Lauderdale and Miami farther south. Hotels, condos and palm trees lined the two-lane street. Most of the tallest buildings sat beachside, but rarely went above fourteen stories. Two and three story condos with balconies on the west side of the road had a faux Cape Cod look. Bicyclists peddled leisurely down the wide bike lanes to a welcoming stretch of public access beach near the Solana hotel site.

The first thing Rose saw when they reached the site was her truck, parked beside the street, outside the eight-foot chain link perimeter fence surrounding the hotel. She'd left it inside yesterday morning, where the rest of the construction crew parked.

She frowned. "That's my truck. Jimmy has my extra set of keys, but why would he park it there? Would you pull over?" He did and she climbed out. A large white envelope stuck to the windshield, held in place by a piece of duct tape. She frowned, snatched it off, and tore it open. The letter on cream-colored Vernon Construction stationery, said that her *services were no longer needed* and they would mail her last paycheck. Carl Vernon signed it.

"Well, I'll be damned," she said. Astonishment morphed into irritation. Employers had fired her before, for just and unjust reasons. She'd *never* seen anyone fired the day after an on-the-job injury that didn't involve deliberate criminal activity. It might even be illegal. How stupid could Carl Vernon be? A letter on her truck window? Usually the bosses were smart enough to wait a few months before doing the deed to cut their medical expense loss. It reduced the chance of a lawsuit.

Rose didn't realize that Ryan had climbed out of his truck and was reading over her shoulder until he snatched the letter away from her.

"This is insane. He can't do this." He headed to his truck, taking the letter with him.

"Hey, that's addressed to me," Rose yelled after him.

Ryan turned back to her. Oh, he was a fine looking man. He winked and flashed that irresistible smile again. "Come on. I'll give it back to you when I'm done kicking ass."

Rose went to him, laughing. "Goody," she said. "I love to watch a good ass kicking."

Chapter 2

Ryan clamped his teeth tight to keep from cursing. He'd called Jimmy when he arrived in Duval County. Jimmy sounded odd when he found out Ryan wasn't in Miami; shocked at first, then almost relieved. Jimmy told him of the accident and asked him to stop by the hospital and pick up an electrician hurt on the job. "Name's Norris," Jimmy said without further explanation. Ryan's Miami crew worked twenty women, carpenters, electricians, and painters, even two welders, but he hadn't known there were any on the Jacksonville site.

Ryan glanced over at her. Rose Norris. Rose the electrician. Damn. When had he seen a more interesting woman? She had hair the color of fine Kentucky bourbon. Hair that flashed gold streaks in the sun when she brushed it away from her face. And that slim body with the longest legs—strong beautiful legs. Double damn. He liked her voice, smooth and low pitched, not unfeminine, but husky, as if she'd just made love. Green-eyed Rose with her angular, aristocratic face, her luscious mouth—the woman his idiotic brother fired. At best, she could sue. At worst, the State of Florida could fine him and his insurance company dump him.

He could fix things, though. That's why he'd come up from Miami. The Solana Hotel project had missed deadlines and hemorrhaged money. They'd pushed the projected opening day forward by three months and, from what he could see, that wouldn't be enough. Construction on the seven-story hotel had progressed little further than a steel girder skeleton covered with a light outer skin. Given the elapsed construction time and good weather . . . he should have come sooner. Too many projects going at the same time. He had to get them back under control.

Haphazard piles of materials lay around the site, visible through the six foot chain link fence: concrete blocks, lumber, pallets of masonry supplies. Even from the road he could see gaps in the fence. Sloppy security.

"I apologize," he said to Rose. "I'll take care of this." He clutched the letter.

"You don't have to." She spoke with a firmness that made him believe her words. "I don't want to work on a construction site where I'm not wanted," she said. "Bad things *do* happen then."

"Are you married?" he asked. Now why did he do that? His face burned. He tried to cover his embarrassment and ended up sounding pretentious. "I mean, is there someone I should call and tell about the accident?"

"No, I'm not married. Are you? In case I ever have to call someone."

"No."

Would she think less of him if she knew he'd tried the marriage game and lost? He'd made a tentative connection to the provocative woman sitting by him, and it was more awkward than his first high school date. Of course, in high school, young and foolish, he had the world in front of him, full of possibilities. Now, time forced him to look back on personal failure. Did he dare try again?

Ryan drove to the site's main gate and stopped at the small guardhouse. The large signs to his right bore the usual proclamations: No trespassing. Danger. Hardhat Area.

He rolled down the window. A heavy-jawed goon who probably made parole the day before yesterday stepped from the guardhouse and sneered at him. A blue, barbed-wire tattoo ringed his neck, and, at one time, someone had objected to his face enough to flatten his nose. A soft breeze brought the stink of a body not overly familiar with soap and water.

Ryan presented the Vernon Construction master pass.

The guard glanced at it, but his eyes slid past Ryan to Rose.

"That bitch can't go in," he said in a voice rough as a gravel road. He crossed his arms over his significant beer gut.

"Can you read?" Ryan lifted the pass a higher. "I'm the owner of this company. You know what an owner is? Someone who can fire you?"

The guard glared for a few seconds. "I gotta call," he said. He picked a cell phone out of his pocket, one far too small for a man with such chunky hands. He fumbled at it, muttering under his breath.

Screw that! Ryan drove through the open gate and across the dirt yard.

"I don't want to be a problem," Rose said. "The jerk back there, his name is Grift. He's a mean one. I told you, if they don't want me here—"

"Screw them. I want you." He glanced at her. Damn, he didn't mean to . . . "Here, I want you here."

Rose laughed, slow and soft.

Ryan knew he'd lied to her and himself. He wanted her. He'd met her two hours ago and he wanted her in his bed and in his life.

The white doublewide trailer that served as the construction office stood a hundred yards from the gate. When he parked, he unsnapped his seat belt, leaned over, caught her chin in his fingers and kissed her. Not with passion, but in sudden surrender to his desire to taste that soft mouth.

He released her, leaned back, then couldn't meet her eyes. Great! Now what did he do? "God, I'm sorry. I didn't mean to . . ."

"That's okay." Rose's voice sounded a bit shaky. "Moving a little too fast. That's all."

"Too fast." Ryan grinned with relief. "Ah . . . could you give me a timetable or something? So I won't get ahead of you again."

She smiled, her eyes bright with amusement. "Well, Mr. Vernon, let's start with a couple of beers and conversation. Get to know each other. Then, we talk about a date. How's that?"

Ryan couldn't believe it. He'd just negotiated a possible

relationship. Mr. Vernon. She'd reminded him that he had come into her world a stranger. "Sounds good to me."

* * * *

Rose thought she handled it well. She hadn't expected him to move so quickly. Ryan Vernon radiated honest sexual charm like a space heater warmed a room, and she liked it. His awkward kiss didn't seem premeditated, only impulsive. Impulsive wasn't always good. She needed to slow him, and herself, down.

Raised on construction sites by her widower father, she'd developed a keen insight into the emotions men displayed, or rather, didn't display. Not that she understood them. She'd always noted the confusing difference between their words and their actions, especially when they involved women. "Never build your house on lies," Daddy had said. "Especially if you want it to stand." She was honest, always—and had few second dates.

A movement to the right caught her eye—bad-ass Grift running toward her. Grift hated her. He took it personally when she told him she'd rather screw a stray dog than take her pants off for him. Always belligerent, he usually just sneered and said something ugly from across a room. He hadn't approached her again after that initial rejection, but she kept a wary eye on him. Now he ran at her with fury etched on his ugly face. Grift could hurt her. He couldn't take his rage out on the big, strong boss man. The woman made an easier target.

Rose carefully unlatched the truck door, but didn't open it until he arrived within range. When he did, she shoved the door hard. Grift slammed into it full force with a thick whump of a body on steel. Pain spiked up her arms at the impact. He bounced off, landed on his back, and lay on the ground, spread-eagled and stunned.

Ryan rushed around the truck to where she stood by the open door.

"Way to go, champ!" He bumped her gently with his elbow.

Rose shook her head. This was not good. "I try to avoid fights on the job site since almost everyone is bigger and stronger than me."

Grift groaned and his legs jerked.

"You better come inside," Ryan said. He grasped her arm near the elbow and held it until they reached the trailer door. "I'll see that there's no more trouble from him."

The trailer, originally designed as a home, functioned well enough as an office. This one was old enough to have nut-brown, wood paneled walls and worn vinyl floors printed in a pattern fashioned by a drunken artist. Rose had seen many on construction jobs over the years, since contractors often dragged them from site to site until they fell apart.

"Hello, beautiful," Ryan said as he walked inside.

Lola, the office manager, squealed in delight. She jumped up, raced from behind her desk, and threw herself into Ryan's open arms.

A petite, vivacious, silver-haired woman of fifty-five, Lola ran an office so tight it awed IRS and Immigration agents when they arrived for surprise audits. She consumed Diet Pepsi by the case, had a small screen TV on her desk, and you *did not* interrupt her afternoon soaps, even if you had death or the devil on your heels. Neither the grim reaper nor the Prince of Darkness took precedence over *General Hospital* and *As the World Turns*. She was Jimmy's sister, though the relationship seemed strained at times.

Ryan scooped Lola up in his arms and spun her around. She gave a joyous laugh as he set her back on her feet.

"Oh, am I glad to see you," Lola said. She caught sight of Rose. "Rose! Honey, are you hurt? I took off yesterday. I called the hospital an hour ago, but you'd gone."

"I'm fine." Rose gave Lola a reassuring smile.

"Jimmy called me just as I arrived in town this morning," Ryan said. "Told me he needed someone to pick up his electrician." He shook the termination letter at her. "What is this? Since when do we fire people when they get hurt? And leaving a letter on her truck? That's bullshit."

Lola's face scrunched up as if she'd bitten into a piece of sour candy. "You'll have to talk to your brother about that."

Embarrassed, Rose lowered her eyes and studied the floor. Ryan's anger gave the impression that she'd gone to one of the company owners and whined because someone fired her. She wanted to leave, but Grift had probably regained consciousness outside in the construction yard and she certainly didn't want to face him alone. The trailer had a back door, and she knew a way off the site. She felt her pockets. Yes, she had her truck keys. She'd get the extra set from Jimmy later. If Ryan wanted to contact her, her address and phone number were in Lola's files. She started in that direction when Carl Vernon emerged from his office.

"Damn it, Lola." Rage filled his words. He carried a piece of paper, waving it in the air. "I told you. . ." His voice trailed off when he spied Ryan.

Rose found it difficult to imagine the Vernon brothers raised in the same home—or on the same planet. Both stood well over six feet, blond-haired, but blue-eyed Carl's face appeared closed and wary, while Ryan's brown eyes radiated clear, confident masculinity. They had good bodies, but Rose bet Carl's was courtesy of machine workouts in an air-conditioned gym, not hard labor. Certainly, Carl's thousand dollar suit and three hundred dollar shoes stood in sharp contrast to his brother's denim and worn work boots.

"Carl." Ryan's voice dropped to icy fury. "You will not curse at Lola."

"I . . ." Carl shook his head. "Sorry, Lola. It's something else." He spied Rose. "What's she doing here?" He sounded confrontational, but Rose suspected he used it to redirect his brother's anger. Carl Vernon had never intimidated her.

"I brought her," Ryan said. He waved the letter at his brother. "I want to talk to you."

"And I want her off this job site." Carl said. "Lola, call Grift. He can escort her."

"Grift isn't going to touch her, Carl." Ryan crumpled the letter into a ball and tossed it in a wastebasket by Lola's desk. "Now, you want to do this here or in your office?"

Carl whirled and marched back toward the end of the trailer.

Ryan reached out and touched Rose's hand. "Don't you go anywhere."

Rose laughed. "Okay."

"He likes you," Lola said after Ryan left. She grinned at Rose, apparently delighted. "I've told Jimmy to get Ryan up here to meet you for the last six months, but the stubborn ass kept putting it off."

"He's just concerned because I was hurt, that's all." Rose didn't want to say much until she knew what might happen with Ryan. The incredibly persuasive man remained a question mark in her mind. She barely knew him. Raised voices drifted from the back, but she couldn't make out the words.

* * * *

Ryan followed Carl into his office. A gang of unsupervised two-year-olds must have had a wild romp through the room. Papers were scattered on the floor and the wastebasket overflowed. Skewed mini-blinds on the window added to the atmosphere of chaos. Way out of character for neat-freak Carl who had driven everyone in the family crazy over the years with his obsessive need for order. Ryan frowned. Oh, yes, something was terribly wrong here in Jacksonville.

"Okay, Carl, tell me why you're firing her." Ryan wanted that matter cleared up first. He wasn't letting Rose get away that easily.

Carl tossed the paper he'd carried into the outer office onto the desk. "She's too much trouble. The men hate her—"

"Jimmy doesn't hate her. Neither does Lola. Their opinions count. Yours doesn't. I don't give a flying fuck what anyone else thinks."

Carl leaned up against the edge of his desk. He wouldn't meet Ryan's eyes. "She's incompetent. That's how she got hurt."

"Bullshit. She stays. Now, tell me why this hotel is six months behind schedule. You've got Jimmy and Lola to manage—"

"I manage this job!" Carl's face reddened as he shouted. "Those two old snoops—"

"Are here to keep you in line. The only reason you're running things, making twice what any other manager would make, is because they agreed to watch over you. And that nasty son-of-a-bitch Grift, I want him gone. I want him off this property before dark."

* * * *

"Sit down," Lola said. "Jimmy told me your heart stopped."

Rose sat on the lumpy, secondhand couch. Lola sat beside her.

"I don't remember anything except going to work, at the panel, and waking up in the ambulance," Rose said. "I'm fine now. Why fire me, Lola? Does someone think I caused what happened?"

Lola shook her head. "Honey, I don't know. Jimmy went into Carl's office earlier this morning. They yelled a lot, for a long time, and Jimmy stomped out. Then Carl tried to get me to write the letter to fire you. I refused. He did it himself."

"It doesn't matter," Rose said. "I told Ryan, I don't work for people who don't want me. I meant it. Once I get out of here and back to my truck, I'm gone."

Lola laughed, but it sounded forced, almost desperate. "Don't be in such a rush. I tell you, Ryan's sweet on you."

"Right. How is that going to look? You know the gossip I get now. I'm going to exchange Jimmy for Ryan? One boss for another? Working my way up in the company? Bedroom promotions?"

"Rose! I know you and Jimmy aren't that."

"No. Love the man, but I guess—"

The explosion shattered the day like a crack of lighting: immediate, intense, and razor-sharp. It slapped at the trailer like a giant hand and rattled dishes in the kitchen. Frames holding permits and pictures crashed to the floor.

Rose jumped to her feet. Carl and Ryan ran from the back, but Lola sat wide-eyed and frozen, her hands clenched into fists in her lap. Ryan ran out the door first, with Carl right behind him. Rose went to the door, but she stopped. She didn't have to go out to see the fire. Her truck, engulfed in furious red flames.

"What happened?" Lola spoke softly from behind her.

"Not sure. My truck's on fire. Maybe the gas tank." The dispassionate sound of her own voice surprised her.

Lola came to stand beside her.

Rose's vehicle burned, along with several thousand dollars worth of tools. All insured, but painful to lose anyway. Some of the tools were her father's, the ones he had used when he taught her his electrician's trade. Two vehicles parked near the truck burned too, along with several palm trees. A deep sense of foreboding overcame her.

Too big, too loud—the blast didn't come from the gas tank. Years of experience on construction jobs where they blew old buildings to rubble with dynamite told her it took more than gasoline to make that big a bang. First the *accident,* now this. Who hated her enough to kill her? "Please don't let anyone be hurt," she said softly.

Chapter 3

Ryan slowed as he neared the flaming torch that had been Rose's truck. Pieces of debris and hot metal fell from the sky, as if the blast opened a hole in hell. He could do nothing except wait for the fire trucks.

Windows had shattered on cars parked on the street a hundred feet away. Two that were closer to the actual explosion burned. A clump of men gathered to watch the unfolding disaster.

"Anyone hurt?" Ryan asked.

The men eyed one another and shuffled their feet. One started to turn away, but Ryan grabbed his arm. "Tell me!"

The man jerked his arm out of Ryan's grasp. He stood with his feet apart, ready to fight. "Who the hell are you?"

"Ryan Vernon. Now, talk to me."

"Jimmy," said one of the other men. A small Hispanic looking fellow, he glanced around, obviously uncomfortable. "Man was crying. Like baby. Had a box." He cupped his arms as if he held something. "Saw him. Went to truck, opened door, climbed in and . . . boom." He walked away, head down and shoulders hunched. The others followed him.

"No." Ryan said the word softly, then clamped his teeth to keep from screaming.

Carl had followed and stood beside him. He must have heard the part about Jimmy.

"What the fuck is going on here, Carl?" Ryan clenched his fists until his fingernails cut into his palms.

Carl grew rigid, arms straight at his sides, his eyes wide

with disbelief. He backed up a couple of steps as if that would protect him. "I need to see if anyone's hurt." He whirled and hurried away.

A gust of wind blew heat his way and high flames still licked out of the truck frame. The doors? Blasted away with the windows. Ryan didn't study it long enough to see if anything remained of the man sitting at the wheel. He rubbed his hands across his face and breathed deeply to quell a surge of nausea. Heartsick, he went back to the trailer to tell Lola and Rose.

* * * *

Rose leaned against the wall to keep from falling. Her Jimmy? Her friend? It couldn't be. Jimmy had stayed with her at the hospital last night until they made him leave. He had come by earlier that morning and left with a promise to return, but instead sent Ryan.

Lola collapsed. Ryan, the closest to her, caught her as she fell. He laid her across the couch. Rose tucked her own agony inside while she went to the sink and wet a cloth in cold water.

"Lola?" Ryan's breathing sounded ragged and strained.

"Let me," Rose said. She knelt and carefully bathed Lola's face with the cool rag while Ryan held her hands. Lola woke and lay limp and shivering. Rose was afraid she'd go into shock. "See if there are any EMTs who aren't too busy," she told Ryan.

He rushed out and quickly returned with a couple of EMTs who had followed the fire trucks. Rose stood back and let them do their work.

While the EMTs treated Lola, Ryan, grim-faced and reserved, slipped his hand into Rose's and drew her outside.

"Come on," he said. "I need to look for something while Carl isn't around." He crossed the construction site at a fast pace, not running, but covering the ground in great strides, and headed straight for Jimmy's travel trailer. The small tin box was parked under a cluster of green trees the clearing crew hadn't cut and burned—yet. The trees would go soon, leaving the ground barren and ready for landscapers to sculpt bushes and palm trees in a neat, orderly fashion.

Ryan's eyes shed no tears, but Rose heard despair in his

voice, along with pure blind fury.

"My truck? Is it my fault?" she asked. "Did I do something wrong?" She had nothing to base that feeling on, but it came anyway. She wiped her eyes on her sleeve.

"No. It wasn't your fault." Ryan slowed and draped his arm over her shoulders. How nice to be comforted by someone so strong. She'd not had that since her father died. She'd lived an independent life for many years.

"Something else is going on here," Ryan said. "That's why I came from Miami. I don't know what it is—yet."

The door to Jimmy's trailer stood open, swinging loose in a light breeze. Ryan held out his hand to keep Rose back as he peered in.

"Shit!" He barely spoke the word aloud, but Rose heard the vehemence in it. She looked past him. Single men weren't the neatest of creatures, but the trailer's living room went beyond Jimmy's usual careless mess.

Ryan went in and she followed right behind. Whoever had ransacked the place left behind a tempest of damage. Cushions off the couch, cabinets open, the worn recliner tipped over, and books, magazines, and papers scattered everywhere. Easy to do with all attention on her burning truck.

Rose gazed at it, trying to make order out of chaos. "Somebody wanted something."

"Yeah." Ryan booted a cushion aside with a savage kick. He went to where the books from a small bookshelf lay on the floor in an untidy heap. "Look for Don Quixote," he said.

Voices came from the outside.

Rose knelt as they frantically pawed through the books. "Got it." She picked up a worn copy of the Don.

Ryan stepped to the front door.

"I don't care," Carl's voice came from outside. "I need to find—" He stopped short when he saw Ryan barring his way.

"You need to find what?" Ryan demanded.

Rose took that as a cue and headed for the back door. It, too, stood open. Was someone waiting outside? She hesitated. As she did, she glanced into the trailer's single bedroom. The bedroom she'd never seen because Jimmy always kept the door closed. Twisted and tangled white sheets lay on the bed and a blanket on the floor.

"Oh, my God," she whispered. She stepped inside.

Photographs lined every inch of wall in the tiny room in a bizarre wallpaper. All unframed, scattered in a chaotic array, some taped, some pinned with tacks—and all of her. Her thoughts scattered like the patchwork of pictures around her, circling and searching for reason. The room closed in on her and threatened to suffocate her with her own image.

Bewildered, she reached out and touched one photo, drawing her finger over its smooth surface. Atlanta, in her ground floor apartment, curled up in a chair reading a book. From that angle, Jimmy—or someone—had peered into her window.

She stepped back. Rose loved Jimmy, loved him dearly. His love for her had apparently gone beyond friendship into something she didn't understand. Separate loves, different loves—she refused to judge him. Others would do that. Others would see them and condemn, make false assumptions, point fingers at perceived immorality. She staggered out the backdoor and onto the small patio area where she and Jimmy often sat in cheap plastic chairs sharing beer and laughter. On the table by Jimmy's chair was a fifteen-inch long, seven-inch high ceramic statue of a black and tan dachshund.

"Herman," Rose said softly. When Jimmy tied on a good one and had a hangover, he'd take a few aspirins, go out back, and talk to Herman. It became a private joke between them. Talking to Herman meant a serious, but temporary, regret.

Tears leaked from her eyes again, and a hard knot formed in her stomach. In this tragedy, she wanted to hold on to the good memories. She grabbed Herman.

The only way to get back to the office was to sneak through stacks of lumber and other building materials. She moved from pile to pile, crouching and awkwardly crawling behind lower piles, freezing at the sound of voices, until she stepped out near the office trailer. At Ryan's truck, she opened the door, slid the book under the seat, and stowed Herman behind it.

Rose shivered. A sharp, chill wind cut the air around her. Only a couple of hours of daylight remained. Short January days, and her jacket . . .? She'd taken it off when she started work yesterday morning. Rose stared at the unfinished hotel's blank windows. No, she wasn't going back in there today. She pulled the key out of the truck's ignition and locked the doors.

A great number of people focused their attention on her now smoldering vehicle, and a changing wind across the construction yard again brought the toxic stench of burning. She went inside the trailer where the EMTs with Lola were packing up to leave.

One, a young man with boyish looks and thinning hair, cocked his head and grinned at her. "Hey, didn't I have to jump start your heart yesterday morning?"

"Yes. You did a good job. Professional." She didn't remember them, but it certainly didn't hurt to be polite to people who saved her life.

"Thank you," he said with a bow.

The woman with him, a tough muscular blonde, punched him on the arm. "I helped too, hero." They left full of the dark humor, the self-defense mechanism of those who grappled daily with bloody gore and death.

Lola was sitting on the couch, conscious, but grief-stricken and crying. Rose sat down and cried with her.

* * * *

"You need to find what, Carl?" Ryan barred his brother's entry to Jimmy's trailer to give Rose time to escape. Grift stood right behind Carl. His already fleshy face had swelled where it collided with the truck door, and blood splattered the front of his shirt. He gave Ryan a menacing stare, but then broke eye contact as if he feared Ryan might take him up on a challenge.

Carl rubbed his forehead with his fingers, a familiar gesture. Ryan knew his brother searched his brain for a plausible lie.

"Jimmy has important paperwork I need." Carl found a lie, but not a good one.

Ryan leaned against the doorframe. "What kind of paperwork?" Ryan crossed his arms, defiant. "Anything to do with bombs?"

"Damn it, no. Now let me in."

Ryan allowed him to enter.

Carl's eyes widened as he viewed the room. "What the hell . . .?"

"Happened before I arrived. You want to tell me what's going on, now?"

"Nothing. Nothing is, I . . ." Carl shook his head as if he could erase the scene from his mind. He rushed out of the trailer and hurried across the yard as if on some vital mission—or maybe he was running away. Grift trotted along after him like a shadow in the falling sun.

Ryan did a quick search of all the places he knew Jimmy hid things. He found an envelope with a few pages tucked inside in the secret drawer behind the couch. He stuffed it in his shirt to read later. He gazed around the room. It hit him then, the hollow, empty feeling. Jimmy was gone. How could that be? They'd talked only hours ago. Ryan touched the corner of the bookcase. He had a scar above his ear where he had fallen on it, horsing around, wrestling with Jimmy. Ten years old, spending the summer on a job site, learning the construction trade, he'd always stayed with Jimmy, not his father.

His legs gave way, and he sat on the couch. The couch? How many nights had he crashed there during his divorce, drunk out of his mind and sick to death with failure? He drew deep, aching breaths. There didn't seem to be enough air in the room. Jimmy would always be there. He promised. Dad lived in another world, Mama was ill, but Jimmy . . . Ryan exhaled and his mind cleared. He forced himself to stand. Time to go on. His love for the man demanded it.

Ryan walked to the back and into the bedroom. Stunned, his gaze went from photo to photo, as if that would make his mind accept the enormity of the thing. Had Rose seen it? Of course she had. He went from puzzled to enraged in seconds.

"Damn it, no." He refused to let the police or some sensation-seeking reporter make evil of it. He snatched one photo off the wall and tossed it on the bed. He tore at the others, ripping and peeling away the evidence of a man so much in love it had become obsession.

A small room, thank God, and in minutes all the pictures lay in a pile. He grabbed a pillowcase and stuffed them inside. The only one he left behind sat on a tiny table beside the bed. Rose, yes, but in a normal display frame. He carried the pillowcase out the back door, praying no one would see him, and hid it under a pile of debris to retrieve later.

Then he headed back to the office where the police had descended en masse. They'd be furious to find Jimmy's trailer wrecked and learn that both Carl and Ryan had gone inside. It would bring serious questions about obstruction of justice and tampering with evidence.

Chapter 4

Rose endured the questions, the police first, and then federal agents. All were civil enough and, on the surface, accepted her answers as the truth. She didn't need to lie. She'd driven her truck to work, left it in the parking lot, and been lying in a hospital bed when someone moved it. And no, she had no idea who would want to kill her or Jimmy. No one asked about Jimmy's photo collection, though, and that spooked her. She'd been struggling to find answers for those questions when they came.

At nine o'clock that night, Rose sat with her legs scrunched uncomfortably in the back of Ryan's truck among the boxes and his clothes. Her body vehemently protested. She ignored it. Physical pain kept her mind from dwelling on the day's atrocities. Part of her said to take a cab home and rest, but the greater part didn't want to be alone yet. Lola sat in the front seat with her back rigid, as if she might collapse when she relaxed. She hadn't spoken in a while.

Ryan left Rose and Lola alone for a few minutes and returned with a knotted pillowcase. He stuffed it under one of the boxes. No wonder the police hadn't asked her about the photos—but they would know something had covered the wall. After he climbed in, he drew a pistol from the console between the seats. It was in a holster, but he pulled it out, checked it, and put it back within easy reach.

Lola lived in a small, rented, ranch-style house tucked in a neighborhood filled with young families and senior citizens; an odd juxtaposition of untidy yards littered with colorful plastic toys and neatly trimmed shrubs and keep-off-the-grass signs.

Ryan and Rose went in with her. He searched her house and checked her locks.

Though Lola often protested that she didn't decorate, the house radiated warmth and charm. She'd arranged comfortable and expensive furniture in a way that invited people to sit and relax inside soft sage-green walls. Her china cabinet held real china and crystal, and the dining room table had the polished shine of fine wood. Multiple photos covered one wall, a collage of everything from snapshots to formal sittings. Rose didn't want to be nosy, but Lola displayed them for anyone to see. Her mind went back to Jimmy's collection and apparent obsession. She shut off those thoughts and concentrated on the ones before her.

Lola's photos, mostly of Ryan and Carl, spanned the years from infant to missing front teeth, and on to a cap and gown. She also noticed one of a much younger Jimmy standing side by side with Lola. A larger more prominent photo caught her eye. At first glance, it appeared to be handsome Carl, but this man was older.

"That's Charlie, Ryan and Carl's father." Lola had come to stand beside her. She pointed to another photo of an attractive woman wearing an impressive diamond necklace. "That's Abby, their mother."

"That's a good one of you and Jimmy." For some reason, the picture made her feel better.

"My thirty-fifth birthday party." Sorrow still filled Lola's voice. She pointed at two photos. "Jimmy gave me these last month. He said . . ." She choked, then cleared her throat. "He said he wanted you to be part of our family."

Rose knew one of the photos. Jimmy had someone take it at his birthday party. Too many beers for everyone, and he had dragged her into his lap and told her to smile. The other? A close up of her staring into the distance, lost within herself. A good photo, but she cringed and wondered how many pictures Jimmy had taken of her without her knowledge.

"How do you do it?" Rose asked. "Look at all these memories every day." Oh, God, why did she project her own life on someone else? "Lola, I'm sorry. I didn't mean . . ."

Lola hugged her. Her silver hair brushed under Rose's chin. "Oh, I have memories that hurt me. They're in my heart. There are only good memories here."

Lola insisted that Ryan return and stay with her after he drove Rose home. Rose considered it an excellent idea. She liked the man, but she didn't want to be tempted to get seriously involved too soon. Temptation involved having him alone in her apartment with nowhere else to go. They had Jimmy's death and her so-called accident to deal with before their relationship went further. Ryan finished his check of the house and made Lola lock the door behind him as he and Rose returned to the truck.

They rode in silence for a while, then Rose said, "Don Quixote is under the seat." She reached behind and retrieved the long, heavy, dachshund statue. "I hope you don't mind. On my way out of the trailer, I picked up Herman. I guess I shouldn't have, but I wouldn't want someone to throw him away. Sometimes, after work, we'd sit out back and have a beer. Jimmy would belch and declare, 'think I'm gonna be talking to Herman in the morning.'" Tears pooled in her eyes again. "Part of me hated him being nice to me. I heard it all: foreman is playing favorites, she's sleeping with him. The bigger part loved him."

"I used to do the same thing," Ryan said. "Talk to Jimmy—and Herman. Five years ago, my marriage crashed and burned like a cruise missile. Jimmy kept telling me it would get better, and it did. You keep Herman, Rose."

"Thank you."

"I'll pick you up in the morning, get you a truck and new tools," Ryan said when they arrived at her apartment building.

"You don't have to do that. I have insurance on everything. And a car." She pointed at the front row of the apartment house parking lot. "That's it, the red Taurus."

"Bombs make insurance companies nervous," he said. "Could take a while to get your money. You can pay me back."

Ryan's voice changed, softened with sympathy. "I got the photos from the trailer. Love seeing your face, but I think I'd better burn them. As for why he had them . . ."

Rose felt the hollow place in her heart shift. "I didn't see it. Him caring for me that way. Was I that stupid? That blind?"

"What would you have done if you'd known?"

"I don't know." Rose clutched Herman in one hand and with the other stroked his cool, hard surface as if she petted a living animal. "Try to be what he wanted me to be."

"I think you are what he wanted you to be. I think Jimmy loved you, but he wouldn't take advantage of you."

"Take advantage? He—"

"Was twice your age. And that wouldn't have mattered, that age difference, if you wanted him, loved him, the same way he wanted and loved you. But you didn't." He reached over and laid a hand on hers where they clutched Herman. "You need rest. Tomorrow will still hurt, but we have to find answers for all the questions."

What would she have done if Jimmy had asked for sex? The idea never occurred to her. Jimmy certainly gave her no hint of desire for more than friendship.

Ryan searched her small, third floor apartment as he had Lola's house. She followed construction jobs from state to state and didn't decorate, keeping only the bare necessities and photos of her father and mother. A couch, chair, two bar stools, the bed and a chest of drawers, all vintage thrift store furniture, made the place comfortable. She kept it as neat and clean as she kept her tools, but it suddenly looked shabby after riding in Ryan's fine truck and going into Lola's house.

"I'm going back to Lola's," Ryan said. He ran a hand through his sandy blond hair, then massaged the back of his neck. "I'll probably stay at her house for a while."

Ryan laid his hands on her shoulders. "I couldn't get the cops to tell me shit." His hands slid down her arms. "Maybe it would be best if you left town. I'll get you on at another job site. You might be safer. I'll pay—"

"No." Rose would not yield on that. "I stay here until I know what happened."

He smiled. "A kiss, then. I'll give you warning this time." His lips brushed hers, gentle and sweet, only for a moment, but oh, she liked his mouth. There was warmth there, warmth that could lead to passion.

"See you tomorrow," he said.

"Yes. Tomorrow."

* * * *

Ryan returned to Lola's, his mind racing over a jumble of memories. When he arrived, he found her sitting on the couch, staring at the wall of photos. He sat beside her. He grew up with Lola and Jimmy, both always there when he needed them. Neither Lola nor Jimmy had children, so they always made do with the Vernon boys.

Lola sniffed and wiped her eyes. "Did Jimmy ask you to come to Jacksonville?"

"No. You remember Rory? My friend who talked like he had marbles in his mouth."

"Yes. He stayed one summer with you and Jimmy. I think it was New Orleans."

"That's him. He called me. He's a CPA for a big accounting firm here in Jax. One of the banks doing the financing is making noise about the delays."

Lola gave a shuddering breath and Ryan feared she'd cry again, but she didn't. He didn't want to make it worse for her, but he had to ask. "Lola, why didn't you call me?"

Lola scrunched her body tighter, drawing her arms close to her sides in a pure defensive pose. When she spoke, she wouldn't meet his eyes. "Jimmy said he had things under control."

Damn it. That was not what he asked her. "Honey, I learned about trouble in my business from someone in a bank."

Lola said nothing. He wouldn't push her, upset her more, but he'd have no problem battering Carl for answers tomorrow.

Ryan hated to do it, but he told Lola of the wallpaper of photos in Jimmy's trailer. "There will be questions. I'm sure my fingerprints are all over the place."

"Did Rose see them?" she asked.

"Yes. It . . . disturbed her. I told her I'd burn them. She loved him, Lola. He was her friend, father figure, I guess. He was obsessed with her. That couldn't have been good. For either of them."

Lola's sobs racked her body again and he wrapped her in his arms and held her until she cried herself out. When she stilled, for her sake, he changed the subject a bit. "Rose seems to feel guilty. I have trouble believing what's happened is her fault."

"It's not." Lola straightened. She sounded as firm and decisive as always. "Rose is strong and smart. She's worked and lived in a man's world most of her life, and dealt with the shit that comes her way." She gave him a warm smile. "You, Ryan Vernon, could do worse than that electrician."

"Yeah." He leaned back. "God, I don't know what happened. I walked in that hospital room and there she was. We made some . . . connection. That's the only word I can think of." He held out his hands as if to ask her to understand something he himself couldn't.

"It works that way sometimes." She smiled at her wall of pictures. "Want advice from an old lady?"

"Your advice is always good, Lola. And you're not that old."

"Oh, I feel old. But Rose, you don't rush her. She's independent and skittish as hell. Don't know if she had a relationship go bad, or what. She never talked to me about her past."

Ryan remembered his first hasty and inappropriate kiss.

"And there's another thing about her," Lola continued. "Rose doesn't lie. Doesn't play games. She's always candid. Remember that when she tells you something you don't want to hear."

Lola stood. "Your bed is made and there are clean towels in the bathroom. Rest. God knows what will happen tomorrow."

Ryan went to the bedroom. Neither of them would sleep much. And tomorrow? More trouble, more sorrow. A bit of light had seeped into his life with Rose. Somehow, he had to make the most of it. Yes, a shower and bed would be nice. When he removed his shirt, the envelope he had retrieved from Jimmy's trailer fell to the floor. He picked it up, started to open it, and Lola called him from the living room. He stuck in on the dresser behind a lamp. He'd look at it later.

Chapter 5

Rose started toward her bedroom. God, she needed to rest. Maybe she could sleep.

The doorbell rang. Had Ryan returned? He'd only been gone fifteen minutes. The second she turned the knob she realized her mistake. Weariness equaled carelessness. A tall, obese man shoved his way through, sending her reeling backwards. Another smaller man followed him, closed the door and leaned back against it.

She dashed for the bedroom. She had a phone in the bathroom and could lock herself in. The big man grabbed her arm and jerked her back. She snatched her arm out of his grip, but then he stood between her and the bedroom.

He moved toward her and she backed up.

"Now, you be cool," he said. "We just want to ask you questions. My name's Cochran. This is my partner Bedlow." He gestured at the door. "We're private investigators hired to look into this bombing."

Cochran's face flushed. He wheezed with every breath, a prime candidate for a heart attack. Bedlow, his much smaller companion, glared at her from narrow rat eyes set in a pale pinched face. Both wore ill-fitted suits, probably purchased from the Salvation Army Thrift Store. If they were actually investigators, private or otherwise, she was a ballet dancer.

"Who hired you?" Rose backed away and searched for something to use as a weapon, but her spare apartment had few such objects. Sweat formed on her body as she fought fear. Calm. She had to be calm. She'd survived more than one brute of a man backing her into a corner.

"Who we work for is none of your business," Cochran said. He shook a finger at her as if she were a child.

"It is my business." She spoke with a much force as she could muster. "You forced your way into my home."

Bedlow remained standing with his back to the door. Cochran flopped down on the couch with a great sigh. He sank deep into the worn springs and thin foam. It would probably take a winch to get him up.

"Did Jimmy have a safe deposit box?" Cochran asked.

"How would I know?" Bedlow blocked the door, but she hadn't seen him lock it. Knowing her own strength, she could take the smaller man—unless he had a gun. The pair looked like clowns—dangerous clowns. She forced herself to remain calm.

Cochran kept up the questioning. "He ever give you any papers to keep? Come on now, we need to find out—"

"Why?" Rose demanded. "What are you looking for? What does it have to do with Jimmy?"

Had they been the ones who searched Jimmy's trailer?

Cochran's coat flapped open and yes, he had a gun under his arm. He jerked the coat closed and clasped his hands across his rounded belly, his sausage fingers locked together. His pinkie kept breaking free to wiggle like a small worm.

"How'd you do it?" Cochran asked.

"I beg your pardon?" She cocked her head and widened her eyes, feigning curiosity.

He leered at her. "Con old Jimmy. Bet he liked having a young piece like you in his bed."

Rose didn't bother to answer that one.

Cochran pointed a fat finger at her. "Guys who work on that job, they say you and Jimmy got it on real good."

"Ah, the guys." Rose laughed. She tried to act indifferent as she eased closer to Bedlow. "Bless their nasty little hearts. They talk about me, but I don't mind. They enjoy it so much and I'm sure it brightens their dull, shitty, insignificant lives."

"Jimmy tell you any of his secrets?" Cochran asked. His voice carried a hint of conspiracy. "Show you his hiding places?"

" No! He did not."

"You and Jimmy faked your getting hurt so you could sue the company." Bedlow suddenly spoke from his position by the door. His voice squeaked, eyes narrowed until they appeared to be only slits under his eyebrows.

"That's possible, I suppose," Rose said. "But with your superior private investigator powers of observation, I'm sure you've noticed that I'm not injured."

Cochran growled like a dog and his face burned a deeper shade of red. "You stupid bitch. You're really pissing me off." He coughed and his wheeze increased in intensity.

In one smooth, rapid movement, Rose rushed Bedlow. She grabbed him by his jacket, slung him around and threw him at Cochran. He landed on his partner. Bedlow gave a sharp cry as they both tumbled to the floor.

Rose threw the door open and raced down the hall, into the stairwell, and down the stairs. She'd have started screaming the minute she ran out the door if ninety-eight percent of the apartment complex hadn't consisted of senior citizens who either couldn't hear her or couldn't do anything except get hurt if they tried. Once she got outside, she could outrun them and find a way to call the police. The sound of feet thumped down behind her.

Bedlow. No way could Cochran run that fast. She raced down the steps at reckless speed, trying to gain distance.

Too fast. Panic, damn it. She'd panicked. She'd held fear at bay in the apartment, but it washed over her when she ran. She miscalculated at the bottom of the stairwell. Instead of going out, she'd gone into the building's ground floor mechanical room.

Trapped! She desperately searched for something to use as a weapon. The maintenance people kept a tidy house, though, and they locked everything away in cabinets or closets.

Footsteps echoed down the concrete stairwell. Rose balled up her fists. She'd attack the instant he entered the room.

He didn't. The exit door opened and slammed shut. Bedlow had gone outside! He'd taken the logical and predictable path. If he'd glanced to his right, he'd have seen her.

The door would lock behind him, and he'd have to go around front to come back in. What about Cochran? She waited, stood tight against the wall, and listened. Yes! He huffed and wheezed his way down and followed Bedlow outside.

Rose raced back upstairs. Each hallway had a fire alarm and when she reached her floor she snatched the handle on one and yanked it. Her terror had caused her to run right by them on the way down. The alarm blared its fog-horn voice through the building. Rose doubted the two men would hang around, but neither would she. She rushed into the bedroom, grabbed her suitcase and backpack and filled them with the essentials. She heard sirens in the distance and increased her pace. She was ready when the sudden pounding came at the door.

"Fire Department," a male voice yelled. "Anyone there?"

This time she peered through the peephole. She opened it to a fireman in full gear who ordered her to evacuate the building. With her backpack on her shoulder and carrying her suitcase, she made her way back down the stairs along with the other grumbling residents. She again carried the steadfast Herman tucked under her arm.

A frugal person who lived a simple life, she left nothing of value, sentimental or otherwise, behind. No lease, and she'd paid her rent through the next month. She could collect her remaining belongings later.

One of the fire fighters stopped her as she filed out the door with everyone else.

"You were ready to go ahead of time," he said. This one was sharp. And suspicious. They'd probably already determined it was a false alarm.

Rose lifted the suitcase. "Important stuff. Papers, photos. I took lessons from my older and wiser neighbors. I prepared." She nodded at the seniors filing out of the building. Many of them carried something, a box, a bag, a suitcase.

He cocked his head, still suspicious, but he let her go.

Rose thought about leaving as she climbed behind the wheel of her car. She could drive north or west, any direction that would take her a thousand miles from Jacksonville.

It wasn't an option. Someone tried to kill her. Someone killed Jimmy. Now this Cochran and Bedlow arrive with their threats and demands. In spite of the cool night air, sweat covered her body. She drew deep breaths and fought for calm.

Ryan Vernon was a question mark, but a nice one. They'd made a tenuous connection in the short time they'd been together. Rose glanced at the clock. Almost midnight. She slid the key into the ignition and turned it. The engine started smoothly.

Then she realized what she'd done. She groaned. Stupid. What if there'd been another bomb? Relief rolled over her like one of the waves on the beach.

Rose drove to Lola's house, parked at the curb, and crawled into the back seat where she had a blanket and pillow. The blanket wasn't much, but it would keep the chill off the January night. She kept her keys ready to set off the horn alarm and fell into an exhausted and dreamless sleep.

In an instant, she opened her eyes to the pale light of the coming day and Ryan rapping on the window glass. She sat up slowly and opened the door. Oh, damn. He wore only a pair of jeans. His bare chest, strong, powerful . . . God, how could she not want him?

* * * *

Ryan woke at daylight as he always did. He moved through the silent house, thinking about coffee, when he spotted the red car at the curb. He recognized it instantly. Rose.

He rushed out to it, but stopped when he spied her lying across the backseat, a pillow under her head and blanket tucked up to her chin.

She'd curled her body up in far too short a space for those long legs, and she'd be stiff when she stretched them out. In his mind, he could see her sleeping peacefully in a bed—his bed.

He rapped gently on the window. She woke instantly, sat up, and opened the door.

"What happened?" Ryan asked.

"Had a problem at the apartment. Fire alarm went off and everyone had to evacuate." She ran her fingers through her disheveled hair. "It was late. Didn't want you to come by this morning and think something bad happened." She stretched and he watched her body move, graceful as a cat. She grinned and his day became brighter.

"Come on in and have coffee," he said.

She climbed out, but caught her foot in the blanket and tripped. He grabbed her as she fell into his arms. She laughed and clung on to him while she untangled herself. He loved the feel of her so close, her hands on his arms and her body close to his—ah, so sexy.

"Hope that coffee's not decaf," she said. The sun rose then, and her tousled hair caught the light. Sleep fled from those wide green eyes, and that mouth, so close.

"No," she said as he leaned to kiss her. "Toothbrush first."

"I can arrange that. Coffee, toothbrush, and a kiss. Anything else?" She gently pushed away.

"Not yet," she said softly.

Ryan agreed. He wanted more, but he wanted it to be right, not something coming on the heels of disaster.

* * * *

Rose sighed at the bitter and wonderful taste in her mouth. Lola insisted she eat something, too. Heavenly, after a day and night from hell. As she sipped her first cup, she told Ryan and Lola about Cochran and Bedlow.

"Do you want to call the police?" Ryan asked.

"Not yet. I want to know what they're looking for."

Rose intended to call the police eventually, but for the moment, curiosity consumed her. She didn't dwell on it, but the idea of vengeance remained. "Did Don Quixote tell you anything?"

"I forgot about the Don." He rose and walked to the back of the house. He returned with the book, laid it on the table and began turning the pages.

Lola poured Rose more coffee.

"Thanks," Rose said. "You have a newspaper? I need to look at rentals. I don't want to go back to that apartment."

Lola's face brightened. "I think I know just the place. Come with me."

Rose followed her out the backdoor, through a gate in the side yard fence, into the backyard next door. A thin, stooped, incredibly old lady stood there. She wore a faded floral print housecoat and clutched her walker with both hands while she sneered at an equally aged, but obese beagle sitting in front of her. The placid dog ignored her.

"All right, Brutus, time's up." the old lady said. Her deep voice didn't match her frail appearance. "Move it, you cat-humping son of a bitch. Squeeze your ass and dump those turds."

"Hi, Annie," Lola yelled.

Annie jumped, pivoted her body, teetered on the walker, then straightened. Rose eyed the wrinkled mouth and yellowed skin of a heavy smoker.

"You out mighty early," Annie said, though she didn't sound surprised. She broke into a liquid coughing spasm that left her hanging on to the walker and gasping for breath. Lola simply waited it out. Finally, Annie's breath slowed and deepened to a moderate wheeze. An expression of disgust crossed Lola's face.

"Where's your oxygen bottle, Annie?"

"Back porch," she gasped. "Too heavy to tote. You come to ask about my health?"

"No. Your health is bad because you've lived a long and sinful life," Lola said. "Sooner or later you're going to die, probably sooner because you smoke when the oxygen is on. I want to know if the cottage is rentable." Lola pointed at Rose. "This is my niece."

Rose wondered about the distance of the cottage from the place where Annie simultaneously smoked and used oxygen.

"You can go look at it." Annie cocked her head, squinted her eyes, and studied Rose. "Nice looking piece, ain't you, honey?" She grinned at Rose, giving her a good view of her toothless mouth. "Key's under the mat."

Annie carefully maneuvered her walker around. Brutus the reluctant beagle sat by the back door. Unfortunately, he had done his business and dumped his turds in her path. She stepped on one and squashed it flat. Oblivious to the smell, she shuffled her way back toward her house, pushing her walker ahead of her.

"Wow," Rose said.

"Oh, yes. Definitely a wow. She can't help it. She grew up in a strip club her daddy owned. After that they had a traveling show. Not much she hasn't seen or done, I suspect. Hopefully she won't croak before you get to hear her stories. They are filthy and incredibly funny."

Rose followed Lola down a stone path to a simple, white frame cottage among a few nice oak trees. It had deep green shutters and a steep roof unusual in that part of Florida.

Lola opened the door. "Annie's son built this for her, but she moved in with him instead. His wife tolerated Mom for a couple of years, then she said 'enough' and caught a bus out of town. The old woman has outlived both her son and daughter. She ambushes men when they come around and makes some interesting propositions. The electric and cable people send females to read the meter or do a repair."

Rose liked the cottage. One bedroom, bath, with a combined kitchen, dining room and living room a little larger than her former apartment, it seemed clean, well lighted and well built. It smelled musty and unused. A few cans of air freshener and a few hours of open windows would cure that. Worn mismatched furniture, but it was clean and still serviceable. It looked like her apartment and every other place she'd lived in her nomadic life.

After seeing Lola's place though, she wondered if she settled for too little. She made good money and rarely spent it. She could have something better than the apartment she'd lived in since she came to Jax. A door by the kitchen opened to a patch of scraggly grass and two parking spots accessed by a narrow alley.

"This is good," Rose said.

"Yes," Lola agreed. "It's perfect."

When they returned to Annie's house, the old lady clung precariously to the walker as she balanced on one foot and scraped Brutus's business off her shoe with a stick. Brutus sat there watching with what Rose knew had to be amusement—even if it didn't show on his sweet beagle face. Annie expressed her displeasure with a steady stream of four-letter words.

"All right, Annie, how much?" Lola asked, shouting again.

"Huh." Annie's head jerked up. She hadn't heard them.

"How much?" Lola repeated.

Rose pressed her lips together to keep from laughing.

Annie studied her, her mind probably working to determine what an outrageous sum she could charge. "Rent is for one person. You get a boyfriend, you pay more."

"That's fine," Rose told her.

Annie eyed Lola with a grin. "Who's that fella you brought in with you last night?"

"My godson." Lola's face remained calm. "He's staying with me for a few weeks. That's why Rose needs her own place."

"From what I saw this morning in your front yard, *her own place* needs to be a bit farther away. Atlanta, maybe."

"Jesus, woman!" Lola's voice exploded in irritation. "Is watch my house all you do?"

"When there ain't nothing on TV." Annie gave them another toothless grin. She nodded at Rose. "Five hundred a month, first and last—cash. No checks, no pets, no kids. Includes utilities. Unless you get that man—which you most likely will. That's a hundred extra a month."

"I'll have to go the bank," Rose said.

"Pay before you move in. Now, this here is fine conversation, but my show's already started." She maneuvered the walker in the back door with a serene Brutus waddling ahead of her.

Chapter 6

Ryan flipped the Don's pages one at a time. Whenever Jimmy wanted to leave Ryan money or a private note, he always stashed it in the Don. The only thing Ryan found was a picture of Herman. He frowned. Herman was a joke; why take a photo of a ceramic dachshund? He glanced at the clock. Eight a.m. The news reports covered the bombing, but the police hadn't released any names. He picked up the phone and called O'Malley at home. A multitude of Vernon legal issues had made O'Malley a wealthy lawyer. His love of the family made him a friend.

"Hey, O'Malley," Ryan said when the lawyer answered the phone. "Got bad news. It's about Jimmy."

"What's he done now?" O'Malley sounded slightly annoyed.

Ryan told him the whole story, except the part about his personal feelings for Rose. He needed more time to define it. O'Malley didn't interrupt. "So, that's it," Ryan concluded. "We don't really know what's going on yet."

"Oh, God." O'Malley let out a sigh as if he'd been holding his breath. "How will we manage without Jimmy? How's Lola?"

"Stunned and frightened." Ryan didn't add that he felt the same way.

"Be careful," O'Malley said. He sounded impassive, but Ryan knew better. "I'll be there tonight."

"You don't have to—"

"Yes, I do. You need to know a few things."

Now what was that all about? It couldn't be good. Ryan knew better than to demand answers. O'Malley would speak in his own time—or not at all. "All right. If I'm not at the job site, I'll be here at Lola's. You have my cell number."

Lola and Rose returned smiling. Not a bad thing. They could remember their sadness and grieve later.

While Rose went to her car to get clean clothes for a shower, he and Lola sat and talked. He told her what O'Malley said.

Lola's smile faded. "This whole thing is terrifying. I hope it's not Jimmy's fault."

"Me, too. But I think a windstorm of trouble has arrived. We have to stick together."

"Like family?"

Ryan agreed. "Like family."

Lola shook her head. "We are in serious trouble."

* * * *

The hot shower water eased Rose's aching muscles, but she made it as cold as she could tolerate before she shut it off. She needed to be alert. She dried, dressed in one of her better shirts and a newer pair of jeans. Yesterday's safety pinned shirt went in the trashcan. The blow dryer did nice things to her hair as she brushed and flipped it up for volume. She drew it back to pin it at the nape of her neck, but loosely so it would look softer than her usual tight utilitarian twist. No heavy makeup, but a light powder on her face and she wiped a touch of pale pink on her mouth. She cast her doubts aside and admitted she did it for Ryan and wanted him to see her as an attractive woman.

Rose packed her bag and returned to the dining room. The slight widening of Ryan's eyes delighted her. He'd used Lola's second bathroom to shave and dress. Big, strong, handsome, he still had that exciting smile for her. She poured more coffee and sat beside him at the table.

"I'm going to the job site," he told her. "I want you to go with me."

"Love to, but I need to run by the bank, get money, get new tools and—"

"No, Rose. Please, I want you to go with me." He sounded sincere, almost hungry, needing her to be with him. Logic and reason said he was still moving too fast, but Jimmy's death propelled them forward.

"I . . ." She bit her lip, uncomfortable with what she needed to say. "Maybe it's better if I don't show up with you again."

"Come on, Rose." Lola threw her hands up. "I know what you're thinking. Do you care what some dirty-minded jerk on the site is going to say? You never cared what they said about you and Jimmy."

"No," Rose agreed. "I didn't. I do care about the police." She studied Ryan. "Did they ask if Jimmy was jealous because I cheated on him with you? Bet they asked you if you and I were lovers."

"They did." Ryan grinned. "I told them not yet. I told them it was too soon, that I'd just met you and you were still grieving for a man you thought of as a father. Of, course, they talked to certain parties who saw me kiss you in front of the office, so I doubt they believed me."

He leaned forward, gently linked his fingers with hers. "This is a bad time for many things, but stay with me. We don't have Jimmy, but we have Lola. Now we need to go whip Carl into shape."

Rose gazed into his deep brown eyes and everything inside of her quivered. She tried to concentrate on simply breathing, but it didn't work. She was falling for a man she'd known for twenty-four hours. That didn't happen to her. She was too cautious. So why couldn't she speak? What was it about the man that he could strip away her independence and make her tongue-tied as a child? All she managed was a nod of her head.

"Good." Ryan released her hand and stood. "Let's go."

"I'm going to stay here," Lola said. "Give me your car keys, Rose, and a check, and I'll go to the bank and square things with Annie." She lowered her head a minute. "I need to tell her about Jimmy, too. She never watches the news. He liked talking dirty and swapping, or maybe inventing, stories with her. And I need to make arrangements. I know what he wanted for his funeral."

There probably wasn't much left of Jimmy to bury, but doing things in their proper order would help them all cope with the loss. They needed closure. They had to say goodbye.

* * * *

Rose watched Ryan as he drove onto Beach Boulevard and

headed east. He drummed his fingers on the steering wheel, and occasionally made a fist and bounced it off the seat beside him. Restless and uneasy, he was not the calm, confident driver of yesterday.

"Hey," he said. "You got coffee and a toothbrush, but I haven't had my kiss."

"Drive, Ryan. Safety first. I'll save it for you. And add a little interest."

He slowed to pass a patrol car where it stopped a speeder. "Jimmy went to work for my dad before either Carl or I was born. Did he tell you that?"

"Yes, but he didn't talk too much about personal things. Neither did Lola, but she was always friendly. They never told me about you." She left unsaid that Jimmy probably didn't talk about Ryan because he, like Lola, believed she and Ryan would find each other attractive. One wanted that meeting, the other did not.

"I spent summers with Jimmy," Ryan said. "He was family, him and Lola."

"Don't know much about that kind of family," Rose said. "I'm an only child. A drunk driver killed Mom when I was eight. My father worked the construction sites, rarely more than a year or two in one place. I traveled with him. I went from school to school. In the summer, he taught me about electricity. I could strip wires before I was ten years old."

Rose's father had filled her life, acting as both parents. When there was something he felt uncomfortable doing, he would find someone to help her. At his request, a nurse on one of the construction sites taught her about her periods.

Later, she realized Daddy had used his daughter to emotionally replace her mother in his life. He didn't abuse her in any way. He simply wanted her undivided attention and he received it—until he died. He left her alone at eighteen, wise in the ways of survival in the world, but with no idea how to make friends, develop relationships, or fall in love.

Traffic eased across the St. Johns River and turned onto A1A. As they approached the hotel site, Rose turned her eyes away from the blackened patch of asphalt and burned trees.

Ryan started cursing under his breath.

"What's wrong?" she asked.

"We have company. Bad company." He nodded at the office trailer. Parked in front sat a long white Lincoln Town Car with midnight tinted windows.

"Who's that?" Rose asked.

"Esteban. I should have known. Javier Esteban y Cirilo. Central American drug runner, gunrunner. He tried to muscle in on the company a couple of years ago. I muscled him out. I know good people in Miami, Hispanic, black, white, and then there's scum like him. He's killed, murdered . . ." He slammed his hands on the steering wheel. "Son of a bitch!"

Ryan parked beside the Town Car. "There's the tool truck." He nodded at the red and white truck not far from the trailer. "Go get your stuff."

Tiny shivers of dread raced along Rose's nerves. "Let me go with you."

"No, Rose. This is too close and personal for me. It'll be okay. Esteban isn't stupid enough to try something here. Hey, what about my kiss?"

Rose popped her seat belt. She rose up to get closer to him, caught the side of his face in her hand, and pressed her lips against his. She threw more passion into that kiss than she intended. His arms closed around her. Oh, the warmth of another human being, the sensation of a body so close. Close enough to touch, close enough to hear the sharp intake of his breath. It fascinated her. It terrified her. Such weakness to want something so much. Light flashed behind her eyes, a brilliant fire.

Ryan held her tight against his hard muscled body. She broke the kiss because she had to breathe. She trembled as he slowly released her.

They sat there for a few moments, then he said, "I was going to do something. I can't remember what." His voice murmured, deep and husky, like he'd awakened from a deep dreamless sleep.

Rose brushed a strand of hair from his forehead. "Miami, guns, drugs."

"Right! Esteban. I'll get rid of him. Then we can . . ." He stopped.

"Yes," Rose said. "We can do that." She slowly drew away from him. Four years ago a man had entered her life, and her wonderful love affair ended in disaster. Should she try again? Yes. Oh, she might lose, but she might win, too.

* * * *

Ryan felt incredibly alive. Rose's pink cheeks complimented the expression of total shock on her face. So, he got to her, too.

"Go," he said. "Get your tools. I'll see you when I finish here."

He drew a deep breath and tried to focus on what he had to do. Kick Carl's ass and get Esteban off the construction site, not necessarily in that order. But, oh damn, his mouth still tasted hers. When had a woman kissed him that way? Never his wife. She'd stopped kissing him six months after they were married. He forced Rose's image out of his mind.

His gun was still in the console, still loaded. A useless thing since he was alone and Esteban would have people carrying small armories under their suits. He went up the steps and into the trailer to meet the devil.

Two of Esteban's bodyguards faced him.

"This is private," one said. "Get out."

"Fuck you." Ryan spoke with a light, amicable voice that denied the insult.

"That's enough," said a voice from the hallway.

Ryan knew the voice. Leandro, Esteban's right hand.

Leandro stepped into the room. He nodded in greeting.

"Leandro," Ryan said.

Few people knew Leandro's origins. He had appeared at Esteban's side ten years ago. Everyone agreed that he was a singularly dangerous man. He couldn't be much over thirty, but his shadowy reputation carried tales of careless cruelty and carnage. What marked him above others was his constant and unremitting loyalty to Esteban. His looks set him apart from most men, too, amber skin, dark eyes, and a movie star's face.

"Please join us," Leandro said. He spoke formally with the slightest of accents. As usual, he wore a black suit that probably covered any number of weapons.

Ryan walked toward him, and the two goons moved aside to let him pass.

Leandro barred Ryan's way. "You are armed?"

"Leandro, I'm not going to do anything stupid." Ryan had fought him and Esteban five years ago when Esteban tried to intimidate him to purchase an interest in the company. A battle that ended in a draw, but they had taken measure of each other's strength. They'd had a few skirmishes since then. One of those ended in tragedy.

"I agree," Leandro said. "Stupidity is not one of your faults. Stubborn denial, however, is. You may pass, but know that I am standing at your back."

"My back? That's your preferred method, isn't it?" Ryan walked by him. He doubted insults would have an impact on Leandro. Certainly they wouldn't anger him. He'd never seen the man actually angry. People simply died or disappeared after crossing him.

When he entered Carl's office, Carl sat in his executive chair behind his executive desk looking dejected as a dog in the pound, sentenced to die. Like the dog, he turned hopeful eyes on Ryan, begging for a reprieve.

Ryan shook his head. "You never learn, do you?"

Carl's face stiffened, maybe drawing courage from his brother's presence. "I simply thought for once, business could be business."

Javier Esteban sat in a chair across the desk from Carl. A tall slender man, of indeterminate age, he wore a light-colored designer suit and his fingers flashed more diamonds than a queen's tiara.

"Ah," Esteban said. His mouth made a gleeful, but incredibly overbearing, smile. "The younger, but wiser, brother has arrived to save the Vernon family honor."

"I have. Get off this property, Esteban." The ghosts of Mario and Celia Sanchez and their children haunted Ryan. A family sacrificed to show Esteban's power. Esteban liked power and never hesitated to demonstrate his own to that end. Not a direct threat to an opponent who challenged him, but to the people that opponent cared for. Like Jimmy cared for Rose.

Esteban leaned back, obviously gloating. "This property, as you will note on the contract lying on your brother's desk, is mine. Perhaps it is I who should order you to leave."

Ryan glared at Carl. A trickle of sweat ran down Carl's forehead and he wiped at it with a shaking hand.

"However," Esteban continued, "since I, through my representative, and you, through yours, have agreed to collaborate and construct this fine hotel, I shall be lenient."

Had Carl cut a deal with Esteban to build the hotel and Esteban used an intermediary to get the contract past O'Malley's review? Somehow, that seemed too simple. "Show me the contract," he said.

Carl tossed a multi-page, legal-sized document at him. Ryan read fast, paragraphs at a time, and knew when he finished it was O'Malley's usual methodical and efficient language, language that held up in court many times.

"Olivarez Corp," Ryan said. "That's you, Esteban?"

"I have the good fortune to own controlling interest." Esteban gave a regal nod.

Ryan tossed the papers back on Carl's desk. "Okay. I'll agree. The contract is legal and enforceable. What do you want?"

"My hotel, of course. I am concerned about the delays."

"Has to be more. You don't think that small. You want to bankrupt me by sabotage?"

Esteban smiled. "No. You are a formidable adversary and I would not deprive myself of the interesting challenge you present at times. However, do you realize that you are, without a doubt, the most reputable builder of larger buildings in the south? The profit margin on this venture is incredibly slim and I simply wanted the best."

"You had the best." Ryan kept his voice low, desperate to remain in control. "No matter how incompetent Carl is, Jimmy and Lola could have pulled it off. Why kill Jimmy?" He held up a hand. "Never mind. I don't need your lies."

Esteban's voice remained gracious. "As you wish, but the

fact remains that this contract, which you have acknowledged is legal, states that this hotel will be completed by a certain date. The contract allows three extensions of time, two have already been granted. I have a great deal of money to lose here. Of course, I will need to have my people come in to watch over things." He didn't speak of the suggestion that he was involved in Jimmy's death.

"I'll finish it on time." Ryan met Esteban's eyes straight on. He didn't feel the need to be gracious at all. "Now let me give you a few more details of this legal contract. It includes a standard O'Malley clause. It says that your *people*, your representatives, and I include you in that, cannot come onto this property, which is now my construction site, without giving me forty-eight hours notice. And when you or your representatives do come, you or they are to be accompanied by my *people* at all times." That particular clause had saved Vernon Construction days of harassment by owners who thought they knew how to build a better hotel than the professionals.

Esteban stopped smiling.

"You want to go to court, Esteban? Challenge it? You can, but that might void the whole contract. Probably tie this project up for months, even years. It will cost us both of us an incredible amount of money."

Esteban stood. "I shall review my options."

"You do that." Ryan faced him. Stubborn denial, Leandro had said. Yes, that was good. "I have a hotel to build, Esteban. And I have a murder to solve. Somehow, I think the two are connected. The bomb was a mistake. Science is better now. Not like the good old days when you could blow up anyone you wanted. The Feds are involved, too. They're going to be looking at you, I'll bet."

Ryan didn't add that the Feds were probably getting warrants for Vernon Construction's books, too. He'd already called and warned his accountants that they were about to earn their exorbitant fees. Esteban rose and nodded pleasantly, as if to a friendly acquaintance, and left the room.

Leandro followed, but he stopped at the door. "I was told

you are angry about that family," he said. "Sanchez, wasn't it? The mother, father, little boy. And the girl, what was her name?"

"Elena," Ryan almost choked on the word. "She was fourteen." He fought to keep his voice steady, knowing he was a heartbeat from making a horrific mistake. Is that what they wanted? If attacked, Leandro could and would kill him in the space of a single heartbeat.

"Ah, yes, Elena." Leandro's expression grew reserved. "Very sweet. Such a tragedy." He walked away.

That didn't temper his rage, but it left Ryan free to deal with Carl. "Why? Just tell me why."

Carl shrugged. His eyes shifted to the wall, not to his brother. "I needed the money. I want Brianna back, my kids."

"Brianna loves you. You don't need money for her."

"Yeah, but it would be better and . . . Oh, fuck. I owe this guy in Vegas. Plus interest. Who's Sanchez?"

"Sanchez was my foreman on the Charter One site. Nice guy, wife, kids. A good friend. They found the whole family in a canal. All shot in the head. Except Elena. She . . ."

Ryan couldn't bring himself to say it. Whoever killed them brutally raped and tortured Elena. Probably Leandro, or at least on his orders. And most likely, her father had been forced to watch. Ryan jerked his jacket off. "You stupid fuck. Get out of that chair and talk to me."

Chapter 7

Rose walked the hundred feet from the office to the red and white Mega Tool Company truck. A large rectangular room on wheels, its back doors opened wide to expose workmen's wares. Titus, the franchised owner and salesman, made his rounds of construction sites, like a modern day tinker. He had graduated from Harvard then traded his suit for a pair of jeans and a salesman's life. Titus was an excellent salesman. He gave Rose a great white-toothed grin as she approached. Why not? He knew he'd be making money today. Good thing she paid off her credit card last month.

A couple of the crew stood inside looking over the merchandise, and several others gathered around, staring at her. Among them was Sam, the jobsite Crew Supervisor. He'd been with Vernon Construction for years. Sam was always sociable, but occasionally he'd muttered under his breath about women on the job.

"Rose." Sam's solemn voice caused the others to press closer. He wore thick, black-frame glasses, had a sun weathered face. His big, rough hands were stuck in his jacket pockets.

"Sam, I don't know what's happening." Rose wished she could reassure him.

"Know those bastards from Miami," he nodded at the office. "Boss Man ran them off down there."

"Boss Man. You mean Ryan?"

"Only one now that Jimmy's gone. Looks like you're getting to know Mr. Vernon real well." Sam winked at her.

Rose's job site image had taken a massive hit when she arrived with Ryan. And that kiss . . . She'd gone from being the foreman's girlfriend to the owner's girlfriend.

"Sam, I'm not—"

"Aw, Ms. Electrician," Sam said, obviously enjoying her discomfort. "Saw you give him a little courage in the truck."

Rose knew denials were useless. "Ryan Vernon doesn't need me to give him courage, Sam. You ought to know that. I'm the one who needs courage. Someone killed me Monday, at least for a few minutes. Now I'm going to buy tools and climb back on the same horse again. You wouldn't know anything about how that accident happened, would you?"

Sam's brows knit into a deep frown. He glanced at the building as if it were haunted. "Wasn't no accident. Told the police. Someone hooked those wires you were pulling to the number three generator out back. You was on the panel when they fired it up. They took fingerprints, but everyone here probably touched it."

"And you don't know who would commit such a dastardly act?"

"I'd say Grift, but he wasn't nowhere near here until 'bout three o'clock that day. Least nobody noticed him."

"How many didn't show up for work this morning? Bombs have a way of spooking people."

"A few quit. Not my regulars. Won't miss 'em. Got a call from Abraham in Tallahassee. Boss Man started dragging in crews from other sites last night." Sam grinned at her. "You're pretty tough." He kicked the dirt slightly with his well-worn boot, suddenly seeming shy. "Glad you're okay."

"Thanks, Sam. Now, let me give Titus three months wages so I can go back to work."

"You don't have to do that," Titus said beaming. "Already taken care of. Courtesy Vernon Construction. Lola called and said to give her an invoice." He waved his hand at a toolbox. "Got you a complete Master E's set, including . . ." He handed her a bright yellow hard hat with the Mega tool logo imprinted in red. "That's your new, improved, super strong, super lightweight, Sunday bonnet. Service is my middle name."

"Greed is your middle name, Titus. I know the markup on your toys."

"Yeah, but this is for free." He handed her an instrument the size and shape of a cell phone. It had a something like a pencil sticking from one end. "This the best, state of the art."

Rose smiled. A Non-Contact Volt Detector. She already had one, she'd used it that eventful morning, but she understood. "Thanks, Titus. I take back what I said about greed."

Everyone laughed, and for a moment, it seemed as if things had returned to normal.

Rose pulled her wallet from her jeans pocket, opened it, and handed her credit card to the enthusiastic tool salesman. "Here, Vernon Construction doesn't owe me anything but a paycheck."

Titus protested and Rose didn't blame him. Lola had the power to bar him from the site if he crossed her. Rose insisted, though, and he finally let her pay. She needed to call her insurance company. She paid a hefty premium to cover everything. All she had to do was figure out how to explain the bomb that blasted the truck and her tools to shrapnel.

The sun rose higher in the hard, clear, ice-blue sky, and promised to warm the earth considerably by noon, even with the salty breeze from the Atlantic. Too much heat for the denim jacket she wore, so she walked over to leave it in Ryan's truck. She hoped her other one, the one she wore Monday morning when Mr. Electric grabbed her, was still inside the hotel. Her cell phone was in the pocket. She opened the truck door, tossed the jacket in, and as she closed it, two big men walked out of the trailer. Men with watchful eyes, eyes that searched for danger. They looked like classier versions of Cochran and Bedlow. One went to the driver's door of the long, elegant Town Car, opened it and slid in behind the steering wheel. The other opened the rear passenger door, obviously waiting for someone.

Two more men followed them out. One could have been smooth, debonair Ricardo Montalban, stepping out of a 1950's movie, the kind her father used to watch. Impeccably dressed in a light beige linen suit, he had jet-black hair combed and neatly styled, and a face smooth enough he could be a poster child for his plastic surgeon. Supreme personal vanity, she'd bet. Wealthy older men, and he was obviously that, did not need to resort to the deception techniques of older women. He stopped when he spied her, then stepped across the short distance between them.

"Good morning, Ms. Norris. I am Javier Esteban. I am told you had an unfortunate accident Monday. Have you completely recovered?"

"Yes, I have." What was his interest in her? And how did he know her?

"Excellent," Esteban said. He had a condescending air about him. "I am the owner of this magnificent structure Mr. Vernon is constructing, and I am, of course, concerned about the safety of the workers."

Rose covered her surprise with a courteous smile. "Thank you. Appreciate that."

Esteban nodded graciously. Rose caught a hint of a sneer, though, the raised chin . . . an aristocrat's tasteful show of contempt for a common laborer. She'd seen it before.

The man who accompanied Esteban stepped closer. Rose tried not to stare, but she couldn't help it. His dark suit created a direct contrast to Esteban's light threads. He wasn't tall, barely six feet. He moved with the power of a lithe, lean wolf racing after a deer. When had she ever seen a man so perfectly handsome? He had dark hair, just long enough to give him a bad boy look, dusky golden skin, and the cold dead eyes of a man never touched by moral sensibility or mercy.

Rose clenched her hands into fists, let her fingernails bite into her palms, and held her ground. She would not be intimidated.

The wolf's voice had the consistency of thick cream. "I am Leandro." His tongue touched his bottom lip as if he would taste her. "You have the eyes of a cat."

Unease forced truth into Rose's words. "You have the eyes of a psychopath."

Esteban clasped his hands together close to his heart. "Oh, dear, Leandro. It would seem that this one knows you."

"You want something?" Rose asked Esteban. "Besides an update on my welfare?"

"Ah, I can see the honorable Mr. Vernon has told you what

an evil man I am. I simply wanted to meet the woman Mr. Beecher loved so much. You have courage and beauty. I could understand a man dying to keep you safe."

"Or killing to make you his." Leandro's mouth curved in a half smile; a beautiful man who gazed at her as if he wanted to consume her, body and soul.

Rose spoke directly to Esteban and jerked her head slightly in Leandro's direction. "Hope he's had all his shots. A mad dog can turn on its master."

Esteban raised an eyebrow. "Perhaps. But a dog and his master may work together to accomplish great things at times. One will have weakness where the other has strength."

Rose's voice matched Esteban's earlier contempt for her. "You mean as in brains and brawn? Or beauty and the beast?"

"Oh, he is beautiful, my Leandro. I see him stalking you. He'd like to be *your* beast." Esteban's voice was smooth and more amicable this time.

"Are you jealous?" Rose had taken note of the look Esteban had given Leandro when he'd called him beautiful.

Esteban sighed. "Yes. Most jealous. Tragically, he does not share my interests. But he has other talents I make use of." He nodded politely, and walked to the Town Car.

Leandro drew closer, and Rose's heart rate soared. Psychopath, she'd named him. The air suddenly seemed thinner and harder to breathe. Her skin flushed hot, then cold, as a slight sheen of sweat formed. Fear swelled, but with it came something unbidden—desire. Leandro's fingers brushed the inside of her arm below the elbow and trailed down to her palm. He exuded an odd heat, as if life burned faster inside him than any other man. She stood frozen as a prey animal hearing the hunter's approaching footsteps.

"There are women who beg to come to my bed," he said in that fluid intoxicating voice.

"I believe you. But I won't be among them."

"No? I feel your desire. I smell it as the scent of flowers on a warm night." Leandro laughed, deep, soft and low.

Fear—and desire—made her reckless. She challenged him.

"Tell me, Esteban's darling, were you born to serve him, or did you crawl down to his level of immorality?"

His fierce onyx eyes locked on hers. "God gave me the soul of a priest. Men taught me the pleasures of immorality. Lie to yourself if you wish, *mi dulce*, but I will have you."

He walked away and left her standing there knowing something powerful and deadly had passed her by—this time. He climbed into the Town Car, but as he did he smiled again, like a man who knew her secrets and would use them to cut her to the bone. She wanted him, that angel-faced killer. How could she? A good thing had entered her life with Ryan Vernon, and it was as if her body had declared war on her rational mind. The Town Car drove away. Rose wondered if there was a scale to rate wicked men. If so, who would be higher on the list? Esteban? Leandro? Men such as Grift had tried to hurt her in the past, rough men with their intentions clearly written on their faces and in their body language. The smooth criminals she'd just met were clearly out of her league. Extreme caution was required. Total avoidance was best.

Rose wanted to go back to her tools, back to her job. Work, that's what she needed—a maze of wires to sort and place in the proper order, followed by good clean exhaustion. Of course, a couple of days of pure, heart pounding, barbaric sex might have the same effect. That kind of exhaustion would cure any intoxicating desire for a dangerous and arrogant Leandro.

The trailer office door popped open and Carl Vernon flew out like a wrestler tossed out of the ring by his slick, sweaty, muscle-bound opponent. He hit the dry ground hard, but with a good clean roll. He jumped back to his feet. Ryan charged out the door to meet him.

Those in the crew who'd been standing around moved in closer for a good view of the fight, calling out bets. Obviously, they'd seen such battles before. How incredibly annoying. The brothers probably wouldn't kill or seriously injure each other, but her tentative plans for a sexual marathon with Ryan dissolved with each blow Carl landed.

Chapter 8

Rose filled the plastic bag with ice, tied the top, and handed it to Carl. He and Ryan sat on the tailgate of Ryan's truck. Blood spotted Carl's pure white shirt and his fine dress pants were torn at the knees.

"How come he gets ice first?" Ryan asked.

"He looks worse than you do." She scooped ice into a second bag.

"That doesn't mean you won." Carl laid the bag against the side of his face. His knuckles looked as if he'd lost a boxing match with a brick wall.

"Bullshit." Ryan accepted the bag from Rose and pressed it against his chin. "Damn it, you little bastard. You knocked a tooth loose." He didn't mention his lower lip, cut and swollen like a sham doctor had screwed up a collagen shot.

"You hit me first," Carl said. He didn't really sound angry, only matter of fact, as if repeating a pattern.

"No, I didn't." Ryan's objection had the same *been there, done that* tone. "I bounced you off the wall."

"I think you both need to go to the emergency room," Rose said. "I'll drive."

"No!" They spoke the word simultaneously.

Rose planted her hands on her hips. "Yeah, they probably have more urgent things to do than patch up a couple of brawling boys. How about a doc-in-a-box? At least get pain pills."

Carl lifted the ice bag from his eye. Rose frowned. The thin bloody line of the cut ran from the outside corner toward his temple. "That eye needs to be checked. I think your eyeball might fall out."

Ryan examined the cut, too. "It does look nasty. Will you drive him over there?"

"May as well. I doubt I'll get much wiring done."

"That's okay. I have other crews coming in. Be here by tomorrow. I need to talk to everyone here now." Ryan handed her the keys to his truck.

"Would you get my new tools locked up somewhere?"

"I'll take care of it." His lips brushed her cheek. "I'm sorry for this. I wish . . ."

Rose shook her head. "Wishes don't change things."

Ryan helped Carl into the truck and fastened his seat belt. Both Carl's hands had swelled like bread dough in an oven. Rose arranged a couple of ice packs on them. Ryan drew her aside when she walked around to get behind the wheel.

"That eye looks bad. Pass the doc-in-a-box and take him to the emergency room," he said. "Tell them he fell down the stairs." He laid his hand on her waist and drew her closer.

Rose leaned against him and relaxed. "What if he says my brother beat the shit out of me?"

"He won't. We've done this before. Did you see Esteban when he left?"

"Yes. He spoke to me, knew my name. Acted concerned I got hurt at . . . his hotel."

"Shit! He . . ." Ryan rubbed the back of his neck and blew out a breath.

"And that Leandro...what does *mi dulce* mean?"

"*Mi dulce*? It means my sweet. I'll tell you more about Esteban and Leandro later."

"How did Esteban know Jimmy loved me?"

"I don't know. We should assume he knows everything we know, and a lot that we don't know."

Rose nodded. Slick, urbane Esteban and deadly Leandro. Deadly? Oh, yes. But also beautiful and desirable, like a flower luring an insect with its sweet honey odor.

Static Resistance and Rose

* * * *

Rose sat in the emergency waiting room for four hours while various doctors made sure Carl didn't have head and eye injuries. At least this time she wasn't the one behind the double doors. The waiting room, new like the rest of the hospital, wasn't bad. Comfortable chairs so she could nap. She could usually sleep anywhere. Not true deep REM sleep, but that half-doze that let a person half-rest and wake feeling like pure shit.

She dreamed, woke aroused, and realized how much two days of sexual tension troubled her. Big problem, though, since Ryan wasn't the one who stalked in her dream.

It was three o'clock in the afternoon before an aide rolled Carl out in a wheelchair. No concussion, so they had sent for a plastic surgeon to stitch up the cut near his eye, bandaged it and popped a couple of pain pills in him. They gave Rose more pills in a brown plastic bottle.

Once in the truck, lethargic Carl sat in the passenger seat and swayed gently as it rolled across the asphalt. Rose glanced at the pill bottle. Percodan. How high could Carl fly? High enough to give her some answers?

"Carl?"

"What?" His voice was sluggish.

"What does Grift do for you?"

"Grift?" Confusion filled that word, as if he wondered why someone would ask. "I pay him extra. In case Esteban tries to kill me."

"And why would Esteban do that?"

"Jimmy had something he wants, but I don't know what it is. Jimmy said he had Esteban by the nuts and . . ." He fell silent, as if he knew he'd said too much. "Do you know what it is? What Esteban wants? Can we give it to him to stop this before anyone else gets killed?" He suddenly sounded like a child, lonely and afraid.

"No, Carl, I don't know, but I'll find out." She spoke with a certainty she didn't feel.

"You will." He sighed. "You're so . . . competent. Lola was right. You belong with Ryan. Jimmy wouldn't let . . ." He drifted off, maybe to sleep, or maybe his mind simply moved on to some other subject.

Rose called Lola to ask where she should take Carl, and Lola insisted that she bring him to her. He went along peacefully enough, allowing Rose to steady him while the diminutive Lola guided them to the bedroom. They sat him on the bed, and Rose removed his shoes while Lola unbuttoned his blood spotted shirt. He didn't protest when she peeled it off and pushed him to lie down.

"Isn't this where Ryan is sleeping?" Rose asked. Lola only had two bedrooms.

"He'll have to find someplace else." She pointed at Carl. "This is Ryan's fault." Lola draped a light blanket over the sleeping man, then bent and kissed his cheek. "Poor baby. You deserve better."

That bit of logic didn't quite make sense to Rose.

"Well, you do have a couch," Rose said, irritated. Why was Lola pushing her at Ryan?

"*You* have a couch, too," Lola said. "I cashed your check, moved you in, loaned you sheets and towels, and stashed a six-pack of beer in the refrigerator. Your keys are on my kitchen counter and your car is behind the cottage."

"Ryan can't stay with me, Lola. Not yet." She followed Lola out of the bedroom.

"And why not? Don't tell me you don't want—"

"I want. Oh, do I ever want. I also want things to last a while. I'm not sure living together is the best thing right now. I've known him a little over twenty-four hours. Relationships that start with a disaster don't always end well."

"You don't know Ryan. I listened to him last night. Listened to him talk about you. He isn't a man who commits easily, but when he does, he's steady as one of his buildings."

"I don't commit easily either, Lola. And it's *way* too soon for that kind of commitment. Sex, getting to know one another, that's fine. But living together is not that easy."

"That worries me, your independence and restlessness. But honey, you're almost thirty years old, and it's time you let some of that go. Damn Jimmy to hell. I've been bugging him to get Ryan up here, mostly to meet you, but he . . ." Lola rubbed the back of her neck. "Selfish, always selfish, that was Jimmy. Oh, Rose, maybe you should run like hell, from Jacksonville, from Florida, and most of all from the Vernons."

Chapter 9

Ryan grabbed another bag of ice and headed back to the office. He needed to make more phone calls. One of them, damn it all, to a dentist. He vaguely regretted hitting Carl, then decided not to. He'd simply regret hitting him so hard. He'd give Carl credit though; after thirty years of brawling, Carl had come close to winning this time.

He stared at the hotel. Five million. He'd go at least five in the red to complete it, not to mention pulling crews off other jobs. And having to deal with Esteban. He decided he didn't regret hitting Carl at all.

Sam approached him. A good man, Sam. Loyal, dependable, certainly as good as Jimmy in knowledge of the trade.

"Boss Man," Sam said.

"Sam. Good to see you." Ryan didn't want anyone to call him Boss Man, but it was better than what he was sure his employees called Carl. "Sorry I haven't been able to talk to you and the crew sooner."

"You been busy. Got calls from the other crews," Sam said. "They're on their way. Christ, what a mess."

Ryan asked him about what had happened to Rose and what he knew about the bomb. It wasn't much. The police had told him that Rose's accident wasn't an accident at all. Her encounter with Cochran and Bedlow seemed to prove that, though he couldn't be sure. When Sam finished, Ryan asked, "You told all that to the police?"

Sam nodded.

"Anything you didn't tell them?"

Sam pursed his mouth, as if considering his words before he spoke. "Jimmy was acting strange. Been doing it for six months, I'd say. He kept losing track of things, material orders, work schedules. Man used to live and breathe the job. Drank more. Some mornings we wouldn't see him until nine or ten. Especially when . . ."

"Come on, Sam."

"Especially when Rose would sit with him for a few hours after work. I'd see them there, sitting behind his trailer. Talking, drinking beer. He wasn't . . . I mean . . ."

"How do you know?" Ryan had to smile.

"Because I seen it before. Man and a woman on a job, if they're together that way, it shows." He grinned. "Like this morning in your truck."

Ryan laughed.

"Something *was* happening with Jimmy, though." Sam sobered. "All of a sudden, maybe a week, week and a half ago, Jimmy started following her. On the job, sometimes I'd see him pull out after her when she went home. Stalking, almost. Seemed like he was serious afraid of something. Course, if he hadn't been close to her Monday, she wouldn't have been chewing on you this morning."

"He was afraid for her?"

"Sure seemed that way."

"Thanks, Sam. I know I can depend on you." He clapped a hand on Sam's shoulder.

"You gonna find out what happened, right?" Sam asked.

"You bet."

Sam started to turn, then stopped. "Boss Man?"

"Yes, Sam."

"That Rose, she's a good one. She's got bal . . . guts. She's tough. Still a fine looking woman, though."

"I know." Ryan said. "That's why I let her chew on me."

Ryan wondered if Sam thought strong, gutsy women shouldn't be beautiful. Not that Rose was beautiful in a Barbie Doll way like his ex-wife. Maybe the simple fact that Rose knew the trade, understood the basic mechanics of steel and concrete, and the details of electricity, made the connection for him. Those long legs and sexy, athletic body didn't hurt, either.

He pressed the ice bag to his throbbing jaw and headed into the office. Halfway there, he realized that he was in love with a woman he'd known for approximately twenty-four hours. He'd never believed it happened outside the movies, those romantic comedies his ex-wife always dragged him to see. He vowed to remember Lola's words. *Don't push her. Don't rush her.* He prayed what he had with Rose would survive the coming days. It would. He'd make sure of that. His confidence faded as he reached the office and the Feds arrived with more questions.

* * * *

When Rose arrived back at the construction site, two black SUVs with US government license plates were sitting in front of the office. She parked the truck, and in spite of the fact that it was three-thirty in the afternoon, retrieved the tools she needed and went to work. She didn't think she could stand another round of questions yet. She hoped Jimmy was a victim and not the cause of all their problems. What had he told her at the hospital that night before he left her? That it was his fault and he was going to fix things. Now he'd left them with a deadly mystery.

Rose dug deep and found the courage to go to the mechanical room and face the panel that bit her on Monday. There were no windows that deep in the building. Lights illuminated the work area, but left the corners of the room in darkness.

The damned panel and its damned wires seemed incredibly menacing. It glared at her like an evil eye. The hairs on her arms prickled. She drew deep breaths, sucking in oxygen. With her feet firmly planted on the concrete, she glared back.

Her fingers only hesitated for a second when she touched the bare wires. Victory! She was there at four-thirty when Ryan arrived. The swelling in his jaw had receded, but his lip didn't look like it could tolerate a kiss.

"You missed the Feds," he said.

"Darn. I just hate that."

He laughed then winced. "How's Carl?"

"Better than you. *He* has pain pills. The hospital didn't buy the falling down the stairs story, but they had the overflow from a pile-up on I-95 to deal with. They didn't make a fuss. The Feds grill you hard?"

"Yeah." He scowled. "I need to talk to Carl before they get to him, though."

"He's at Lola's. She wanted me to take him there."

"Good. Put your tools away and let's go. O'Malley is supposed to be at her house by seven."

"O'Malley? Your lawyer?" Rose had heard the name before. Jimmy had both cursed and praised the man.

"Yes. He knows *all* our secrets. I told him about Esteban. God, he was pissed. He spent so much time keeping things straight when we had problems with him before."

"Did the Feds ask about Esteban?" Rose unbuckled her tool belt.

"No, and I didn't enlighten them. I doubt Esteban's name is anywhere on anything worth noticing. That's why I need to talk to Carl. Esteban orders people killed as easily as I give orders to my crews. But a bomb? Not his style at all." Ryan slipped his arm around her and drew her close. His solemn expression told her he was going to give her bad news. "One of the guys I talked to said that when Jimmy climbed in the truck, he carried a box."

"You think he made a bomb?" she asked. "It went off too soon? I don't believe that. Even if he had actually wanted to kill someone, a bomb might hurt innocent people. That's not my Jimmy." Rose gently brushed his lip with a feather touch of her finger. "No kisses for you for a while, buddy."

He pointed at his cheek. "Lay one here, sweetheart."

Rose kissed his cheek.

"Mmmm . . ." he said. "This is nice, but we need to go. Lola said we should be at her house by five-thirty."

"Yeah, but we'll disappoint the audience if we leave too soon." She nodded to her right where Sam and a couple of the other men stood grinning at them.

Ryan waved at them. He seemed perfectly at ease with their

budding relationship. She wished she felt the same. Oh, she liked the big man, wanted him, but she didn't know if she was ready for that final leap of faith into love. Especially after her reaction to Leandro earlier in the day.

Rose carefully stowed her tools in the toolbox and carried them to the large walk-in wire cage set up on the hotel's ground floor. Luck was with her and her jacket with the cell phone in the pocket was where she left it Monday morning. She already missed her truck. Maybe she could get away tomorrow afternoon and buy another one. Not as fancy as Ryan's, but a custom job where she could have toolboxes built into the back rather than bolted in the truck bed.

* * * *

Rose dipped out more barbecue beef dripping with spicy red sauce and grabbed another slice of bread. Lola had a feast delivered and spread out on the table when she and Ryan arrived.

Ryan ate slowly, trying to chew on one side of his mouth. He still appeared hungry when he gave up. Carl sat sipping iced tea, listless, his head occasionally drooping with pain. The bandage covered his entire eye and had to be uncomfortable. He'd refused more pills, saying he'd need them to sleep that night.

"Have you been boring Rose with any of your Carl and Ryan 'boys will be boys' stories yet?" Ryan asked Lola.

Lola shook her head. "No. I haven't had time. I'll get to it."

It made Rose uncomfortable, sitting there awaiting the arrival of O'Malley, the family lawyer. No matter how Jimmy had felt about her, she wasn't family. She offered to leave, but both Lola and Ryan insisted she stay.

"Carl, this is the time you need to tell the truth," Lola said.

"And answer questions." Ryan lifted his tea, seemed to have second thoughts about placing it against his lip, and set it down. "Why didn't you tell me about that contract and Esteban?"

Carl stared at the wall for a moment, then turned back to Ryan. "Jimmy persuaded me to do it. He said that, in the end, it would show you that I could make a deal. Hold up my end of things. God help me, he said he had Esteban under control." He gave a sigh that bordered on a sob. "A couple of weeks ago, I got the idea that something had gone terribly wrong, but I was used to doing what Jimmy told me to do. I've done it all my life. As you so often remind me, I'm a figurehead, and Jimmy and Lola are the real power on the construction site."

Ryan winced, and Rose could tell Carl made a point.

"Why did you fire Rose while she was in the hospital?" Ryan asked.

"Jimmy told me to," Carl said. "Ordered me. I've never seen him so adamant. He drove her truck off the site while I wrote the letter. Jimmy said she wasn't to come back there, no matter what. He said he had to protect her and getting rid of her was the only way."

Rose's barbecue dinner burned in her stomach. She wanted to curl up in a ball like a baby.

The bell rang, and Lola peered out the window, then opened the door.

"O'Malley," she said and stepped back, only to be scooped up into his arms. O'Malley, an incredibly muscular six-foot, seven inch giant, held Lola tight, his face close to hers. His shiny bald head and size made him look like a TV wrestler. Such a man, a lawyer, could sway a jury by simply standing too close. Major intimidation.

"Ah," he said. "My little Lola."

At the sound of his deep voice, Rose realized he was crying. For Jimmy. A pang of loneliness surged through her. These people, family, she didn't understand it. She rose to leave, to go out the backdoor, across the yard, and to her new place. It wasn't home, but then she'd never had one of those. Home had never been a place, but a person—her father.

Ryan stood, caught her hand and drew her close. "Stay with me, Rose. Don't leave."

Indecision raged through her. The small bit of stability in her life had disappeared. Jimmy was gone, and her job, the routine that was often the redeeming attribute when relationships went astray, had radically changed. She gazed into Ryan's eyes and saw the sincerity, the longing. She nodded and accepted his request.

O'Malley approached, still carrying Lola. He frowned at Ryan, then spied Carl. "Carl, I approve. You're getting better at fighting back."

Carl gave him a sheepish smile.

"Put me down, O'Malley," Lola said. Her voice had a vivacious tone, one Rose had never heard from her before.

"But little Lola," O'Malley lifted her higher. "I might step on you."

"Then you better watch where you stomp your size fourteens."

O'Malley gently set her on her feet. He gave Rose a steady, assessing look. "May I assume that the young lady Ryan is holding prisoner is Ms. Michelle Roseanne Norris?"

"I'm Rose." She frowned. This man, like Esteban, spoke with familiarity.

O'Malley nodded and smiled. "Oh, Jimmy told me all about you." Those words coming from some men might sound like a leer. With O'Malley, they sounded like Jimmy had nothing but praise for her.

O'Malley nodded at Lola's big screen TV. "I presume you have a DVD player?"

"Yes, I do. Are we going to watch a movie?"

"Yes, a tragic movie, full of irony, that anyone who knows this family will understand."

They went to the living room and Rose sat beside Ryan. Some of her discomfort eased, but she remained wary. Lola offered drinks, wine and beer all around. Rose chose a beer, one that tasted good and slid in a cold wave down her throat.

O'Malley removed a DVD from his briefcase and placed it in the player, but didn't start the show.

The doorbell rang again.

"Good," O'Malley said. "We can begin."

Lola gave a yelp of joy when she answered the door. She darted out to embrace the visitor. When she returned, she led an attractive young woman with copper colored hair and pale ivory skin. The woman left Lola and went to Carl, who sat with his face down, ignoring everything but his pain. She knelt beside him, and he met her gaze.

"Bri?" Carl's voice sounded thick. "What are you . . .? You shouldn't be here."

"Oh, God," the woman said. She started to grasp one of Carl's hands, but spied the swelling and settled for caressing his cheek. "Your eye, is it . . .?"

"It's not the eye, just the skin beside it." He leaned toward her, obviously wanting her even as he'd denied her.

The woman glared at Ryan. "Did you do this?" she demanded.

"Yes, Brianna," Ryan replied. He spoke with no guilt in his voice. "He deserved it."

"Don't, Bri," Carl said. He bent down and rubbed his cheek against hers. "He's right. This time he's right. I deserved it."

Brianna sat beside him on the couch. She slid her arm through his and Rose could see tears in her eyes. "It wasn't your fault, was it? That Jimmy . . ."

"I hope not. I did a couple of stupid things, though." Carl kissed her.

"Rose," Lola said. "This is Brianna, Carl's wife."

Rose nodded at the woman and envied that spectacular hair.

Brianna smiled and cocked her head, her face filled with curiosity. "Rose. Yes, last time I spoke to Jimmy, he talked about you. Somehow, I thought you were older."

"Jimmy was a great guy," she said. "He was a good friend."

Brianna seemed to absorb that information and tuck it away in her mind for future reference. Not a stupid woman, this one. Except that she had married Carl.

"Now," O'Malley said. "The reason I'm here. Six months ago, Jimmy came to Miami and said he wanted to change his will. He was always levelheaded, when he was sober, so I accepted his request and made the arrangements. I had a psychiatrist and a physician, the best in Miami, examine him to be sure he was mentally stable. All examinations were recorded and are on the DVD." He sat down and picked up the remote.

"This will is on paper too, properly signed, witnessed and recorded. It will stand." O'Malley picked up the remote. "Let's get started, then I'll answer any questions." Jimmy's smiling face appeared on the screen.

Chapter 10

Jimmy sat in a chair with O'Malley to his left and two other people behind him. "Are we ready?" he asked.

"Yes," O'Malley said. He introduced the men behind him as doctors in various medical fields. "Be sure you give the pertinent details first," he said to Jimmy.

"Pertinent. Sure." Jimmy rattled off his name and a significant number of facts about himself. "That it?" he asked.

O'Malley nodded.

Jimmy sat back and grinned into the camera. "Okay, boys and girls, here I am sitting with a shrink and shyster who say I'm sane and legal. I want to do this right. I haven't told no one, but I'm pretty sick. Body sick, not mind sick, at least according to the shrink. I had my will all made out, had it for years, but now I'm changing it. Not much, but it's important to me." He spoke to O'Malley. "I have to say it all? Not just the changes?"

"Yes, Mr. Beecher, you do. At least, the major ones."

Jimmy nodded. "About forty years ago, I got into a card game with a man named Charles J. Vernon. This is for those of you who haven't already heard the story 20 or 30 times. We got to be regular drinking buddies, and Charlie said 'Jimmy, stick with me and I'll make you rich.' Well, that's what he did. I'm no billionaire, but I was careful.

"First of all, let me talk about the two people I'm not leaving much to. Not cause I don't love them, but . . . well, I think they'll understand. Ryan and Lola. Excuse me. Ryan Vernon and my sister Lola . . . make that Lillian Ann Beecher. Lola, you get everything that's in my storage unit. Books, photos, furniture, you got a spare key. Your name is on the lease. Now,

Lola honey, don't throw anything away until you look at everything in every box, every drawer, every book, everything.

"Ryan . . . ah, son, I . . ." Jimmy bowed his head, then raised it. "I got a couple of things your daddy gave me. A watch and his autographed copy of *The Yearling*. He gave them to me the week he died. Said he didn't want to leave me with nothing. Which isn't true because he gave me a lot. But that's another story, another time.

"Now this is the new part. There's a hundred thousand dollars in a safe deposit box at the First Commercial Bank of Miami. O'Malley has the key. And my twenty percent of Vernon Construction. I leave those two things to Rose." He smiled. "Excuse me, Michelle Roseanne Norris. Rose the electrician. Beautiful Rose.

"Now, knowing Rose, she's gonna say she don't want it, but I'm depending on O'Malley, Lola, and Ryan to be sure she accepts it." He held out his hands in an appeal. "Please, Rose, take it as a gift. Honey, you hold the twenty percent of the company and Ryan and Lola will make you rich, like Charlie Vernon did me." Jimmy sighed. "The rest of the will is the same as it has been for years. There's a fund at the First Commercial Bank of Miami. It's for Brianna Vernon. About two million dollars. Maybe more since it's earning interest. You're a sweet girl, Bri, and in case you can't straighten Carl out, this will make sure you and your kids have what you need.

"Everything else I have, stocks, Certificates of Deposit, bonds, property in Miami, about five or six million dollars cash, and anything O'Malley knows about that I don't, I leave to Carl Vernon. Carl, I'm sorry. I did wrong by you, and money won't make up for it, but it's all I got." He glanced at O'Malley, then back at the camera. "That's it then."

The DVD played on, O'Malley and the doctor asking Jimmy questions to determine that he was of sound mind and not on drugs.

O'Malley shut it off. Silence filled the room like a swelling balloon.

Rose touched her face and realized tears lay there. She left the room, walked into the kitchen and out the back door. This time, no one stopped her.

She went to the cottage, her new home. Not a home, though. She unlocked the door and walked in. Lola had indeed unpacked her things. Rose found her suitcase in the closet, opened it, and started to repack.

Georgia, Alabama, Tennessee, which one? She had Master Electrician licenses in all three, and would have no trouble getting a job somewhere else. Summer was on the way. Something near the mountains might be good. A slight noise made her turn. Ryan stood in the doorway.

"Tell me why you're leaving. Please." He sounded desperate, maybe as desperate as she felt.

"I can't deal with this, Ryan. If he'd left me Herman or some token out of friendship, a couple of thousand dollars, I could take it. But not . . ."

"Rose, he loved you. You loved him. What's the problem?"

"The problem? You, Jimmy, Lola, Carl, even your lawyer, for God's sake. You people are tied up in each other's lives, and Jimmy has tried to force me to join you. He thinks..." Rose drew a deep breath. "He thought he would buy my way in. He wanted to buy me the family I never had. Damn him to hell . . . no, I don't mean that."

"No, you don't. He meant you well, Rose."

Rose went to stand in front of him. "I want you, might even love you soon. But I can leave. Right now. I am leaving."

"Fine. I'll go with you." He laid his hands on her shoulders.

"What? You have responsibilities here. You have family. I don't."

"Are you leaving because you're afraid of family? Of being loved?"

She pushed his hands away. "I'm afraid of being caged. I know how it works. My father dearly loved my mother; he never recovered from her death. Daddy stayed inside that trap, the net of love, and mourned all his life." Rose never wanted to love anyone that much—to hurt that much.

She turned away from him and sat on the bed. Ryan sat close beside her. He felt so solid, his shoulder against hers. He lifted her hand and kissed her fingers, wincing as they touched his lip.

"I think I'm going to love you, too, Rose. When I walked out of that hospital room yesterday, away from you, I had a company electrician to find. I didn't look for him. I waited for you to come out, to see you again. When I asked one of the nurses your name, learned who you were, I didn't know what to do. I saw you, and you filled up my mind and my heart."

"You barely know me." Her voice wavered and sounded insignificant. It matched how she felt inside. She wanted to embrace what he offered, fall joyfully into his arms without misgivings, without doubt. Nothing in her life had prepared her for that kind of event. "How can you trust me with so much?"

"You barely know *me*. Give me a chance. If you really need to leave, let me go with you. Lola can run the company."

"The hell she can," Lola said from the doorway. "You stop this nonsense right now, Rose. You can stand against the meanest, dirtiest version of Grift, but you're going to run away from people who care about you? You're made of better stuff. At least Jimmy thought you were." She walked away.

"Oh, God," Rose said. "Guilt. She's doing the guilt thing."

"Yeah." Ryan draped his arm around her shoulder and hugged her. He kissed her ear. "Lola is a pro. Stay with me, Rose. I swear, I promise, not to hold you any tighter than you want to be held. All you have to do is tell me to back off. You did that once, remember."

"I . . ." Rose glanced up. O'Malley stood in the doorway.

"Have you convinced her, yet?" the lawyer asked. "We have other things to talk about."

"Oh, for . . ." Ryan buried his face in Rose's hair. "You're right. Family is a trap. Why else would I put up with him and Carl?"

Rose smiled. She leaned against him. She wanted to love him, didn't she? And God help her, his family. Walking into a trap, knowing what it is, and doing it anyway. She rationalized and made the excuses. She realized that she didn't have anything more exciting to do with her life. No plans for a fantastic alternative future peeked over the horizon. If she left now, she might never know what happened to Jimmy. "Okay, Ryan. I'll try it."

"Good," O'Malley said. He crossed his arms over his massive chest. "Now, Rose, if Ryan gives you any trouble, you let me know. I'll take care of it. You get married and I'll write you a pre-nup that will clean him out if he tries any shit."

"Married! Now wait a minute. Nobody said anything about getting married." Rose cocked her head and studied O'Malley. "Pre-nup for me? Isn't that a conflict of interest?"

"Honey, these Vernons have so damned much conflict one little divorce isn't going to make a bit of difference. Now let's go. We're not finished here."

The three walked out her door to find her new landlady, Annie, again urging her plump beagle Brutus to complete his business. This time she carried her oxygen bottle hooked to her walker, and had an unlit cigarette stuck between her lips. She removed the cigarette and gave them a toothless grin.

"Rented the place for one, remember?" Annie nodded at the men. "You have company, you pay more."

"Oh, it's such a nice place. I'm showing it off. This is my brother." She laid a hand on O'Malley's arm. She nodded at Ryan. "And this is—"

"Her fiancé," Ryan said.

Annie eyed O'Malley. "Big one, ain't he?"

"Got it from my father's side of the family," Rose assured her.

"Oh, I can see that." Annie teetered a bit on her walker.

O'Malley, a gentleman, stepped up to steady her. Yeah, a real gentleman. She remembered Lola's warning about Annie's behavior around men.

"O'Malley," Rose said. "Why don't you help Annie get back into her house?" She grabbed Ryan and dragged him away. Family? She'd see if they really wanted to adopt her.

"Mind the dog turds," Annie called after them.

Rose was still laughing when she reentered Lola's house—after she had scraped the dog shit off her shoes. She told Lola what she'd done, and Lola laughed so hard she had to sit down.

Laughter, clean laughter, laughter to break the tension; it was much better than crying, a gentle buffer to the pain of loss.

O'Malley stormed back in fifteen minutes later and Lola immediately ordered him out again to scrape his shoes.

"You witch," he said to Rose when he plodded back in, shoes in hand. "I'll tie that will up so tight you'll be as wrinkled as that old woman before you get a dime."

"Come on, O'Malley," Lola said. "Bet it's been a while since you had an offer like Annie's. Did she tell you she was good because she didn't have any teeth to get in the way?"

O'Malley closed his eyes and shook his head. Then he grinned. "The money she offered was tempting. Certainly more than I'll make for taking care of this family."

As O'Malley walked by Rose he wrapped his long arm around her and gave her a congenial hug, almost jerking her off her feet. Family. Oh, boy.

Then they all went into the living room where Brianna and Carl sat quietly talking. Brianna held Carl close.

"But why?" Carl asked O'Malley. "Why leave me money? He apologized, but he never did anything bad to me."

Rose noted a missing piece. There was talk of Ryan, Jimmy, Lola, and Mama, but only the barest mention of Dad. Where was Charlie Vernon in all of this?

"Lola . . .?" O'Malley made it a question.

Lola glared at him. "All right," Lola said as she walked to the bar separating the living room and kitchen. She sat on one of the stools and leaned against the bar as if she needed it for support. "You're right, Carl. Ryan was Jimmy's favorite. Nothing equal about the whole situation. You wanted to come to the job sites in the summer, too. I saw it. Bitter disappointment on a little boy's face when he was left behind. Jimmy could have handled both of you, but that selfish bastard . . ." She shook her head. "When you got older, after your Mama died and you started your rich playboy routine, he knew he had done wrong by you. The more you played the bad boy, the worse he suffered. He thought he could have made a difference if he'd taught you what he taught Ryan."

"No," Carl said. "It wasn't that way. Yeah, I wanted to go

sometimes, but Daddy was *always* gone. I couldn't leave Mama alone. She cried. She loved him so much and he was never there."

Lola's face twisted. Rose thought she'd never seen so much misery in one person. O'Malley went to Lola and led her to sit on a couch with him.

Everyone sat in silence for a moment, then Carl spoke. "Is everything my fault?"

"Carl," Brianna hugged him. "Don't blame yourself for things until we understand what happened. It's what Jimmy wanted. You need to rest. It'll look different when you feel better."

Carl nodded. His head drooped. The pain had worn him down.

Rose agreed that everyone needed to rest, herself included. She'd decided Ryan could go with her. He promised not to hold her too tight, and she wanted him. It wasn't a good time, too soon after disaster, but it all came down to trust. She wanted to trust them all, the Vernons and lawyer O'Malley.

They all agreed that no decisions would be made that night. O'Malley offered to drop Brianna and Carl off at Carl's apartment. He left with a promise to be back tomorrow and another that he would call everyone he knew in law enforcement for details about the bomb.

"Why did Carl and Brianna break up?" Rose asked Ryan after everyone else left.

"Money. Carl owes money. That five million? If he doesn't give it to Bri, he won't have it in a year. That's why Jimmy made sure she received her own share. Carl loves her. No other women, no drinking, but he likes to play the big shot."

"I'll bet Jimmy stuck conditions on Carl's money," Lola said.

With a calculating look at Lola, Ryan asked, "Is there any way I could get a *real* answer from you about why he left it all to Carl?"

"Not a chance in hell." Lola crossed her arms and her eyes narrowed. "You're not jealous, are you? About him leaving it all to Carl?"

"No." Ryan shrugged. "I own a successful company. I've made more than that last year alone."

"Who was shorted?" Rose asked. "A hundred thousand for me isn't much compared to all the rest, which, by the way, I had no idea he had. Twenty percent of the company sounds extravagant for a woman he'd known only a year."

"He was going to give it to me." Lola sounded satisfied, not upset. "That's the part of the will he changed. Then I'd leave it, along with my twenty percent, to Ryan."

"I never asked Jimmy for anything." Rose suddenly felt resentful. Regardless of his secret love for her, he should have known she'd hate it. Leave her a little money, yes, but twenty percent of a multi-million dollar company? "Lola, if you want it, I'll give it to you."

"No, Rose, you're stuck with it, bless your sweet heart."

"Why doesn't Carl own part of the company?" Rose asked.

"My father *sold* it to me," Ryan said. "Right before he died. I didn't expect it. I figured Carl would be a partner, but Daddy said no. He ordered me to *take care of* Carl, but that's all. He said Lola, Jimmy, and I could make it, even if we had to drag my big brother along with us."

"We have. We will continue to do so." A satisfied smile crossed Lola's face. She went to Ryan. "You staying here tonight or do you have other plans?"

"I . . ." Ryan stared at Rose. She heard his unspoken question.

Rose caressed his cheek, trailing a finger down to his chin. She'd accepted his word and agreed to stay in Jacksonville. It seemed that giving in to desire would be the next step. Yes, she could live with that.

Lola diplomatically left them and went to the kitchen.

"You sure you're ready?" Ryan asked. "I'll stay here at Lola's if you're not comfortable."

Rose smiled. "Oh, I'm ready. I'm cautious, but still ready."

"Oh, got burned, did you?"

Rose heard sympathy in his voice. "Incinerated."

"You feel comfortable enough to tell me about it?"

"Ah, you want to know about my disaster? I show you mine, and you show me yours?" A good enough way to begin, to get to know one another. "You've probably heard something like it before. Building trade mythology. Five years ago, I met a man on a high-rise job in South Carolina. A carpenter, actually."

"A match made in construction heaven." Ryan's words told her he had heard similar stories. Rose knew such liaisons were becoming common as more women entered the building trades.

"I lived in one of the trailers they had on site," she told him. "You know, where they let you live for free to act as night and weekend security. I let him move in with me. I didn't think it was true love, but we were on our way. I was a bit reluctant, but everything fit."

"Shall I guess?" Ryan brushed a strand of stray hair from her cheek. "He went home to take care of his aging parents a couple of weekends a month."

"Nope. I wouldn't have bought that." Rose said. "He owned half a business with his brother. And maybe he did. He called me a couple of times a day when he was gone. Then one Monday morning, I got up about six to make coffee before we went to work. Someone started banging the trailer door."

"His wife."

"Yeah. She was pretty cool. She said, 'You have something that belongs to me.' I told her not to worry she could have it back. He was in the bathroom, buck naked, taking a leak, when I caught him."

Rose stopped speaking for a moment, reliving the scene in her mind. "I grabbed him. He didn't fight. We played rough at times and I guess he thought I wanted a little morning wake up. I shoved him down the hall and threw him out the front door. He landed at her feet. That's when I saw not only the crew standing around laughing—I expected that—but three kids, about six to ten years old, standing behind their mother."

"Oh, God." Ryan shook his head. "I try to pay for my regular people to take their families with them. Keeps them out of trouble."

"I know. Jimmy wouldn't have tolerated it. I felt bad for those kids seeing their father like that. Kids are fragile."

85

"Rough place to be. How did you handle it?" Ryan asked.

"I tossed him a blanket off the couch, asked her to bring the kids and come in. She did. In shock, I guess. I locked the door, locked him out. I apologized and said I didn't know about her, but I was wrong anyway. She packed his things while I fed the kids juice and toast. I told them it was all a game we adults played sometimes, and none of it was their fault."

Rose halfway expected Ryan to reciprocate with a story of his own, but he didn't offer. He studied Lola's picture-filled wall, seeming lost in his own thoughts, or perhaps memories.

Lola returned to the room. "Sorry, kids, but you're going to have to postpone the honeymoon. Sam just called. The office and Jimmy's trailer are on fire."

Chapter 11

Ryan slammed on the brakes, narrowly missing a car that suddenly stopped. Six lanes of highway, light traffic, and everyone wanted to be in front of him. He swore under his breath.

Rose didn't swear, but he heard a curse in her gritty voice. "At the risk of sounding like a cowardly backseat driver, I suggest you slow down before you kill someone's child. You can't extinguish a fire by getting there a few minutes earlier to piss on it."

Chastised, he eased off the gas.

Lola didn't live far from the hotel, but every driver in Jacksonville seemed to be going in that direction. Once he reached A1A, it would probably thin out.

"If it's the trailers, it won't be a problem," he said. "But if it reaches the hotel . . ."

Rose reached out and stroked his arm. "Depends on how soon it was reported."

"And the police will be back." Back with more damned questions he couldn't answer.

"Sucks, doesn't it?" Rose gave an exaggerated sigh. "Everyone is a suspect until cops find evidence."

"Damn it, Rose." He squeezed the steering wheel tight and gritted his teeth. "Stop sounding so fucking reasonable. Do you know how irritating that is?"

"Yes. However, it's a minor irritation compared to going to jail for reckless driving." She sat back and crossed her arms, staring straight ahead.

The truck's speed had increased as he spoke. He slowed to drive the speed limit. Rose was ominously silent.

"Does that mean anything?" he asked. Damn, was he ever going to get to know her before more disaster struck?

"Does what mean anything?" she asked.

"You being so quiet."

"It means I don't have anything to say."

"What if I want to know what you're thinking?"

"You ask." She relaxed and shifted in her seat so she could turn more toward him. "I'm too direct sometimes. I didn't have a mother to teach me how to play boy/girl word games. As to what I'm thinking, I keep going over the past few days, trying to make some sense of it."

"Let me know if you do."

Flashing red and blue lights appeared in the distance as they turned south onto A1A. Ryan silently prayed. Let it be the trailers, please let it be the trailers. Barricades closed the entire street, so they had to park and walk.

As they approached, Ryan relaxed. The hotel was dark. Only the trailers burned. The leaping flames outlined the tall shape against the sky as smoke swept around it.

Sam met them when they reached the perimeter set up by the police. He'd been working late in the office trailer.

"What happened?" Ryan asked.

"Don't know. I heard a noise, kind of a big whoosh. The whole back of the trailer was on fire. I got out, called 911. Then Jimmy's place started, too." Sam coughed thick and heavy. "When they got here, I told 'em to hose the hotel first, not the trailers. Is that okay?"

Ryan swallowed. Dependable Sam knew what to do. "It's perfect. Trailers are shit, that building . . ." He relaxed until he realized that the police officers who had worked the bombing would be bearing down on him soon—and Rose had disappeared.

* * * *

Rose stepped away from Ryan. He'd be the best one to deal with the situation. She could stand back and watch. She frowned. Was that Esteban's white Town Car parked in the shadows on a side street? Would Leandro be with him? Excitement and curiosity edged in, and she didn't fight it. She could look, couldn't she? No harm in that.

It was easy enough to edge away from the crowd of people watching the fire and walk in that direction. Leandro leaned against the car in what Rose decided was a far too casual pose. The back door was open, but the inside remained a black hole.

Leandro smiled at her as she approached. The dancing flames from the fire cast shadows on that perfect face. She moved forward cautiously until she reached speaking distance.

"You wish to speak with the psychopath?" Leandro asked. "Esteban's dog?" His voice held subtle, secret laughter, as if he knew exactly what she wanted.

Rose swallowed. "Yes. I want to apologize. I was rude this morning. You frightened me, but bad manners are inexcusable."

"And you are no longer afraid?"

"I wouldn't go that far," Rose said. The urge to flee conflicted with an urge to move closer to him.

"You are wise," Leandro said. "Perhaps you should leave this city now. Disassociate yourself from criminals such as Esteban and myself."

"I'm not that wise." She wanted to stare, but if she gazed straight into those dark eyes, she might get lost—she would be lost.

Leandro eased closer, too close. He reached out and trailed a finger along her cheek.

She stepped back. "No."

"Then why did you come?" He was laughing at her again.

"I wanted to tell you . . ." She made another step back and the distance increased her control of the situation. "Those two clowns, Cochran and Bedlow, they seem like a mistake you wouldn't make. Bombs and bonfires, too. They attract too much attention." She nodded at the flames.

Leandro said nothing, but the glowing firelight caught in his eyes, and they narrowed a bit. Did he not know about Cochran and Bedlow?

"You lurking in there, Esteban?" Rose spoke into the pitch black of the car. Good. Spell broken and she was back in stride.

Esteban moved from the darkness of the Town Car's interior to the door, but he didn't step out. "My dear, I do not lurk. And I am not responsible for this," he said in a low voice. "I have millions of dollars invested here, and I would not jeopardize that much money, even for the extraordinary pleasure of irritating Ryan Vernon." He sounded logical and reasonable, and it would be easy to believe him, but she'd bet the man's lies were smooth as thin ice on a frozen lake.

Leandro shifted his weight, so slight a movement she almost missed it. Ryan marched toward them. He didn't appear happy.

"Step away, *mi dulce*," Leandro said.

Rose did, not because he told her to, but because she knew she'd hinder Ryan. To her surprise, Esteban climbed out of the car and took her place. "I will deal with this, Leandro."

Leandro's mouth tightened, but he said nothing.

Ryan stopped in front of Esteban, fists clenched. "You may be an evil bastard, Esteban, but you cannot be this stupid."

Esteban nodded. "I am more evil than you can imagine. And no, I did not order arson to complicate matters."

Ryan glanced at the fire, ebbing under the power of the Fire Department's relentless assault. He turned back to Esteban.

"What do you need to complete this project? Money?" Esteban asked. Ryan shook his head. "Time. I need more time."

Esteban gazed at the hotel, apparently contemplating how much or little he would offer. "Will eight months be sufficient?"

Ryan nodded. "It will—if there are no more accidents. Which there shouldn't be because I'm going to order twenty-four hour security—with cameras." He rubbed his forehead, as if attempting to keep a headache away. "The police are here now. You should leave so I don't have to explain how you're involved in my construction job."

Esteban smiled. "You are your father's son. Oh, I see you

are surprised. Yes, I knew him. When we were both young." He slid back into the car and Leandro followed.

Before he closed the door, Leandro smiled at Rose. "Another time, *mi dulce*." He probably intended it to piss off Ryan. From the expression on Ryan's face, it worked.

Chapter 12

At two a.m., Rose sat on the couch at Lola's house and listened to Ryan calling his Miami security firm, ordering surveillance cameras and personnel to guard the Jacksonville site. The endless questions from the police had left them all exhausted. They seemed to push the idea that Ryan had set the fires. Ryan patiently explained that little of monetary value had been lost in bomb or fire. She heard him raise his voice once. "I am not going to file an insurance claim over two fifteen-year-old trailers and a few piles of fucking materials."

O'Malley had arrived from his hotel to stand with Ryan, and eventually the cops left him alone. Ryan called Carl and told him about the fire, but insisted he stay home with Brianna.

Rose closed her eyes and remembered how long it had been since she slept. A few hours in the backseat of her car. Now she'd hit the wall of total exhaustion. She stood and swayed. Could she make it to the cottage? Where were her keys? She searched her pockets.

Lola laid a small hand on her arm. "Come on. You can lie down here. You don't need to go out there alone."

Lola led her to the bedroom where Rose sat on the bed and shucked off her boots. The boxes from Ryan's truck sat stacked in the corner where he'd placed them before they left for the job site that morning. Her things remained in her car. She wished she could go to the cottage where she could strip off her jeans, but Lola was right. She didn't need or want to be alone. The instant her head hit the pillow, she fell asleep.

When she woke, streams of sunlight poured through the

window. Ryan's big warm body lay against her back, his strong male arm around her. His calloused, long-fingered hand gently cupped her breast. He breathed deeply and rhythmically in her ear.

Rose sighed and he woke. She removed his arm and rolled over to face him, stretching out her body against his. He smiled at her, his eyes still heavy with sleep. Darkness lay under them, evidence of how exhausted he must be.

He wore only a pair of jeans so she let her fingers curl around the fine hairs on his chest. His heart beat increased under her fingers.

"We've got to stop meeting like this," she said.

"Like what? With clothes on?" He slipped his hand under her shirt and around her breast. His thumb rubbed a circle on the nipple, and all her nerve endings screamed for attention.

"Oh, shit," she said. "Don't do that unless you mean it."

"I'm dead serious, sweetheart, and—"

The door open and Carl walked in. "Come on, brother, O'Malley's here with news and . . . oops. Sorry, Rose."

"Get out." Ryan spoke, but there was no force in his words.

Carl frowned. "What? You're too tired to threaten me? Maybe you should rest a while longer."

"No." Ryan sat up and smiled at Rose. "Sorry."

"Don't worry. I know your intentions were good."

"Honey, my intentions are anything but good. My intentions involve . . ." He sighed. "No point in talking about it."

* * * *

Rose filled one of the mugs on the counter with Lola's strong black coffee and sat at the dining room table with the others. Ryan sat close beside her. Disturbingly close, close enough that his arm brushed hers and he could lay his hand on her thigh. She didn't know how much more she could stand before she dragged him into the bedroom, an uncomfortable feeling since she wasn't sure if it actually involved him or an overload of sexual tension running amok in her body.

No one spoke for a minute. Then O'Malley said, "I've contacted people. The Feds aren't focused on Florida.

Something is happening along the Canadian border with New York. But, as far as this is concerned, they're halfway looking at unions."

"What?" Ryan sounded astonished that anyone would suggest such a thing. "I've never had problems with unions."

"No," O'Malley agreed. "But I'm willing to let them go that way. It might give us time to straighten out this mess. Especially with Esteban involved. I'm worried about that. As for Rose's electrocution, they've run out of leads, and it's almost off their radar. They've pretty much written it off as a man resenting a woman working in a man's job, but the case isn't closed yet."

"Ah," Lola said. "Long live the male chauvinist pig."

The men chuckled.

Rose winced. "Not funny, guys. One of those oinkers tried to push me off a five-story building once. They also locked me in a basement for a weekend and welded my tool boxes shut."

Ryan sat up straight. "On one of my jobs?"

"No. Well, they did the toolboxes in Atlanta. I didn't want to fight. I let that one go."

In Mississippi, she'd surprised the would-be pusher, the man who wanted to kill her, and beaten him unconscious. The whole incident, his visible attempt and her battle to stay alive, was videotaped by security. They fired her—not the man.

Ryan shook his head. "I'm sorry, I'll—"

"No. Don't start. I can take care of myself. You're not Jimmy or my father."

"Which brings us to the crux of our problem," O'Malley said. "Jimmy. Carl, let's start with you."

Carl's fingers curled around the coffee cup sitting in front of him. He told O'Malley what he'd told her, Ryan and Lola about Jimmy's behavior. "The Solana Hotel deal went through all the channels, jumped the regulatory hoops, we made the low bid." Carl glanced at Ryan. "I'll remind you that I've done this before, done it right, and made the company money. Olivarez Corp's rep signed, and a few months later, someone pointed out that Esteban was the owner." He pushed his coffee away. "I could have called it quits right then, but I needed the money. If the deal went down, wound up in court, Olivarez would sue us, and I'd be in real trouble. I figured O'Malley's contract would hold. Olivarez is legitimate, regardless of who owns it."

"What went wrong?" O'Malley asked.

"Jimmy came to me about six months ago. He said he knew about the deal with Olivarez and Esteban. He said to keep my mouth shut, he was about to take care of old debts. There would be plenty of money for both of us. He was . . . acting strange. Like he was twenty-five and going to live forever. I thought . . ."

"What?" Ryan demanded.

"I thought it was Rose. He had a young girlfriend and—" Carl shook his head when Rose started to protest. "I saw him looking at you. You saw what you wanted to see. It wasn't a lover. I think he respected that."

Rose's eyes watered, and she wiped them with her hand. "I loved Jimmy, but—"

"Rose, this isn't your fault," Lola said. "I loved him too. When I watched him coming apart this last year, I let it happen, hoping it would get better."

"Did he specify how he planned to take care of these debts?" O'Malley asked. "What kind of debts? Or how they involved Esteban?"

"No, but in spite of what he said, I don't think they involved money," Carl said. "Jimmy never cared that much about money, anyway. At least not to spend it. It frightened me, though, so I paid Grift extra to hang around as a body guard."

"Jimmy was blackmailing Esteban?" Ryan asked. "With what?"

No one spoke.

Ryan sipped his coffee, silent for a few moments. "The problems aren't going to go away," he said. "Security should arrive this afternoon at the site. But that doesn't mean we won't be careful. Rose, since she's been a target, Lola, because someone might think she knows something. You too, Carl."

"Me?" Carl's eyes opened in surprise, causing him to lay his hand against the bandage. "I thought you'd fire me."

"No. I may kill you tomorrow, but I won't fire you today. Tell me, what do you plan to do with your inheritance?"

O'Malley chuckled. "Carl's taken care of. I'll pay the man in Vegas so he won't get his arms and legs broken, and Brianna and I will manage the rest. We'll give him an allowance."

Carl's mouth pursed, but he said nothing.

"Lola," Ryan said. "Talk to me about materials on the site. Or the lack of materials. We could have lost a lot more last night."

Lola rubbed the back of her neck and closed her eyes for a moment. Then she said, "Four months ago, Jimmy started leaving for three and four days at a time. Sometimes he'd drink himself into oblivion, but other times…he'd just disappear."

Rose frowned. She'd noticed that he'd been gone more than usual. The drinking? About the same, but she wasn't around him all the time.

Lola continued. "I was worried and ordered material on a need-to-use basis. Costs more that way, but at least we didn't lose much."

"Damn it all." Ryan shoved his chair back and stood. "And neither you, nor Carl, thought I might need to know about this?"

Only Carl met Ryan's eyes. "We kept waiting for him to go back to being our Jimmy, the one we knew."

Ryan returned to his seat. He'd obviously let go of his anger, or successfully suppressed it. Rose liked the practicality of a man who could focus on action and not the past. He was quite capable of emotion, she'd seen that, but he kept it in its place.

Ryan asked Rose to tell them all about Cochran and Bedlow. "I'll bet it didn't take much to buy those two," Rose said. "A couple of dog biscuits, maybe a ball to fetch. I only met Esteban yesterday morning, but I don't see *him* hiring such idiots." She didn't speak of Leandro and her suspicion that he hadn't known anything about Cochran and Bedlow. Ryan might ask her why she went over there in the first place, a question she couldn't answer.

"I can't see that either," Ryan said. "But until we discover another player in the game, we're going to assume it is him.

Jimmy was blackmailing him, and that's not something he would let go easily." He leaned back. "We're going to build a hotel for an incredibly immoral man, who will, if he can, cut all our throats. I've bargained with the devil for an extra eight months. I may lose a few million, but a lawsuit would cost more. I have more crews coming in. Lola, you set up a new office. Use one of the rooms in the hotel. Try to cut a deal on lodging for the incoming crews. As of today, we work two eight-hour shifts, six days a week.

"Carl, coordinate with Lola. Order and do a regular inventory of every single piece of material and equipment that comes onto the site. Organize the work crews and keep their shifts moving." He grinned at Rose. "Now, what should I give our new business partner to do?"

Rose frowned. "I suggest you tell her to go pull wires through a hotel."

Ryan threw his arm around her shoulder, dragged her to him, and kissed her.

Irritated by his smug surety, she pushed him away. "Now what the hell am I supposed to do? Giggle, sigh, and tell you how wonderful you are?"

"No . . ." He hesitated. "Would you do that?"

She gave him a level stare.

Wariness crossed his face. He shook his head.

Satisfied that she'd settled that issue, Rose said, "Then I think I'll go take a shower and go to the job site. Until O'Malley coughs up that hundred thousand and you and Lola make me rich, I have to work for a living."

"I'll get everybody's money as quickly as I can," O'Malley said. "Unless one of you heirs wants to contest?" He gazed around at them. "No? Good. Saves time. There is one other thing I learned from my source. The police won't tell you yet. This is difficult."

O'Malley leaned forward and a frown wrinkled his forehead. "Whatever Jimmy carried in that box, it wasn't a bomb. The bomb was under the hood, wired to the starter. Jimmy had loaned his truck to someone to go pick up materials, and there wasn't a company truck on site. He used yours, Rose, because it was convenient and he had a set of keys. That makes two attempts on your life in two days."

"I don't understand," Rose said. "Why would anyone want to kill me?"

O'Malley gave her a look of sympathy. "If Jimmy had something Esteban wanted, he might have tried to kill you as a warning. It would be a case of, 'see what I can do to people you love.' That would explain Jimmy's orders to fire you and get you away from the site. But remember, the thing that someone wants, the prize, is probably still out there. Jimmy, for all his bad judgment, wasn't stupid. It seems unwise, burning those trailers, but maybe it's a ruse to get us off guard. Now, we have to make one more decision. Do we wish to take everything we know, which isn't much, and turn it over to the police and let them do the investigation? That would be the logical thing to do."

Ryan straightened. "You want me to tell the police that I'm building a hotel for a gun running murderer with connections to every two-bit dictator in Central and South America? If we're voting on this, I say no."

"*We* haven't done anything illegal," Lola said. "The deal to build the hotel is legitimate, isn't it?"

"It is." O'Malley agreed.

Lola sounded frightened. And defensive. Rose wondered what she knew that made her wary of the police.

Carl offered his opinion. "Jimmy said he was ill. He probably made some serious errors in judgment."

O'Malley nodded. "Oh, yes, that's possible. He wasn't mentally unsound, at least when he changed his will, but I think he allowed emotions to cloud a reasonable thought process. Rose? What about you? You're now part of the business. You might want to consider running again, but give us your opinion first."

Rose gazed around at them. Did they always live on the edge of catastrophe? "I think it's a bad idea keeping things from the police. They're the professionals. I know they're overworked. Feds and locals, two jurisdictions. Cold, clear evidence is what they need. I'll go along with looking for evidence for a while, but I can't lie to the police—or anyone else. I get nervous and throw up."

Lola reached out and laid her hand over Rose's. "Jimmy loved you for your incredible sense of honesty."

Rose didn't have a choice on the honesty thing. Lying wasn't an option for her. It hadn't been since her lie as a young girl drew her mother into the path of a drunk driver. The thought, the mere suggestion of falsehood on her part drove her to physical illness.

O'Malley rose. He towered over them. "Decision made. No police. And I hope none of us will have to lie about anything. That said, you all realize that it will be incredibly difficult to stop in the middle and say, *oops, I made a mistake* and send for the uniforms. At least not without serious consequences."

Lola went to O'Malley and, as he had on that first day, he scooped her up like a child and hugged her. She clung to him as if his solid body mass would see her through anything. A look passed over his face, and Rose thought she had never seen such longing. O'Malley was in love with Lola.

"I'm going back to Miami," he said. "You have all my phone numbers. I'll let you know if I learn anything more. I'll be back for Jimmy's memorial."

"I'll walk you to your car," Lola said.

"Okay." He headed for the door with her still captured in his arms.

Lola laughed and whispered in his ear.

He suddenly stopped as if startled by what she said. "Really?"

Lola kissed him tenderly on the mouth, and he carried her on out.

"It's about time they got around to that," Ryan said. He squeezed Rose's shoulder. "Where's Brianna, Carl?"

"At my apartment. She's worried about the kids, but I can't get her to go home."

"You should take better care of her."

Carl hung his head. "I know."

Rose stood.

"Where are you going?" Ryan asked. A bit of fear tinged his voice.

"To my little cottage. I need to take a shower and get into clean clothes."

"Want me to come and wash your back?"

Rose caressed his cheek. Oh, she wanted that. Wanted his hands on her, wet and soapy, gliding down her body. "Well, you could—"

Ryan's cell phone rang. He sighed and flipped it open. "It's Sam. I better see what he wants." He winced and smiled at her. "Be there in a bit."

"Yeah, yeah. See you later." She'd have to get used to that if she wanted to be with him. He owned a big company and that could be a 24/7 job. She left him and headed out Lola's back door and to her cottage.

Dodging Brutus's business cards was much easier in daylight. She opened the back door and walked in. A nice place. Clean and quiet. Ryan could stay with her, and she'd be comfortable. She thought he would, too, at least for a time while they sorted things out. While he spoke of making and losing millions, he wasn't a pretentious man who needed luxury around him all the time. Even his truck, while splendid, was not the best money could buy. Twenty percent of Vernon Construction? A nice gift, but owning it . . .? How would she escape if she needed to run? She'd never in her life owned more than she could carry with her from place to place. Jimmy had thrust her into a new world.

The back door of the cottage opened onto the alley, and through the window, she could see her red Taurus parked close against the house. Lola had aired the place out, and the smell of fresh flowers greeted her when she had opened the door. Herman's long dachshund body graced the slightly scarred wooden coffee table in front of the couch. She needed to retrieve her remaining possessions from her old apartment.

Rose discovered soap, shampoo, and a couple of towels in the bathroom, again courtesy of Lola. Lola had provided for her with the same precision she used to run the business.

"Lord, let there be hot water," she said as she twisted the

shower knob. Ah, an answered prayer. She made her shower quick, not knowing how long the warmth would last. The bed called her, tempted her, but she had other things to do.

The decision to avoid the police made her uneasy, but Ryan and the others seemed confident in their own ability to deal with the situation, which made her wonder about how they had operated in the past.

"Damned hotel," she muttered as she laced up her boots. She sighed. With clean underwear, a denim shirt, jeans and socks, she could face the day. Her cell phone gave a quick double beep. The battery . . . oh, shit. She'd left her house charger at the old apartment. At least she had one in her car.

The sun hit her in a warm, pleasant wave when she walked outside into the alley. January, almost February, and the nice weather held. By June, she'd probably wish she had a job somewhere far to the north. If she stayed with Ryan—and he stayed at the hotel—she'd spend a whole summer in the Sunshine State. She grinned. Lord, let the man be worth it.

The alley, a narrow semi-paved lane, cut through the block. Masses of vegetation grew along a patchwork of ragged wood and wire fences, and clumps of weeds, protected from the mild winter by the pavement and closeness of other vegetation, sprouted in potholes.

Rose opened the car door, sat in the driver's seat, dug out the cord, and plugged the cell phone into the charger. She flipped it open. There was a message. From Jimmy. It had come at 2:36 p.m. on Tuesday afternoon, an hour before he died. She swallowed and rubbed the bridge of her nose, keeping her eyes closed tight, drawing the image of his face to mind. She punched the buttons and held the phone to her ear.

"Rose, honey, you listen real good." Jimmy choked, then cleared his throat. "I've done something stupid, and I'm going to try to fix it. Don't know if I'll make it, but . . . never mind. Two things are important, baby. The first is Herman. You take care of his little ass."

He stopped talking, and she could hear his labored breathing. "I . . . oh, damn. I love you. I never minded getting older, until I met you. Now I hate it. I hate playing your father when I want to . . . shit! I'm screwing it up again." He drew a sobbing breath. "That's it, Rose. Remember me. Remember I love you."

The message ended. She stared at the phone. *I love you.* He'd never said those words to her face. Had she simply not paid enough attention to him? Now, too late, she remembered the times he hugged her just a little too hard, the times he looked away suddenly so she didn't see his eyes. She leaned forward and rested her forehead on the steering wheel. She loved him, but she couldn't have desired him the way she did Ryan.

Rose climbed out of the car, closed and locked the door.

She turned and came face to face with Cochran and Bedlow.

A single moment of cold-sweat panic raced through her, then she locked it down. Action was required here, not fear. She had done this before.

"Hey, guys," she said with a bright smile. "Been to any good fires lately?" Cochran was the closest. She made a fist and slammed him in the gut as hard as she could. The fist sank deeper than she expected. Cochran gasped and staggered back. She spun away and ran.

Bedlow tackled her.

She slammed to the ground with brutal force. She managed to keep her face from the asphalt, but one elbow took most of her weight in an agonizing blow. Arms circled her and Cochran's hand slapped across her mouth. Gagging, she sank her teeth into a fat finger and tasted blood. Cochran gave a sharp cry and jerked the hand away.

"Fire! Fire!" she screamed, knowing that people didn't always respond to a cry for help. Bedlow hovered over her, struggling to keep her pinned down. She drew her fist back and punched him square in the face. She couldn't get much advantage, but she felt the satisfaction of busting his lips against his teeth. Teeth that cut into her knuckles. She screamed again. Could anyone hear her?

Cochran had recovered. The fat man ignored his bloody finger, and grabbed her by the hair and one arm. He dragged her back and she couldn't get to her feet.

Bedlow struggled to stand, holding his hand against his face while red liquid dripped between his fingers. Good, she'd marked both of them.

Her feet were free. She drew her leg back and slammed her boot into Bedlow's knee. A direct hit. He howled, staggered back, and landed on his ass.

A windowless delivery van rolled up beside them and stopped. She heard the driver climb out and Cochran shouted, "Help me, damn it!"

Cochran still had her arm and her hair. She twisted her body around desperately trying to catch hold of his balls. She could crush those babies.

A man, probably the van's driver, grabbed her free hand. It was over.

They rolled her over on her stomach, and the driver pinned her down. She managed to keep her face off the asphalt, but pain seared her shoulders as they twisted her arms and secured her wrists with thin plastic.

Bedlow was on his feet, limping, but moving toward her. "Bitch!" he snarled. His foot slammed into her ribs. Had he not been injured, he would probably have killed her. She tried to scream again, but pain reduced it to pathetic squeak. Cochran slapped a piece of duct tape over her mouth.

They dragged her to her feet. The van's back doors gaped open. Cochran and the driver picked her up and threw her in. Tossed her like garbage into an empty metal box. Only it wasn't completely empty. She landed hard. A blinding shock of pain hit her like a nail driven into her skull. It eased, though, as she fell into darkness. She barely heard them close the van doors.

Chapter 13

Ryan heard her scream the minute he stepped out Lola's back door. He'd taken a few minutes to shower and shave and now cursed himself for not going to her sooner. He raced across the yard toward her cottage, but the cries came from the other side. He ran around, only to come upon a four-foot high chain link fence. Not a problem, he'd scaled many of those, some much higher.

Her cries stopped.

He ran straight at the fence, caught the top bar in his hands and vaulted over. A bush on the other side caught his boot as he landed, and he crashed to the ground. He rolled back to his feet and fought his way through more bushes.

When he emerged, he saw two men climbing in a car. Cochran and Bedlow—Rose's description fit. A white utility van sped out of the alley, and the car carrying Cochran and Bedlow headed in the other direction. He couldn't catch either.

An enormous black Escalade raced down the alley, forced Cochran and Bedlow's car aside, and rammed it through a fence. The Escalade rolled up beside Ryan.

"Get in," Leandro said through the open window. "We'll get her."

Ryan knew Rose would be long gone before he could get his truck or even call the police. He didn't have a tag number, and there were probably thousands of white vans in Jacksonville. He threw open the passenger door and jumped in. Leandro had the Escalade rolling before he closed the door. Leandro wanted Rose; a situation Ryan had become painfully aware of last night. *Mi dulce*, he'd called her.

"You were watching her," Ryan said as he snapped his seat belt.

Leandro whipped the Escalade around a corner. The white van sat half a block ahead of them at a light.

Leandro smiled. "She's the key to this mystery, don't you think? Otherwise, why would someone try to kill her? Or, perhaps I simply enjoy watching her."

Ryan shifted in his seat, staring intently forward at the van. What mystery? Didn't Leandro know what Esteban knew? Could there be a schism between the two men? Esteban suddenly didn't trust his own man enough to tell him about being blackmailed?

"Can you catch him?" Ryan asked. "I want her out of there."

"Not yet. If she's alive, which I assume she is, she will be safe until he reaches his destination. If she's dead, there is no hurry. We need to capture the driver and take him to a place where he can provide us with more information. Then we will take the appropriate action."

Leandro's calm logic matched his uncompromising single-minded pursuit. If Ryan had his cell phone with him, he would forget the family agreement not to involve the police. But if he did that, Leandro would probably kick him out and drive away. Then he'd never find Rose.

Still alive? Probably. Somebody wanted something, something they sent Cochran and Bedlow to retrieve. They thought Rose knew where it was and would keep her alive—for a while.

The van left Lola's subdivision and drove onto Beach Boulevard. They followed it to A1A and into heavy traffic. Two cars separated the vehicles. The van driver obeyed the speed limit and didn't seem to be in a hurry. It passed through a yellow light and the cars between them slowed to a stop.

Leandro cut to the right onto the grass, passed them and, without hesitation, ran the red. With superb agility, accompanied by the screech of tires, he cut across four lanes of moving traffic that had already entered the intersection.

Leandro held the wheel with confidence, and his eyes never left the road except for an occasional glimpse in the mirror.

It surprised Ryan to hear him speak.

"She's yours, then," Leandro asked, "this exceptional woman with cat's eyes."

"I don't own her." Ryan crossed his arms and kept his eyes on the van.

"And if I ask her to go with me?" He glanced at Ryan. He appeared amused and sounded patronizing. "If she says yes?"

"I'd say she had poor taste in men." Ryan tried to force indifference into his voice.

"You would be correct." Amusement again.

"She won't go with you, Leandro. She's stronger than that." Ryan hoped his voice didn't carry the apprehension roiling in him like a great storm. The idea of her with this abhorrent man sickened him.

"You're right," Leandro said. "She is very strong. I suppose I'll have to seduce her." He ran another light, again accompanied by a symphony of tires on asphalt.

Ryan said nothing. He knew Leandro was deliberately antagonizing him. Leandro apparently didn't consider him worthy of caution. Ryan had never killed a man, but he wanted to kill Leandro and make the world a cleaner place.

Leandro laughed softly. "Now, you are thinking murderous thoughts. You should learn to guard yourself better. Of course, an honest man such as yourself has no reason to hide his emotions."

Ryan still said nothing. He'd deal with the condescending bastard later. He tensed at every light, but Leandro managed to keep close as the traffic eased. The van turned right onto County Road 210. They followed, but it didn't pick up speed. The land gradually morphed from subdivisions to open pasture and lowlands. They rolled on a couple more miles, then turned right again, heading back north on a narrow, unmarked paved road.

"We have to stop him now," Leandro said. He leaned forward, his eyes narrow and intent. "He's going to Bayliss."

"What's Bayliss?"

"A . . . gathering of people. A place where common

criminals, mostly transients, live in tents and trailers."

"Common criminals. As opposed to sophisticated criminals living in mansions in Miami?"

"Certainly. These are lower animals." Leandro chuckled. "No discretion, no finesse. Of course, they are numerous and well-armed lower animals."

The van's driver gave no indication that he knew they followed him. Leandro drove up behind it, waited until there was a clear stretch of road, and pulled out as if to pass. The van obliged him by slowing down to let him by.

Leandro moved slightly ahead. He eased the Escalade to the right. With a slight scrape of metal, a gentle collision, he nudged the van off the road and into a shallow ditch. It moved forward a few feet, as if the driver planned to roll back onto the road. Leandro quickly pulled the Escalade over and stopped, blocking its path.

"Get out with me," Leandro said as he shut off the engine. "Keep your hands in sight and see if you can soothe the driver I so callously ran off the road. We have to get him out of the van."

Ryan popped his seat belt and opened the door. Part of him wanted to balk at Leandro's commands, but the more rational part said that Leandro was a master of the deception required here. Ryan's style usually involved a head-on, bare-fisted brawl.

Leandro met him at the back of the Escalade. They approached the van and the driver studied them through the open window. A solid panel separated the driver from the van's cargo area.

The driver appeared distracted, but not injured. He had a puffy, florid face and a two-day beard stubble. As Ryan approached, a soft breeze brought the rancid odor of an unwashed body.

Ryan tried to sound concerned. "Are you hurt?" he asked. "Oh, God. We're so sorry."

"I'm fine," the driver said. He frowned but spoke without belligerence. "Just need to get back on the road. Got a package to deliver."

"We need to give you a ride, buddy." Ryan nodded at the back of the van. "I don't think you're going anywhere on that wheel." The wheel was fine, but Ryan would bet the driver didn't know it.

Leandro had eased closer to the vehicle, but kept a distance from Ryan. The driver could focus his attention only on one of them, and he probably would focus on the larger man.

The driver opened the van door and stepped out. He carried a pistol.

Leandro moved incredibly fast. He'd anticipated violence. With one smooth motion, Leandro grabbed the driver's gun wrist and wrenched his arm behind his back.

Reflex—the driver jerked the trigger. The small caliber pistol gave a loud pop, and a clump of dirt jumped where the bullet cut into it. Though the driver was a far bigger man, Leandro drove him to his knees and silenced him with a brutal fist to his head. The driver collapsed and lay unconscious, face down on the ground.

Leandro held the pistol.

Ryan didn't wait to see what happened next. He raced to the back of the van and jerked the doors open. The stink of oil and gas hit his nose. He gasped. Had Rose suffocated in that dark prison?

She lay on her side. Blood sheeted down her face and neck. Ryan jumped in beside her. The bastards had twisted her arms behind her back and secured them with a plastic tie. Thank God he'd stuffed his knife back in his pocket when he'd dressed. They'd bound her now swollen wrists too tightly. With the utmost care, he slid the knife blade between the tie and her skin. She moaned.

"You'll be fine, honey." Ryan spoke with a conviction he didn't feel.

He held her arms so they wouldn't jerk when he freed them, then cut the tie. He raised her and cradled her in his arms. "Rose, oh honey, I'm sorry." He'd been busy, talking business over the phone, when he should have been with her. He carefully peeled the tape from her mouth.

Rose choked and licked her lips. She clung to him with bloated hands. Pain roiled in her eyes. He lifted her and eased her to the back of the van. Careful, awkward movements, but he couldn't stand it if he hurt her more. He sat her on the edge with her feet on the ground.

She drew deep breaths as she hunched over, arms across her breasts. Her swollen fingers hooked into claws. "I'll kill them," she said. Her voice broke.

"Don't trouble yourself, *mi dulce*." Leandro appeared. "I'll take care of that for you—eventually." He spoke casually, as if telling her he'd open a window or mail a letter.

Ryan fought jealousy when her gaze softened and she gave Leandro a faint smile.

Leandro handed Ryan the Escalade's keys. "Take her to the hospital. Please find a plausible story for what happened, or we may never find those who did this. I'll be along later."

Ryan accepted the keys. Rose was his first concern at that point, and he'd deal with the outcome of what Leandro would do to the driver later.

When he lifted Rose to her feet, she staggered and clung to him, barely able to walk. He held her tight and supported her. It agonized him to see her hurt and docile. That wasn't his Rose.

The van's driver was nowhere in sight, but Leandro had come from the opposite side of the van. He'd probably dragged the man back there, out of sight from the road.

Ryan opened the Escalade's passenger door, lifted her, then gently secured her seat belt. "God, Rose, you've worked for us and you've had nothing but hurt for it." His fingers brushed her cheek.

She wrapped her arm around him and pressed her bloody face against his. "But what if I'd never met you?"

"You might have had a more peaceful life."

"I don't want peaceful. I want you."

Ryan decided he didn't care what Leandro did to the driver.

The van's rear doors slammed. Leandro climbed behind the wheel and started the engine. The back wheels spun on the soft dirt, spit a few black clods into the air, but then the tires caught and he drove away. Ryan turned the Escalade around and headed back toward Jacksonville and the hospital.

Chapter 14

"Norris, Michelle Roseanne." The perky young man in blue scrubs who had wheeled her to the scan room on that eventful Monday morning shoved the curtains aside. Still intolerably energetic, he tossed his clipboard on Rose's emergency room bed. "Honey, we have *got* to stop meeting like this."

Painful as it was, Rose lifted her head to speak. "I took your suggestion seriously about getting run over by a dump truck."

"I can tell. Well, let's go check out the damage." He began unhooking her from the monitors. Ryan hovered close, his face taut with concern. It brought an aching memory of Jimmy doing the same.

"Did you call and ask Lola to bring me some clean clothes?" she asked. She wanted out of there. A hospital twice in one week was more than she could take.

"I called her," he said.

The doctors and nurses in the emergency room had questioned her after they separated her from Ryan. Had he hurt her? Should they call the police? She reassured them that she had fallen. The lie made her gag and shiver, but given her condition, it seemed very realistic. That didn't explain the swollen hands and abraded wrists, but she kept a *mind your own business* attitude, and eventually they walked away shaking their heads at her stupidity.

* * * *

Four hours later, Rose sat on the side of the emergency room bed, dressed in her underwear and a hospital gown. White curtains shielded her from the rest of the Emergency

Room sick and wounded.

Uncertain of her injuries, they'd cut her shirt off. Lola was supposed to bring her another one. What a mess. The laceration on her head had bled like a bitch. The doctor had numbed it, trimmed away a little hair, and closed it with multiple stitches. A two-inch puncture on her shoulder required more attention. It didn't hurt because they'd numbed it too. The pain would come later. One of the nurses made her swallow pain pills and promised her drugs to take home with her. Percocet or any other morphine derivative usually sent her off on a frightful, out of control high, but this time she welcomed the soothing fog.

Her jeans and socks lay on the bed beside her, and her boots on the floor. Ryan had gone to deal with the paperwork for her release.

She picked up her jeans, and they slid through her fingers like liquid and landed on the floor. When did denim get that soft? She studied the blue cloth puddle under her feet. Well, they looked fine down there, didn't they? Her mouth split in a goofy grin as her brain succumbed to drugged euphoria.

Rose glanced up at the sound of a low chuckle.

Leandro stood watching her.

Now there was a fine sight, with his expensive, sophisticated black suit and enticing movie star face. He cocked his head and gave her a seductive smile. It should be against the law for a man to be so desirable, to look so much like an amorous young god.

"Hello." Rose gave a lethargic wave. "I'm drugged and not responsible for what I drop. Or say. Or do."

Leandro walked in and stood in front of her. "I promise not to take advantage of you, *mi dulce*."

"Hah! So said the lion to the lamb." She cocked her head, entranced by his presence. "Your name means lion. One name. Do you have another one?"

"One name is enough." He brushed her hair from her face and kissed her forehead. She leaned into that kiss.

Rose sighed. "Oh, I'll bet that one name strikes terror in the hearts of many."

"Are you still afraid?" He laid a finger on her cheek.

"Yes."

"Afraid of me? Or yourself? Of what you might do?"

"All of the above." Rose placed her hand on his chest and rubbed it across the fine white fabric. She liked touching him. She could see dark passion flame in his eyes. Could she rise to that level of desire?

Rose studied his face. A thin, almost invisible scar skimmed the corner of his mouth. Leandro the lion wasn't perfect after all. She touched the scar with her finger and moved on to trace his lower lip. He drew a quick breath and shuddered.

He suddenly broke contact and knelt in front of her. He picked up her jeans. With the greatest of care, he lifted each foot and slipped it through the legs. Then he stood, placed his arm around her waist, and helped her stand.

The closeness, the power of the man, slim and tight, all muscle and bone, set her trembling. She leaned against him for support. Wallowing in drug-induced pleasure, she fought a fierce urge to wrap her arms around him and lay her cheek against his. She could do that. He wasn't as tall as Ryan. He smelled faintly of fine cologne, not sweet or sultry, but clean as air after a rain.

Leandro carefully drew her jeans up to her waist, then zipped and buttoned them. His breath brushed her cheek in a warm caress as he lifted her back to her seat on the bed. With the same graceful care, he knelt again and slipped her socks on, caressing her feet as he did. It sent delicious sensations racing up her legs. She bit her lip when he stopped to slide on her boots. When he finished, he rose again to face her. Close, much too close. Where was Ryan? Why didn't he come and save her?

"Why were you following me?" Rose asked.

"You are part of the mystery."

"Oh." She prayed he hadn't sensed the disappointment that spiked in her. Had she wanted him to be there for some other reason?

"Someone tried to kill me," she said. "Twice."

"I did not." Danger slipped into his voice.

Rose studied his eyes. They had none of the killer cold she'd seen in them when she met him, but she'd bet the killer hadn't gone away. "You're a professional, Leandro. If you wanted to kill me, I'd be dead."

Leandro's lips brushed hers, gentle as a feather. "But I want to please you, not harm you."

"No. I can't." Her denial carried the soft caress of a summer breeze. It said no, but she heard yes in her voice. He probably heard it, too.

"Tell me why." He sounded thoughtful.

Rose told him the truth. "You are such a beautiful man. You're like fine chocolate. Smooth as silk. If I get a taste, I'll want more . . . and more. I don't want anything, or anyone, to own me like that."

"Surely you allow yourself small amusements on occasion."

A bit of clarity seeped into her mind. "You are *not* a small amusement."

Ryan parted the curtains and walked into the room. He gave Leandro the Escalade keys. "Lola is coming to pick us up. Did you . . . ?"

Rose wondered what he was going to ask. Did you kill someone, Leandro? She started to speak, but then the need faded and drifted away.

Leandro shook his head. "The driver was hired to take her to Bayliss. Someone with money, but no name, was to meet him there. You saw the two who kidnapped her?"

"Yeah. Their names are Cochran and Bedlow. They tried something like this before." Ryan pitched his voice lower. "The van driver. I . . ."

Leandro smiled and the psychopath rose in him. Gone was the beautiful seductive man who helped her dress, the one she had compared to fine candy. "The driver is not a . . . problem. I shall find this Cochran and Bedlow and discuss the matter directly with them. Do not trouble yourself. Nothing I do will touch you." He glanced at Rose and the psychopath faded. "Or you, *mi dulce*." He released her hand. She hadn't noticed that he held it. "Rest," he said. "You have a hotel to help your lover build." He parted the curtains and left the cloth walled room.

Ryan moved close to her. "You don't have to stay with me. If you want to go . . ."

"I want you, Ryan. I'm sorry I'm so weak."

"You're drugged. That's why drugs are bad. They ease the pain, but leave you a little short on logic." Ryan drew her into his arms, and she clung to him.

Drugged into personal weakness? A good excuse. Rose wanted to be with him, not Leandro. Leandro was exquisite, but he wasn't for her. Leandro lived a complex life, and if she went with him, she'd be lost in a maze, a maze where she'd soon lose her way.

"I was so scared when they grabbed me," she said, remembering what happened. "I fought, but it wasn't enough."

Ryan lifted her swollen hands and kissed them. "Rose, I swear, you may have to fight again, but you won't do it alone."

Rose smiled at him. "We talked about that, remember? You trying to take care of me. While I was packing my suitcase. But I'm glad you were there this time."

Ryan nodded, straight-faced and grim. Then he grinned, that same alluring grin that drew her into his arms that first day. "If he's fine chocolate, what am I? Meat and potatoes?"

"You were spying on me." She gave him a light punch on the shoulder. "See, that's it. I know exactly what he is. You're a lot harder to figure out. One minute you're the strong silent cowboy with a gun in your pocket, the next you're holding me, telling me you'll give up your whole life and leave with me if I want to go. You bully your older brother, take charge, manage things, the boss man, you . . ." She forgot what she was going to say. Damned drugs.

"What I am," Ryan said, "is frustrated."

Rose knew everything would be fine. Leandro was gone. No more temptation. Ryan wanted her and she wanted him. She would make it work.

Lola arrived, bringing the promised shirt so Rose didn't have to wear the hospital gown home. The nurses made her take another pain pill. Oh, that was dandy. It sent her soaring again. She demanded a kiss from Ryan as he strapped her into the backseat of Lola's car. Fearful events forgotten, she smiled and hummed quietly to herself. Occasionally, she waved at other cars. People waved back, especially kids. She liked kids. Liked the way they were always fresh and full of questions. Deep inside she knew she was making a fool of herself, but she didn't care. Her mind cleared and she heard Lola and Ryan talking.

"Are you sure?" Lola asked.

"Yes." Ryan sounded exasperated. "I'm not going to leave her alone again."

"But she might not want you to move in with her yet."

"Are you talking about me?" Rose asked. It troubled her that she kept fading in and out of reality.

"No, honey," Lola said. "You concentrate on people in the other cars and wave at them."

"Okay." Rose giggled. How silly—but how completely appropriate. Ryan's next words cut through the fog and found a pocket of clarity.

"I don't think I could bear it if I lost her," he said. "It's insane, I know."

Rose ceased her waving. She didn't think she could bear it if she lost him either.

"Ryan," she said.

He turned back to face her. "Yes, Rose."

"I think I'm insane, too."

"Oh, good." He reached back and patted her knee. "Maybe they'll let us share a padded room."

Chapter 15

Ryan had watched Rose's alertness level drift up and down like a rising and falling wave. She'd smile, but she'd stopped waving at passing cars. A few logical words tumbled from her mouth now and then—wildly out of context, but logical. He kept an eye on her to be sure she didn't slide out of her seatbelt and fall over.

"What could Jimmy have had that was worth so many lives?" Lola asked.

"I don't know. I never had to think of him in those terms." Ryan hadn't thought much about Jimmy the last few hours. Some part of him didn't really want to blame the man for all their troubles. "I despise Esteban. He's brought me nothing but trouble and grief. He never did anything to make me feel the need to go out of my way for vengeance. I wouldn't mind seeing him behind bars, but blackmail, murder? That's not my way." He let thoughts and memories stew in his mind. "Esteban said he knew my father. Did something happen back then? With Daddy or Jimmy?"

"Not that I'm aware of," Lola said. "But they would have kept things like that from me. They had secrets, those two."

When they arrived at Lola's, he had her drive around to the alley behind Rose's cottage. That way, he wouldn't have to explain things to Annie, the wacky landlady. At least not until later when he'd talked Rose into marrying him and could call himself her fiancé for real.

The back door was still unlocked where Rose had walked out to her car and been dragged away. Ryan clamped his teeth at the memory, then relaxed when the tooth Carl knocked loose bit back. He'd only had one glimpse of those bastards Cochran and Bedlow, but he wanted them, bad. His mind formed malevolent images of breaking bones. He wanted to beat them until they were bloodier than Rose was when he found her in that van.

"Come on, sweetheart." Ryan gently grasped her arms and helped her out of the car.

"Don't," she said. She swayed, a long stemmed flower in the wind, then leaned against him.

"I have to." He held her close. "You can't walk alone."

"No." She slapped her hand against him, but weakness made it a caress. "Don't call me sweetheart. Jimmy calls . . . called . . . me . . . sometimes." She sounded so poignant, so heartbroken. They shouldn't have given her that extra pain pill.

"What shall I call you?" Ryan guided her toward the cottage door. "Let's see, how about babe? Or sugar? Maybe darling or honey bunch. You can be my main squeeze. My turtledove. And I can be a determined suitor, your Casanova."

Rose groaned. He felt her silent laughter as he led her inside and sat her on the couch. He held her straight. "Don't go anywhere, my lady love. And don't fall on the floor."

"Do you need anything?" Lola asked. "I'll go to the store."

"Bandages, antiseptic soap, antibiotic cream. Food, in case she's hungry later. And bring my gun. It's in the console of the truck. Loaded. Be careful."

"I'll take care of it. Now don't blame me if she gets pissed."

"Why would I get pissed?" Rose asked.

Lola laughed. "He might take advantage of your drugged state and make passionate love to you."

"Oh." Rose giggled. "Wicked, wicked man. Wouldn't want that to happen."

Lola left with a smile on her face.

Ryan sat beside Rose.

"Help me up," she demanded. "I have blood and guck in my hair. Gotta wash it."

"Rose, you have a two-inch gash on your head. You don't want to get it wet."

She frowned and tentatively touched her scalp. Her fingers found the bandage. Her face formed a petulant pout. "I forgot. Can I put a plastic bag over it?"

"The bandage, no. Your head, yes. But I wouldn't advise it."

Tears formed in her eyes. God, now what did he do?

"I'm dirty." She grabbed a strand of hair and waved it at him.

"Let me work on that."

A quick trip to the bathroom and he had shampoo and towels. When he went back to her, he found her staring at the wall, smiling, her bloody hair crisis apparently forgotten. She'd remember soon enough, though.

"Come on." He led her into the kitchen and lifted her to sit on the table. "Lie back. I'll hold you."

"Okay, but I'd rather do it on the bed." She gave him a sappy smile. "I've still got my clothes on, too."

"I'll take care of that problem later." Oh, God, how could he not love her?

He laid her head at the table's edge and rolled a towel to cushion her neck. The only thing he found for water was a large pot. He filled it with warm water and placed it on a chair. He could mop the floor later.

With the utmost care, he wet her hair, gently drawing his fingers through the fine threads. Using a folded washcloth, he carefully worked a drop of shampoo around the bandage, soaking and cleaning the strands caked with blood.

Angelic and alluring, she kept her eyes closed as he worked. He spoke to her occasionally, and she smiled.

Ryan hated himself. He'd failed her. She'd come crashing into his life like fantastic fireworks, so desirable, and he'd let her get hurt. She'd made her rules for their relationship, though, and he'd agreed. He couldn't protect her the way he wanted. He couldn't keep her safe and . . . a prisoner.

He changed the rinse water twice, dumping the bloody remains down the sink. When he finished, he used a towel and rubbed her hair dry. She kept her eyes closed until he lifted her and helped her sit up.

"Aren't you going to take my clothes off and wash the rest of me?" Her face carried a dreamer's expression. "Cleanliness is next to godless . . . ness." She sounded baffled. "I think." She held out one foot. "Leandro put my socks on and tied my boots for me. My jeans, too."

Leandro again. Damn him.

Ryan lifted her and helped her stand. "If I get you naked, I'll do terrible things to you. Maybe you should take a nap, and we can talk about it later." He held her and led her toward the bedroom.

"Ryan, what does Leandro want?" She sounded so earnest.

"He wants to seduce you." He had to ask the question, no matter how much the answer hurt. "What do you want from him, Rose?"

"He's pretty." She frowned. "I like to look at him. I like the way he talks. Smooth like cream and honey. I don't want to be naked with him. No. No. That's too scary."

Rose's eyes suddenly became clear and sharp. "I want you, Ryan. Need you. I'm not strong. I get scared. I have to be tough. Construction. Be one of the guys. Sometimes I can't do it."

"Rose, I *am* one of the guys, and sometimes I can't do it either. Maybe that's what we need, you and I. To remember that we're human. No one is perfect."

Rose frowned. "You're too good for me. Big, rich boss man."

She sagged in his arms. Her chin tilted up. Asleep. Good. He laid her across her bed, a bed far too short and narrow for a big man and a long, lean woman. He'd buy a bigger one as soon as he could get out.

Spots of blood dotted her jeans. She couldn't be comfortable. He removed her boots and socks, and with the greatest of care, unzipped the jeans, slid them over her hips, and pulled them off. She didn't wake. He wanted to touch her. Tempting, but he stepped away. He had more respect for her than that. He covered her with a blanket he found in the closet.

After he checked the window lock, he returned to the kitchen to clean up. Not long after he finished, a small tap came at the door. Lola had returned. She had also brought his truck and parked it beside Rose's Taurus.

"I'm moving you out, buddy," she announced as she walked in the door. "Your stuff from the house is on the seat."

"But you were concerned about my crowding her." He accepted the keys she offered him.

"Thought about it. Changed my mind. You can always sleep on her couch." Lola dug in a plastic drugstore bag she carried. "Here." She set a large box of condoms on the table. "Just in case. She hasn't had a boyfriend since she's been in Jacksonville, so I doubt she's protected. Now that you have the important stuff, I'll go buy your groceries."

Chapter 16

Rose woke, her body aching, but part of the narcotic fog had burned away. The memory, ah, yes. Kidnapped, rescued, Leandro kissed her, helped her dress, and she behaved like a shameless slut. Ryan's gentle words, lying on her back while he had tenderly washed the blood from her hair.

Her body? She drew deep breaths and started with her fingers, moving them, then her wrists. Not too bad, so she kept going.

Cataloging her pain, arm with puncture wound, sore when moved; head with stitches, no pain there; ribs, tender and sore. Jeans? Missing. She ran her hand down the ribs Bedlow had kicked. She'd see him again, oh yes, and she'd be ready for him. Bladder, major discomfort. Could she make it to the bathroom? She oriented herself by the dim light from the other room.

Ryan was probably asleep on the couch. She didn't think he'd leave her in the cottage alone. Bracing herself on her arms, she sat up. She swayed, but then things righted. She tossed off the cover. Well, at least she had the on shirt Lola brought and her underwear. She gingerly swung her legs over the side of the bed—and planted them on a body.

She jerked back. "Ryan?" She called for him, panic in her voice.

"I'm here," he said from the floor. He sat up.

"You were sleeping on the floor?"

He grinned at her. "I wasn't going to leave you alone. Bed's too small. I didn't want to wake you."

"Oh."

He sat there on the floor, such a big, wonderful man. She wanted him, wanted to make love to him, and yes, wanted to love him. And she would love him. She kept reassuring herself on that one.

He helped her stand and walk to the bathroom, but she pushed him out while she relieved her straining bladder.

When she emerged, he was sitting on the bed, smiling at her. He'd turned on the lamp. It gave the room a warm glow, pushing darkness away and leaving them in an island of light. His gun lay on the nightstand within easy reach.

Rose sat beside him.

"How do you feel?" he asked.

"Sore." She leaned toward him. "Would you kiss me?"

Ryan caught her chin in his hand and laid his lips on hers, gently, pulling at them. He groaned softly. "I know you're hurt, but I want you so much."

"Maybe if we take it easy." Warmth spread through her. Using his substantial shoulder for balance, she stood and stepped in front of him. She fumbled at the buttons of her shirt, but she managed and it slipped off her shoulders.

Ryan groaned, and his fingers touched the massive bruise on her ribs. He caught her panties and slid them down.

He stood and jerked his tee shirt over his head. She kissed his chest, feeling his heart beat under her lips.

Rose watched as he removed his jeans. Such an attractive man, big and powerful, he seemed indestructible. She felt greedy and brazen as she rubbed her body against his. Hot, so hot. A fine sheen of sweat formed over her skin. She forgot her injuries as other sensations took over.

He lay on the bed, drawing her on top of him. She wasn't a small woman, but she was hurt. How compassionate. His skin was warm and alive against hers, and his breath ragged in her ear. Then she spread her legs and moved her body up to straddle him. Her nervous system jolted with raw sensation as she let him slide into her. Ryan Vernon was big all over.

He seemed determined to wait for her, but she smiled and tightened her muscles. The vibrant link forged between them on that first day struck a powerful note. He lost the battle as his body jerked and he clamped his hands on her thighs.

"Good," she said, after his breathing slowed. "Now it's my turn." She glanced at the clock. "Three-thirty. Three hours before I have to go to work. But I can call in sick. The boss will never know."

"True." His voice was rough and deep. "But let's not tell anyone we forgot the condom."

"Oops, you're such a bad boy. Now I'll have to go get a morning-after pill." Damn, damn; it had been so long, she'd forgotten. "You owe me big time, buddy."

"And how can I pay you?" He cupped her breasts, his fingers teasing her nipples.

She shivered in wanton delight. "Oh, I figure a couple of shrieking orgasms would do it for tonight."

"Do you know how beautiful you are, Rose? How incredibly desirable?"

Rose smiled. At that moment, she did. At that moment, she believed she was the most beautiful, vital, sexy woman in the world.

They made love again, gently, caressing each other, tasting each other, building a connection deeper and stronger than mere physical presence. They made love exploring, listening, trying to learn the rhythm of each other's body.

"Am I holding you too tight?" he whispered.

"No." She understood that wasn't what he meant. "You mean like owning me." She rubbed herself against his muscular body. "No, not now."

Rose wanted to think it would always be so, but she didn't dare dream of that. Luck of the draw, win the lottery, she had done nothing in her life to deserve this man.

"Are you afraid of being owned?" Ryan's fingers locked in her hair. "Or are you afraid that you'll love someone, and they'll leave?"

"Both, I suppose." She snuggled against him. "I'll never lie to you, Ryan. I'm afraid of many things. Being loved and abandoned isn't the least of them. It's right up there with being caged. But if you ever do want to go, to leave me, please tell me. Don't lie. I'll deal with it."

"I've waited my whole life for you. Why should I leave?"

Rose didn't answer his question. There were a hundred reasons he could choose to leave, but she had no intention of counting them right then.

Chapter 17

Ryan waited in the quiet of Lola's living room. It was the second Saturday after Jimmy had died and, while the shock had eased, the painful memory of the catastrophic event remained. He touched the bronze urn that contained a part of someone he loved, a man who taught him about life and offered compassion when everything went to hell, when no good answers were available. They found very little of Jimmy to cremate, but the symbolism carried great weight. The funeral home had delivered the urn an hour ago.

Lola and Rose waited on either side of him.

"Are you sure this is what he wanted?" he asked.

"Yes" Lola sounded grim. "I wrote it down when he told me."

"It is what he wanted," Rose agreed. "He told me. 'Take my ashes to the party, then dump them down the toilet.' I called him a weird old fart, but he laughed." Her voice broke and she wiped her eyes. "You're not going to . . ."

"Dump them in the toilet? No. I'll scatter them on Mom and Dad's graves. That's what I want done with mine, too. We had good parents."

A surprising number of mourners had attended the memorial service at St. Catherine's Church that morning. Following Jimmy's instructions, Lola rented Brody's Pub for the evening to have the party. It would draw the crowd.

Ryan picked up the urn. "Weird, but he always loved a party. Weirder was the priest inviting everyone in the church to get sloshed at Brody's tonight."

"Oh, I thought Father William was a good sport about it,"

Lola said. "I invited him, too. He said he'd be there. Let's go."

O'Malley asked Ryan to ride with him to Brody's. He and Rose had planned to go together, but instead, she went with Lola. Ryan loved so many things about Rose, from her sexy body to how she intuitively understood when he needed to be alone or do something without her. Of course, that meant he had to leave her alone if she needed it, too. Don't tie her down. She's afraid of a cage. If he held her too tight, he'd lose her.

The battle raged in his mind each day, how to protect her without smothering her. At night? No problem. In his arms, she was everything he wanted or dreamed of, sexy, and adventurous. On the job, everyone watched out for her—much to her dismay. She often grumbled about having too many babysitters. He'd had security cameras installed at the hotel site, but what happened when Lola badgered her into going shopping? When she drove to the grocery store alone for a six-pack?

"Something new?" Ryan asked O'Malley as he climbed in the car.

"A few things. Some rumbling in Miami. Esteban seems to be out of town longer than usual."

"I haven't seen him here. Whatever Jimmy had on him hasn't shown up, that I know of."

"Get out of Jacksonville as fast as you can, Ryan." O'Malley's voice carried a warning. "There's some unusual movement going on in Esteban's circles. Dealers and buyers. Strange talk coming out of Panama, too. I don't like you connected to him, legally or otherwise."

"I want to be rid of Esteban." *And I want to be rid of Leandro*, he said to himself. Though the man hadn't shown his pretty face since Rose's kidnapping, the thought of Leandro and Rose worried Ryan almost as much as someone making another attempt on her life. Leandro wanted Rose. A bit of shame rose in Ryan. Leandro had saved her, from the kidnapping, not him.

"How is it going with you and Rose?" O'Malley asked.

Ryan laughed. "I tell her I love her, but she gets a worried look on her face when I do. I'm going to ask her to marry me. Maybe it won't scare the shit out of her. Is that all you wanted?

To ask about my love life?"

"No. You think it will take a full eight months to finish here in Jax?"

"Probably not. Carl is genius at organization on the ground, especially with Brianna hanging around to keep his bad habits under control. We don't let him play with the cash box, though."

O'Malley chuckled. "That's a good idea. Carl is misguided, but basically a good person."

O'Malley's Mercedes gave them a smooth, quiet ride as they followed Lola's car and headed east on Atlantic Boulevard to the pub.

"O'Malley, you know anything about women?" Ryan asked. He hated that he had to ask. A man his age, married and divorced, ought to know something. O'Malley had married, but his wife had died of cancer eight years ago and it devastated him. Now he had Lola and that was good.

"Ah . . . some," O'Malley said. "What's the problem?"

"Leandro. He wants Rose."

"And Rose?"

"I don't know." And that frustrated the hell out of him.

"Did you ask Lola?"

"Yes. Captivated. That's Lola's word. Rose is fascinated with something so deadly, so close. Lola said Rose lost her mother very young, and her father raised her on job sites, still a mostly male environment. She doesn't have much defense against a smooth snake like him."

"Perhaps," O'Malley said. "Rose is open, honest, and while she's probably known bad people, Leandro's deviousness may be beyond her experience. She's also strong-willed enough to reject him, though. And strong-willed enough to do exactly what she wants to do."

"Is there anything I can do?" Ryan hated that he sounded like a kid begging advice.

"Love her. Tell her you love her." O'Malley drove into Brody's parking lot. "And forgive her if she falls. Like Carl. Perfection is a rare thing in this world."

O'Malley switched the car off. "I did learn something about the Sanchez family murder. Sanchez's kid brother went down on a weapons and possession charge. He was looking at twenty years. Sanchez agreed to spy on Esteban for the cops. Get little brother out of jail."

"Oh, hell." Ryan closed his eyes and thought of the urn sitting on the floor of the back seat. Men shouldn't play those games, not ordinary men with families and friends who loved them.

"Now, here's something," O'Malley said. "Esteban ordered the hit on Sanchez, I know that. One of my law clerks dated a girl who worked in Esteban's house in Miami. Right after it happened, Esteban and Leandro had a shouting match that ended in Leandro stalking out. Apparently he wasn't involved in the Sanchez hit and vehemently objected to it."

Ryan fought to keep from making a fist and punching the dash. Leandro had taunted him, implying he had intimate knowledge of those murders for no better reason that to irritate him.

"Having problems controlling that temper of yours again?" O'Malley asked.

"Always." Ryan relaxed. "But I don't usually act on it anymore."

"Haven't beaten the shit out of anyone lately?" O'Malley asked. "Besides Carl. And I think that was a draw."

"I assume you're telling me not to take on Leandro?"

"That's exactly what I'm telling you."

* * * *

Rose grinned as Ryan and O'Malley strolled toward them. O'Malley's eyes stayed on Lola and glowed like the shine on his bald head. Lola smiled and Rose saw love there—and caution, as if they embarked on a precarious journey. How tiny and fragile she must be in his arms.

Ryan came to Rose and kissed her on the forehead. She leaned against him. Precarious described their relationship, too. Love, powerful as it was, couldn't always overcome certain fundamental differences in temperament. Fearful of jinxing things, she rarely admitted, even to herself, that she and Ryan seemed to belong together.

Brody's Pub sat on Atlantic Avenue, east of the Intracoastal Waterway. Bar, poolroom and dance floor, Brody's had it all. Rose had gone there with Jimmy to play pool on Thursday nights. Games and beer, Half-Price Thursdays. Jimmy loved it. "Here's to good old Herman," he'd say with every beer. Alcohol never affected his pool game, though; at least not until after the fourth glass. He won and she won, back and forth, until she helped him out to the truck and drove him home. Tears leaked from Rose's eyes as they reached the front door.

"Can you do this?" Ryan asked. He had one arm around her, and the other arm carried Jimmy's urn.

"Oh, yeah." Rose wiped at her eyes. "Jimmy would be mighty pissed if I didn't."

Ryan opened the door, and they went in to honor the dead.

Brody's was half-full of mourners at seven o'clock. Lola had leased the entire pub and a private party sign hung on the door. Vernon Construction workers replaced the usual crowd. Clark's Surf-n-Turf had received a blank check from Lola to keep food coming as long as people wanted to eat. Ian Brody, the Pub's owner, received a similar generous check and an additional sum to hire bartenders and drivers to take care of those who overindulged. There were vans to get them safely home or to their hotels.

Men and women from Ryan's crews scattered throughout the south had arrived during the last two days, all asking questions Rose knew Ryan couldn't answer. The police told him nothing. They probably still considered him a suspect.

Brody had arranged a place on the bar for the urn, with a spotlight to illuminate the guest of honor. An energetic song about the beauty and virtues of cowgirls danced in the air since Lola ordered the band she hired not to play gloomy songs. The pungent aroma of beer already filled the room.

Ryan insisted that Rose stand with him and Lola as they greeted everyone. Rose spoke to those she knew, and Ryan introduced her to those she didn't. Speculation filled their eyes and voices as they noted her place at the Boss's side. Some of that speculation wasn't exactly friendly.

At nine o'clock, Ryan had the music shut down and yelled for quiet. The legion of construction workers immediately ceased their revelry and silence filled the room.

Ryan started to speak, then had to clear his throat. "This is what Jimmy wanted. Everybody should have a good time and raise a few for him. I know you have questions. I don't have answers—yet. But you need to forget all that now. Now is the time we have a party in honor of our friend." He picked up a glass of beer and held it high. "For Jimmy."

"For Jimmy," the crowd shouted.

The band started playing again, and people drifted into muted conversations. Rose knew it would take a few more drinks to lift their spirits—and hers. She wanted to go to Ryan, ask him to dance with her, hold her, but his people crowded around him, needing him to be the Boss Man, to tell them he'd set things right. He was good at that. Solid steady Ryan, who, like Lola, had the ability to organize and hold the narrow path.

O'Malley kept Lola sitting on his substantial knee anytime she wasn't working the crowd. Rose sat beside him once when Lola conversed with others.

She set her beer on the table in front of her. "What did Jimmy say when he told you he wanted to change his will?"

"Not much. I tried to dissuade him. Changing his will to leave so much to a woman he'd only known a year is not appropriate. The doctors all said he was stable, though. And it was his money. Now that I know you, I understand."

"Thank you, but I wish I'd known he felt the way he did about some things."

"Why? It would have changed nothing. Love comes in degrees. If one must be obsessed, moderation is necessary. Jimmy moderated his obsession with you. My obsession is Lola. I have loved little Lola very quietly for many years. Like a ghost, I haunted her. Her obsession is the Vernon boys and the company. But she has agreed to moderate hers. Perhaps we can both be happy."

"I'm an only child, but it strikes me, as a not so neutral observer, that the Vernon family is a bit unusual. Why don't Lola, Carl, and Ryan talk about Charlie? Was he that bad?"

O'Malley chuckled. "It depends on your definition of bad. He cheated on his wife and ignored his sons, though he provided them with all the material things they wanted. He was a good businessman, an aggressive competitor, talented at making money, not all of it legally, and a general all around-asshole. Jimmy was Ryan's father figure."

"And Jimmy ignored Carl."

"Not exactly. Abby, the boys' mother, kept Carl to herself."

"Then why . . . ?"

"The will? I don't know. Charlie, Abby, Jimmy, they all had secrets. Now Lola is the only survivor, and those secrets are probably safe with her. I'll ask no questions."

Lola returned to her place in O'Malley's lap and Rose left them alone. Certainly O'Malley had secrets, too.

Rose scanned the room. Annie was there in her wheelchair, tube across her face and her oxygen bottle tucked into a holder on the back. Occasionally, she'd shut off the life-giving gas to light up and suck in a good helping of tar and nicotine. Then she'd stub it out and turn the oxygen back on. Other smokers kept a good distance. Rose's landlady had drawn a crowd, thanks to Lola urging people to go ask her to tell outrageous stories of her days and nights in the strip clubs and her years on the road. Annie was happy to oblige as long as they kept the beers coming.

Rose drained her beer, grabbed another, and headed for the pool tables. On her sixth birthday, Daddy had given her a pool cue and box to stand on while he helped her make her shots. He beamed with pride as if she were a child prodigy on a piano or violin. By the time she was thirteen, Daddy would bet money that his little girl could beat them all. She beat most of the challengers, and the others she charmed with her skill and smile. Daddy told her to always smile, win or lose. He'd bribed many a bartender and bouncer to get her inside. In a little over an hour at Brody's, though, she'd beaten the best there and run out of takers.

She started to return the pool cue to the rack when she felt someone behind her.

"I will play with you, *mi dulce*."

Leandro.

Rose turned to face him. "What the hell are you doing here?"

"I came to honor the dead, of course." Leandro's face had an open, bemused expression, one worthy of a slick politician. "I have heard Esteban curse many men, but he saved his special curses for your lover and your friend. Such men deserve my respect."

Rose knew all eyes and ears in the immediate area were on her. Leandro's looks set him apart, even if he hadn't worn an expensive, perfectly fitted black suit that cost more than most men in the room made in a month. A few probably knew Esteban's right hand and gave him the mark of the beast.

"Leandro, you are completely crazy," she said. Then more softly, "I'll play with you, if only to keep that gorgeous face of yours from getting maimed. You'd better play good and play to this crowd. Let's keep these boys and girls entertained."

Chapter 18

Rose nodded at the padded cover of the nine-foot pool table in the middle of the room. "You want to feed quarters to play on lumpy cloth or get the real table? It's expensive, but I'll bet you're rich enough to afford it."

Leandro drew a money clip filled with hundred dollar bills out of his pocket. "I don't have any quarters, *mi dulce*. This will have to do." He offered her the clip.

Ian Brody had brought the ten thousand dollar pool table with him when he retired to Florida. His wife wouldn't let him keep it in their beachfront condominium, and he always said he had to open the pub to have a place to store it. Serious players—those with money—could use it for a fifty dollars an hour and a $500 dollar deposit returned after he inspected it for damage.

Rose accepted the money clip, peeled off seven bills, and returned it to him. She went to pay Brody. As she did, she saw a smiling Ryan approach Leandro. Ryan spoke to him with a genial expression on his face, and Rose knew he'd done it to forestall any problems from the construction worker crowd. If the boss gave approval to Leandro's presence, then they had no excuse to cause trouble.

"Thank you, my love." Rose said softly to Ryan as she returned.

"You're welcome." Ryan gave her an agreeable smile. "It's a façade. It only means I don't want trouble. I'll admit to shameless jealousy and a hefty dose of pure hatred whipping the beer around in my stomach."

"Oh, boy. It turns me on when you're honest." Rose gave

him a quick kiss and walked back to the pool table.

"Would you like to wager?" Leandro asked.

"Sure. Dollar a game. I left all my hundreds at home. You play Eight Ball?"

"Yes, of course."

Brody uncovered the massive oak table and unlocked the cabinet that held the good cues. Then he, too, waited with the audience to watch the game. Leandro touched the head rail, almost a caress, and moved around the table, admiring the absolutely flat and level green cloth. "Such a fine thing deserves better surroundings."

Rose agreed. "It does. Jimmy always called it a nun in a whorehouse."

Leandro won the lag, and she racked the balls for him. All eyes focused on him. He had a sexy, bad-boy smile as he removed the expensive coat and tie. He rolled up the sleeves on his pure white shirt. Full of grace and energy, he did give the crowd a show.

He ran the table the first game, and smiled at her when he pocketed the eight ball. She almost won the second. Almost. No good shots appeared, so she left him with a safety, the cue ball tight against the rail and inches from the corner pocket. Impossibly, he made it and finished the game.

Rose observed the crowd while he played. Because they concentrated on him, they let their faces relax and give expression to emotions they usually guarded. This lithe, beautiful man evoked insatiable desire in women and blatant envy in men, envy that could easily turn to rage. Leandro was fully aware of his face and body, and the prurient sensual effect it had on people. No one, man or woman, could stay neutral around him.

For the first time, Rose saw passion in him, not for sex, but passion for doing something and doing it well. For certain men, the words *just a game* had no meaning. That personified Leandro. His arrogance remained, but he controlled it with patience and skill. She had the skill, but she lacked his drive to overcome all opposition. Still, she managed to win half the games.

Between games, Leandro worked the crowd, speaking genially to the men and offering polite innocuous greetings to their women. Annie rolled in while Rose had the table, and Leandro knelt beside her wheelchair. He listened as she lowered her head and spoke to him, then he laughed. It was an impetuous, good-natured laugh, one that seemed genuine and in total opposition to the idea that he was a soulless master of deception. When he rose to come back to the game, he bent and kissed Annie on the cheek.

Leandro pocketed the eight ball and came stand in front of her. "Let's raise the wager, Rose."

Rose leaned against the table. He used her name and not the now familiar *mi dulce*. Suddenly furious at his condescending smile she said, "Sure. If you win, I'll give you anything you want that I have the power to give."

Leandro raised an eyebrow and his mouth pursed. He didn't look around to see whether anyone heard her proposal.

He nodded, but wariness crept into his voice. "And if you win?"

"You tell me who killed Jimmy and why they tried to kill me."

Leandro lowered his eyes. When he raised them to gaze at her, they carried sadness, not arrogance. "That is a wager too high for either of us to pay, *mi dulce*. At least right now. We would both lose. Let me offer something less dangerous. If I win, you'll give me a kiss. If you win, I'll give you this." He drew a thin gold chain out of his pocket. A single diamond, not enormous, but large enough to sparkle in the light, hung suspended from the chain.

Rose laid the pool cue on the table.

"No."

The game with Leandro had gone too far. And it was her fault. She wanted Ryan. He stood ten feet away, watching. She went to him.

"I'm tired," she said. "Will you take me home?"

"Sure." He laid an arm across her shoulder and drew her to him.

* * * *

Ryan glanced at her occasionally as he drove through light traffic. She watched the road ahead and didn't speak. He'd heard her challenge and Leandro's rejection. The bastard offered a substitute, but Rose wanted the truth, not diamonds. Leandro had made a mistake. Ryan had seen knowledge of that on the man's face as Rose walked away. Leandro learned from his mistakes. He would not make that one again. It was too much to believe he'd given up his plan to seduce Rose.

Ryan decided to take a chance. "You remember when you said I should ask if I wanted to know what you were thinking?"

"I didn't guarantee I'd tell you. But I will. I was thinking about lies and complex relationships. I don't think I've done much of either. I'm twenty-eight years old. All I've ever done since my Daddy died is move from construction site to construction site, wiring buildings. I've had occasional mediocre sex—with the exception of my current lover—and that's it."

"Your current un-mediocre lover appreciates your admiration, and doesn't think *his* relationship with you is complex at all. You must be confusing me with someone else."

Rose shifted in her seat. "Someone with whom I *do not* have a relationship."

"A relationship doesn't always include sex. You're always honest, Rose, so don't lie to yourself. I alternate between wanting to kill him and wondering who he really is."

Ryan hadn't intended to discuss Leandro. He wanted to make her forget him.

"Do you think Leandro killed Jimmy?" Rose asked.

"Not directly, but, like you, I'll bet he knows who did."

Ryan drove down the alley and parked beside her Taurus at the cottage. He shut off the engine, and they sat there in the darkness.

Rose reached out and touched him. "I need to know what happened with Jimmy."

"Yeah." Ryan hated the bitterness and jealousy he heard in his own voice. "Learning what happened from Leandro. That would be an onerous task, wouldn't it? Close your eyes and hold your nose and jump in."

"Knowing too much about Leandro is dangerous, probably deadly, but if you're speaking of sex, I doubt if it would onerous."

"Rose, I love you, but sometimes I wish you did know how to lie."

Chapter 19

Rose wondered if all of February was going to be as interesting as the event unfolding before her. Grift's fist connected with the cop's head. She heard it from the hotel doorway, 30 feet away. A hammer smacking a melon.

The battle in the construction yard had begun when four cops politely asked Grift to get in a car and go with them for questioning. Not an arrest, they'd assured him. Grift apparently didn't see it their way. He violently objected to their request.

A second cop hit Grift with a stun gun in the back of his thick, tattooed neck. A third hit him with a jolt in the gut.

Carl had let Grift return to the job. Ryan had objected, but Grift was an excellent welder, even if he had learned his trade in prison. They needed him. When they asked Rose to make the decision, she had told them it was fine, as long as he stayed away from her. She still believed Grift wasn't smart enough to wire that panel to the generator.

Grift remained on his feet, roaring obscenities at the officers. The cop who went for the gut received a fist in the face for his trouble. He staggered back and went down.

Another cop hit Grift over his thick head with a piece of two-by-four pine he'd picked up from a trash pile. It made a crack as if someone dropped a concrete block on asphalt from a second floor window.

Grift swayed.

One of them hit him again with the stunner, and Grift crumpled to the ground, swinging his fists, lashing ineffectively into the air.

"God Almighty," Sam said. He'd come to stand beside Rose,

as had Ryan and Lola.

"Amen." That was Lola.

"Tough bastard," Ryan agreed.

Rose was surprised she'd been able to take him down with a mere steel truck door. Of course, his own momentum had worked against him then. No one would be sad to see Grift go. Even though they'd let him come back, they'd cut his former bodyguard's privileges. He hadn't liked that. He stayed, most likely because he was looking for revenge, or no one else would hire him.

Two of the cops struggled to get Grift's arms behind his back to handcuff him, but his short, thick limbs wouldn't let his wrists come together. Finally, the cop he hit in the face made it to his feet and to the patrol car. He wiped blood from his nose, opened the trunk, and dragged out arm and leg shackles. The cop Grift hit in the head still lay on the ground, but he was moving.

A man Rose knew as Detective Holloran approached. "Well, that was a piece of work," he said. "You know Roger Vellar, Ms. Norris?"

"Yes. Master Electrician. I worked with him in Atlanta."

"He's wiring a new shopping mall here. He heard about your so-called *accident* and called us. Four months ago, Grift paid him for a crash course in electricity. Roger knew you weren't Grift's favorite person. Not much proof that the bastard actually hooked those wires to the generator, but he's already violated parole," Holloran continued. "We'll get him out of here and back to Raiford. Now we need to find out if someone taught him how to make a bomb."

"Wow," Rose said. Holloran walked away, making a wide circuit around the uniforms who struggled with a semi-conscious Grift.

Ryan draped an arm around Rose's shoulders and tugged her to him, an act made a bit difficult by the fact that she wore a full tool belt. His hard hat bumped against hers. "It's a long way from stringing a few wires to a generator to building a bomb. Grift may have tried to kill you, but someone else built that bomb. We're not any closer to getting answers than we were a few weeks ago. Get your red pen ready, Lola. Security is going to search everything that comes onto this site."

"I take it that means we're not going to make a profit this year," Lola said. "Too bad. It's February and our new partner was probably counting on getting rich by November."

"No I wasn't," Rose protested. O'Malley sent her the hundred thousand dollars Jimmy left her. She sent 15 percent to the IRS. When she'd added the other 85 percent to the remainder of her father's life insurance, it made a tidy sum in her bank account. "I can wait until after Christmas for incredible wealth to start pouring in."

"Anybody seen Esteban recently?" Ryan asked. "I expected him to be around before now."

Rose hadn't seen the man. She hadn't seen Leandro either, not since the night of the wake. She rarely thought about him these days. Too busy with Ryan and work. This was good. Very good. She didn't need someone like Leandro around causing trouble.

Love had finally eased into her life. She trusted Ryan, trusted his kindness and honesty. Jimmy remained in her mind and some nights she would rise from bed and go hold Herman. She'd weep silently, but somehow Ryan would wake, come to her, and gently lead her back to bed. For the first time, she'd begun to think about children and wondered what kind of a mother she'd be. Ryan? He'd make a great father. He hadn't proposed yet, but he'd talked around it, probably trying to determine how she'd react. What would she say if he asked her? When he asked her. Yes, she'd say yes—with a long engagement.

Chapter 20

"Sunday morning," Rose grumbled. "And I'm sorting tools for Monday." Damn Esteban. He picked Sunday to want a tour of the site. So what did she expect? That he and Leandro would be in church, desperately praying to keep their souls out of hell?

She shivered. She'd left her jacket in the truck. A chill clung to the room even though the early March weather warmed things outside. Good Florida weather, though, temperate sunny days and cool nights. She'd rather be sleeping late, naked and snuggled up against the big male body that usually covered most of the bed.

A terrible inconvenience, the requested tour, but as part owner along with Ryan and Lola, Rose felt obligated to come in and spend her Sunday on business.

Since she didn't have a truck yet to store her tools, she kept them locked in a sturdy twenty-foot square steel-wire equipment cage set up inside the large empty space that would eventually be the hotel kitchen. It wasn't a good situation, but with the loss of the office trailer and the smaller tool shed in the fire, they made do using the ground floor as a security and dry materials storage area.

Except for the cluttered area where Rose worked, the building seemed more a hotel now, at least for her part. Major wires were already pulled and panels installed. Sheet rock was up and the plasterers applied hard coat daily. She and the other electricians had finished the main wiring for the heating and cooling units and would start on the kitchen next week.

She crouched on the floor, digging through the steel box. Damn, she had to take time to buy a new truck. She kept her truck toolboxes in perfect order.

She thought about Ryan's marriage proposal last week. Scary, but it felt right. She'd said yes. She finally admitted to herself that she loved him, wanted to be with him, wanted to marry him. He offered her his strength and a stability she'd never thought she'd have. What would people expect of her as the Boss Man's wife? She asked for a long engagement. He'd agreed, not happily, to wait until they finished the hotel to do the deed. If he had his way, they'd be in church tomorrow. It still made her uneasy, not of being in love, but of making a commitment. She needed time to decide if her reticence was caution or terror.

Sex was wonderful, and she finally had an appointment next week with a gynecologist to get her pills. No more breaks in the rhythm of things to get a condom.

"Rose," Ryan called from the door. "You in here?"

Rose stood. "Yes."

He wound his way through pallets stacked with bags of masonry material as he walked across the room toward her. "I'll get Esteban through as fast as I can," he said. "Then we can go home."

"That's fine." Rose stepped up and leaned against him. "All I had planned was making mad passionate love to you, anyway. Nothing important."

"Now that's all I need." He gripped her waist and drew her tight against him. "To be distracted with thoughts of making mad passionate love to your glorious body while I'm with Esteban."

He kissed her, and she rubbed herself against him. He'd become familiar, but she still loved running her hands over the smooth muscle of his body, kissing him, tasting him.

"Hey, Boss." Sam walked in and stopped. "Oops. Sorry."

"That's all right," Ryan said. "I was getting bored anyway."

"Sure you were." Sam chuckled. "Esteban's here. And the dayshift security guards arrived. Finally."

"All right. You go on home, Sam. You shouldn't be here on Sunday anyway. We'll call another security company if this one can't get their people here on time."

"Okay. See you tomorrow." Sam grinned and walked away whistling an unusual tune.

"Bored, huh." Rose slid her hand between them and rubbed across his jeans. "You don't feel bored. In fact you feel—"

He grabbed her arms and pushed her back. "God, don't do that."

Rose laughed. "You go smooth Esteban's feathers, and I'll meet you at the truck."

Ryan kissed her again, capturing her hands in his so they wouldn't wander around his already sensitive body. "Later," he said as he walked away.

Rose closed her tool box back and left the cage. She had her back to the door as she locked the cage door, and she heard a faint footstep behind her.

She whirled and faced Leandro. The sight of him made her want to smile, but she kept her mouth straight. "How come you're not shadowing your boss?"

Leandro shook his head. "He doesn't need me to guard him from your lover. Perhaps *you* should be guarding your lover from Esteban." Leandro laughed softly, and she shivered. He made her feel naked in spite of her jeans and work shirt. He stepped closer, and she forced herself to stand still. "I see you are working diligently to uphold the Vernon family honor," he said. "I understand you are soon to be a part of that family."

Rose knew Jimmy's will and her ownership status was now public knowledge. Could Leandro know about Ryan's proposal? She gave him a speculative look. "I've agreed to accept the share of the company Jimmy wanted me to have, if that's what you mean."

"And have you made a commitment to the owner?" His dark eyes narrowed.

"Ryan? That's none of your business."

"Then will you have dinner with me tonight?"

"No."

"The circumstances surrounding our meetings always seem to be difficult."

Leandro moved in close, too close. Again, the heat of him, the sheer energy, burned at her. She stepped back and could go no farther. Her spine pressed against the tool cage's thick wire. He laid his hands on the wire, trapping her. She locked her fists behind her back to keep from touching him. He brushed feather kisses over her cheek and mouth. She closed her eyes, intoxicated with his presence, breathing the scent of him . . . what was she doing? Only minutes ago she'd kissed the man she loved, promised him another night of passion.

* * * *

Ryan watched Sam walk to his truck, wave, and drive away. Then he went on to where Esteban talked with Lola, slick and refined in his light-colored suit. Ryan tried to remember a time when he'd seen the man dressed otherwise and couldn't. He rarely noticed what men or women wore unless it was outlandish or, in the case of a female, how much cleavage or leg she presented. He'd never seen Leandro in anything but black. He glanced around. Where was Leandro, anyway?

Ryan's mind ran to Rose. He fought the urge to go back to her. He didn't think Leandro would hurt her. As for anything else, including the man's stated desire to seduce her, that was her choice. He loved her, but he'd made his promise not to hold her too tight. Her decision. Leandro was a mistake, a dangerous mistake, for an independent woman like Rose, and a choice he hoped she wouldn't make. But she had already made her choice, hadn't she? When she accepted his marriage proposal?

"Hello, Esteban." Ryan stuffed his anxiety down and climbed into the illusion that he was glad to see his partner in this unholy mess. "You ready for a guided tour?"

"I am. It need not be extensive, though. I understand the interior elevators are not yet operational."

"Not inside. You can ride up the outside of the building on the construction elevator if you're not afraid of heights."

"No. I prefer to stay on the ground."

Ryan scanned the area, trying to decide where to go first. He frowned. The closest security camera had a tiny red light flashing under it. That meant it was off line. Damn. Now he'd have to take the time to call and get it reprogrammed.

Esteban and Lola followed as Ryan led them across the new asphalt toward what would be the lobby. He pointed out the new entrance and sea-blue tiled portico area. "That will be ready in . . . give it a month," he said. "Over half the rooms are finished except for carpet."

"I am pleased," Esteban said. "I think you will not need the eight months you requested."

The building did look good. The newly designed hurricane window panels on the outside appeared part of the vertical, modern design rather than safety and property damage control. He'd built fancier buildings, but this one was stable and would hold guests for many years. He'd already sent most of the additional crews he brought in back to their regular sites.

The Balsam-Beech Security van sat parked near the building, its back doors standing open. Ryan didn't see the guards. If he found them, he could have them call about the camera. He glanced up at the camera on the building. The red light flashed on that one, too. Were they all down?

As he passed the van, one of the Balsam uniformed guards stepped around from the front. He thought he knew them all by now, but this one was new. Ryan started to speak when he noticed something in the guard's hand. His mind registered the word *taser*, just as a tremendous white-hot pain burned across his arm and shot through him as if his blood suddenly boiled. He collapsed, his mind wandering in a labyrinth as the pain shrieked along his nerves.

Lola screamed. A single gunshot, close, loud, then everything around him became a jumble. He knew that men surrounded him, but his eyes refused to focus. He thought they wore Balsam uniforms, but couldn't be sure. One twisted his arms behind his back and tied them tight. Ryan tried to fight and must have had some success because his captor muttered foul words.

* * * *

Leandro drew closer. Rose breathed the scent of him, her gaze riveted on that wonderful face.

His hands gripped the cage on either side of her as his body pinned her against the wire. A warm ache filled her, a sense of urgency, while her mind screamed in outrage and called her an unfaithful slut.

Leandro's mouth pressed against hers in a gentle kiss. A gentle kiss that quickly became demanding. What an unbearably soft mouth he had. Her fingers slid under his coat yearning to drag him closer and touched . . . a gun.

The world cleared around her and she twisted, desperate to escape.

"No." The word burst from her in an explosion of breath.

Leandro instantly released her.

A firecracker popped—too loud.

Leandro whirled and ran out of the room. He had his gun in his hand before he reached the door. Rose searched for a weapon and found a two-foot pipe wrench in a pile of tools some idiot had left on a pallet of cement. Nine pounds of cast steel; not much of a weapon against a gun. Her mouth filled with the caustic taste of acid and old coffee. She swallowed it and raced after Leandro.

* * * *

Ryan fought, but nothing worked. His muscles refused to obey his commands. Helpless, feeble, he'd left Lola vulnerable.

"Motherfucker's heavy," someone said. Were they talking about him? Well, yes, he was a big man and should be kicking their asses, but his body wouldn't let him.

"Get in there, bitch," another voice said. To Lola? What about Esteban?

They lifted Ryan higher. God, they were dragging them into the back of the van. He could see better now. Lola was beside him, sitting up, so she probably hadn't been stunned, but Esteban lay still and limp on the floor. Ryan suddenly had expert insight to the panic Rose had endured that day Cochran and Bedlow kidnapped her. The doors closed, leaving them in darkness.

Chapter 21

Rose ran behind Leandro, twenty feet behind him, because she'd stopped to pick up the pipe wrench. He raced into the construction yard. As he passed between a pair of head-high stacks of building studs, two men slammed into him, one on each side. He reeled, twisted and managed to stay on his feet, but the one on his right wrenched his gun away and tossed it aside. The second, a tall beefy man with a shaved head, twisted Leandro's arm behind his back and forced him to his knees. In spite of the man's size, Leandro dragged his assailant over and threw him down. The man froze, then collapsed.

Leandro faced the first man, the one who'd relieved him of his gun. This one looked more refined, gray-haired and sophisticated, someone's grandfather, maybe. He had a gun pointed at Leandro's heart. Leandro spoke to him—in Spanish—and the man replied in the same. Rose didn't understand the language, but she heard black and merciless hatred in the gunman's voice.

Concentrating on Leandro, the gunman didn't hear Rose approach. She drew the pipe wrench back over her shoulder. With a ferocious swing, she brought the steel down on the forearm of his gun hand. It hit with the thick sound of an ax hitting a block of soft wood. The gunman staggered. By reflex, he pulled the trigger. The gun jerked and gave a thick, heavy whomp. The bullet punched into the dirt. The shooter gaped at his arm. His mouth opened as if he wanted to cry out in excruciating agony, but had no voice.

Rose had already drawn the wrench back again. She aimed for his shoulder, but the heavy steel smashed into his chest, solid metal on flesh and bone. He fell backwards and collapsed.

His weapon slipped from his fingers.

Behind Leandro, the baldheaded man lay on his back, his eyes open wide and unblinking. He would not trouble them again.

Leandro stepped to where his gun lay on the ground and casually retrieved it. He drew something out of his jacket pocket, and screwed it on the end of the barrel.

The gunman Rose struck lay on the ground and gasped for breath.

"No." Rose barely had time to breathe the word.

With no expression whatsoever, Leandro pointed and pulled the trigger. Another muffled explosion and the man fell back. A red stain bloomed on his chest. His legs twitched once, and he joined his companion in death.

"No?" Leandro seemed genuinely surprised. "He wished to kill me. And you. They would leave no witnesses. That is not acceptable behavior." He glanced at her, a smile on his exquisite face. Charming, and at the same time incredibly savage. "I was careless, *mi dulce*. Thank you for saving my life. Let us find the others. Perhaps we—I—should have more caution."

Rose stepped back from him. She wanted to shout, *call the police*! It was far too late for the police, though. Others had decided not to call the police weeks ago, and she'd agreed. Leandro? She'd recognized him on the first day she met him. Psychopath. And yet, in a most disturbing manner, she'd allowed him to kiss her, touch her, make love to her with words. He was true to his nature. She was a hypocrite.

Leandro smiled, as if he heard her thoughts. She lowered the pipe wrench and laid it on the ground. It sickened her to look at it. When he walked away, she followed. They moved carefully around the now silent site, finding no one.

What had happened? Fear bubbled up in Rose. Where was Ryan? As they approached the construction trailer, they saw a man leaning against a plain, smoke-gray sedan. A lean figure in worn clothing, he had the look of a man driven precariously close to the grave by time and alcohol. He seemed unconcerned as Leandro approached him, the gun at his side, but obviously ready.

The man held a small note pad and pen.

"Norris, that you?" He nodded at Rose.

"Who are you?" Rose asked.

"I'm a messenger. Gimme your cell phone number."

"Why?"

"Because somebody has your boyfriend and the old lady. They'll call you and tell you how to get 'em back."

"What about the other man who was with them?" Rose asked. She prayed that he wouldn't say Esteban was dead. Leandro might kill the messenger and leave her with no way to find Ryan.

"Took him, too. Package deal. Now, do I get your number?" He cocked his head and gave her a smile that revealed yellow teeth with significant gaps.

Rose gave him her number, furiously enunciating each digit.

Leandro stepped closer to her. "Perhaps you should go inside," he said softly. "Let me talk to this gentleman alone."

"Won't do you no good," the self-declared messenger said with a grin. "I don't know nothing. I give them this number, pick up my cash, and I'm gone." He opened the car door, climbed in, and drove away.

"When he gives them that number, he's dead." Leandro removed the silencer from his gun and dropped it in his pocket. He slid the gun into the holster under his jacket with ease.

"I must make some calls. There are bodies to dispose of," Leandro said. "Then we will deal with other things."

In a parking lot on a million-dollar spring day, Leandro spoke of gruesome body disposal as another man would speak of taking out the trash. In some ways, she felt safe with him and in others, incredibly vulnerable. In spite of the deplorable desire for him that overcame her when he came close, he remained an incredibly volatile man, a man who could make love and kill with the same impersonal ease.

Rose rubbed her hands on her jeans. Why did they feel so dirty? "If I called the police, you'd disappear and leave me to face them alone."

"Yes, of course." He shrugged, and that now familiar, faint smile tugged at the corners of his mouth. His intense midnight eyes gleamed.

"I don't understand. Who were they?" She nodded toward the stacks of building materials where two bodies lay.

"The attack on me was not at all connected to what's happened to the others. Those men probably followed me and thought to take advantage of the fact that I was alone."

"Why didn't they just shoot you as you ran by? Why take you down first? Talk to you?"

"For them, vengeance required that I know in whose name I would die. It is important to some men."

Leandro's creamy voice filled with superior distain. "Very unprofessional. Very personal."

Rose stared into the distance to keep from looking at him. She knew how he killed. "What did you do?" she asked. "To make them hate you so much?"

Leandro gave a casual shrug. "Oh, one of the multitude of sins I have committed against my fellow man, I'm sure. Or perhaps one of Esteban's sins. But I most humbly beg your pardon. My carelessness almost cost you your life."

"You don't look humble."

She hadn't meant it as a joke, but he laughed. "Humility is difficult for me."

How many men had hated Leandro as he walked through a ruinous life? He killed so easily. One man in self-defense, the other with glacial indifference. No, she did not wish to know the acts that brought about such intense loathing. Very unprofessional, he had said. Very personal. And yet, she knew he was the only one who could help her now. It wouldn't be free, but she would pay the price.

"Will Esteban be angry with you because you weren't near him when it happened?"

"Furious. But it was he who suggested that I go and find you. He wishes me to take you away from your lover. Such a petty, spiteful man, Esteban. Of course, I also wish to take you from your lover."

"Rose already knew that. "Shit! I know what they want."

"And that would be . . .?" Leandro's voice still hinted at inappropriate amusement.

"Whatever Jimmy used to blackmail Esteban. That's all it could be. Surely you know what it is?"

"I am Esteban's servant, but not always his confidant. I'm sometimes forced to come in and clean up his disasters." Leandro appeared disgusted, as if he'd tasted something foul.

"I don't know what or where it is." She raked her hand through her hair. "If they're holding Ryan, Lola, and Esteban hostage and I can't find it . . ."

"They will kill them."

"Do you care if they kill Esteban?"

"It would be . . . inconvenient."

"Inconvenient." She tried to restrain her voice. "Does that mean you'll help me rescue them?"

"You would trust me?" He moved close to her.

Rose swallowed hard. "No, I don't trust you. I don't have good options here. Why don't you have one of those spy things? The ones that track people. You could shove it up Esteban's ass every time he goes out." Oh, great. Control. Her fear now bordered on panic and she was babbling.

"*Mi dulce* . . ." He smiled at her

Rose's cell phone rang. She motioned for Leandro to come closer. He took the opportunity to slip his arms around her and nuzzle her neck. Rose bit her lip to keep from screaming. Leandro wasn't worried about Esteban. Leandro could easily walk away and let him, Ryan, and Lola die.

She flipped the phone open. "Rose."

"Listen, bitch." The voice was deep, rumbling, and filled with menace. "I want them papers. I want them in twenty-four hours, or your boyfriend, the old lady and that old fart go down. You get them, you call this number." He rattled off the digits. "You want to write it down?"

"No," she said. "I'll remember."

"You go to the police, they die."

The phone went dead. Dread filled her. She hunched her shoulders, wanting to curl up in a tight ball. Agonizing helplessness was not a familiar emotion for her.

Rose started to close the phone, then stopped. She hadn't erased Jimmy's last message. She had to listen to it again. Her heart ached at the thought of hearing his voice again, but maybe there was a clue there. She punched the buttons.

Chapter 22

"Ryan?" Lola's voice drifted out of the darkness. It quivered with apprehension. She leaned against him.

"I'm okay." He spoke with a parched throat. They'd tied his feet, too. His body throbbed with each random movement of the van.

"Esteban?" Ryan said.

"I'm here." Esteban sounded breathless.

"Esteban shot one of them. His body is . . ." Lola moved closer to him. They shared the van with a dead man, but he already knew that. He could feel the body when he moved his tightly bound feet.

"They're going to try to use us to get what Jimmy had, aren't they?" Lola asked.

"Yeah, I think so." Ryan twisted, trying to ease the ache of his body, but it made it worse. His hands had grown numb. There was nothing he could do.

Each time the van slowed or stopped for a light, fumes seeped in and burned their eyes. The heat of sunshine on the metal shell radiated in, and sweat soaked Ryan's shirt. Lola had managed to get her knee under his head so he could at least lie on his side. It seemed like hours, but the van did slow, stop, and move again. Ryan heard the rumble of doors and knew they were rolling inside a larger building. Doors rumbled shut again as the van parked.

The van's back doors swung open, and two men jumped in. They grabbed Lola. She blistered them a few choice names as they dragged her out. Two more men grabbed Esteban. He moaned slightly. His body went limp and they had to hold him up between them.

Ryan couldn't move, but he could see directly behind the van's open doors.

"I want to hurt him." A tall, thin man with sharp features stalked toward Esteban. He had a violent, hateful nature clearly drawn on his face.

"No." Another man, possibly the leader, spoke. He had a rough, deep voice that grumbled like a three-pack-a-day man. Ryan couldn't see him.

"Motherfucker shot Joe," the thin man said.

"Too bad." No sympathy from Deep Voice.

The thin man suddenly punched Esteban in the stomach.

Esteban cried out and collapsed—or would have if the two men hadn't held him between them.

Deep Voice came into view, a big man, gut and muscle, who matched his rough words. He grabbed the thin man and spun him around. As the thin man turned, Deep Voice drew a gun from his pocket. A single deafening gunshot exploded in the building. It drifted to silence. The thin man crumpled to the floor.

Ryan's stomach revolted, but he swallowed the bile that surged into his mouth. They would die if no one rescued them. Even if ransom was called for and paid, these men would not let them live to tell of what they'd seen.

"Okay," Deep voice growled. "Anyone else want to argue?"

Apparently no one did. They cut Ryan's ankles loose and two of them dragged him out. He clamped his teeth tight to keep silent and fight the pain. How many were there? The leader, two holding him, two for Esteban, one for Lola, and two dead, the body in the van, and one lying on his back on the concrete, a pool of thick blood forming around him. The smell of fresh blood filled the air in a sickening cloud.

Ryan had seen death before, multiple deaths and injuries from construction accidents, but he'd only heard of such a casual slaughter. Their lives now depended on Rose and Leandro. But what incentive did Leandro have? With Ryan out of the way, he had Rose. He could only hope that Leandro would come for Esteban, and bring Rose with him. Maybe he wouldn't kill them in front of her.

His captors propelled Ryan toward the back of the empty steel walled building. His legs ached, but at least now he could feel his feet. Esteban staggered between the men holding him. His complexion faded to dangerously pale and he breathed heavily through his mouth.

When they stopped at a door in the back wall, Deep Voice spoke to Ryan. "Take it easy, big man. You go in. They're gonna cut you loose. But you remember, I got her." He placed his gun barrel at Lola's temple.

"What do you want?" Ryan asked. "Money? My attorney can deal with you. Contact Leandro. He'll deal for Esteban."

"You don't know shit," Deep Voice said. "Get in there."

The pair holding Ryan shoved him into the room. Concrete block, about fifteen feet square; probably a storage room at one time, it might as well be a tomb. They backed him up to the far wall and freed him. His swollen hands ached, throbbing with each heartbeat. He rubbed them against his shirt, desperately trying to get circulation going. He remembered Rose's hands when he and Leandro freed her. Dear God, had she hurt that much?

Esteban's captors lowered him to the floor. Deep Voice cut Lola loose and shoved her in. Then the door closed, locking them inside their concrete prison.

Chapter 23

"I need to go home." Rose listened to the message again. A sense of urgency filled her. Herman was the key. The photo in Don Quixote was Herman.

"I'll take you." Leandro walked toward a black Escalade parked by Ryan's truck. The same one he'd driven to rescue her in January. He didn't hurry. He seemed to have no sense of impending doom.

Rose rushed after him. "But what about the bodies?"

"I'll have others deal with them." He opened the Escalade door, then closed it after she climbed in. He walked around and opened the driver's door. "Do you have a key to the gate?"

Rose twisted and dug her key ring out of her pocket, snapped off the gate key, and handed it to him. He opened the console and lifted out a phone. Like a cell phone, but larger. He punched multiple buttons on a box set in the console, far more than necessary to dial any number, then started speaking quickly and quietly in Spanish. He listened a moment, talked more, then hung up.

"You don't like regular cell phones?" she asked.

"Yes, but I prefer that some of my conversations not be overheard. This technology is designed for privacy. I assume you know privacy is critical in this situation."

He drove through the open gate, parked, climbed out, and locked it behind him. He laid the key at the base of one of the posts.

"What's your price, Leandro?" Rose asked when he climbed back behind the wheel. "I'll pay it, but what will it cost me to get back Ryan and Lola?"

Leandro didn't speak for a moment. He seemed pensive, even hesitant. Not like Leandro at all. Didn't he know what he wanted? Then he said, "I wish you to spend a few days with me."

Rose frowned. "I'm asking you to save lives and you're wanting sex. Hey, that's a real bargain for me."

"Perhaps I value you more than you value me."

"Fine." Rose tried to sound brusque and businesslike. She was bargaining, after all, for the lives of people she loved. "How many days is a few?"

"Three, perhaps four."

Leandro started the Escalade and turned toward the street. "Don't worry, *mi dulce*, I have resources. We will find them."

Rose tried for calm, tried to think, work out Jimmy's message in her mind. She rubbed her eyes. No tears, not yet. She didn't have time. She knew the odds. If Leandro couldn't rescue them, no one could.

Leandro drove to her cottage and parked in the back beside her Taurus. She didn't speak during the journey, and he didn't encourage her to do so. Her mind kept reliving the scenes of the day. She kept clenching her fists, wanting to strike something or someone, but there was nothing to fight. At that moment, her mind filled with wrath and she hated Jimmy Beecher.

Leandro followed her inside the cottage. He scanned the room with obvious curiosity. It seemed smaller and shabbier in his presence. The mismatched furniture that suited her so well yesterday seemed so old and worn. He probably lived in pure luxury, but he made no comment on his surroundings.

Herman sat in his usual place on the coffee table. Rose picked him up and rolled him over. It was nothing but a statue.

"I don't understand. What could be so important about Herman?"

Leandro took the ceramic piece from her. He examined it, then frowned. "When was it broken?"

"Broken? I don't know."

She took it back and studied it again. A thin line marked the place where Herman's back leg had been broken off. No, not broken. Carefully, almost surgically, removed, glued back and painted, barely noticeable. She twisted the leg and it popped loose.

Excitement rose as she reached inside the ceramic dog and touched papers, rolled tight. But each time her fingers closed on them they slipped farther inside the fifteen-inch body. Frustration mounting, she went to the kitchen, found a towel and folded it around the statue.

"Forgive me, Herman." She gave the towel-covered dog a sharp rap on the corner of the counter, and Herman broke in half. Maybe later she could glue him back together.

She extracted the papers. Rolled in a tight cylinder to fit Herman's body, they didn't want to lie flat. Finally, she had them spread out. Five sheets. One was a property deed; two were personal letters, written in Spanish. She handed the letters to Leandro. The last two sheets appeared to be a short contract. She carried them into the living room and sat on the couch. Leandro followed and sat too close to her.

"You make me uncomfortable when you crowd me."

Leandro leaned against her. "If you relax, I can make you comfortable."

"I won't be comfortable again until I find Ryan. You don't seem worried about Esteban. Does that mean you know where he is?"

"No, it means I care far less for him than you care for your lover."

Rose already knew that. Leandro had no compelling reason to find Esteban. "At least you're honest."

"In that trivial matter, yes." He laid a graceful hand on her knee and squeezed it.

Rose studied the papers while he read the letters. "This is a deed. The hotel property. In 1940, it belonged to Richard F. Hamilton."

Leandro glanced up from the letters. "These are from one Carmen Salveros Hamilton. Carmen is promising to sell the property to one James Brighton, with whom she is ecstatically in love. She expresses her love in a most explicit manner." He chuckled softly. "It sounds interesting. Anatomically challenging, but interesting. Shall I translate for you?"

Rose ignored him. "James Brighton. He bought the hotel property from Hamilton—only the contract isn't signed. And the date . . . that's over fifty years ago."

"Esteban, or rather the corporation, bought the property from a younger man named Harris Brighton. Possibly a son."

"But if the contract wasn't signed . . .? Does that mean Brighton didn't actually own the property? Didn't Esteban's lawyers do a title search? They would surely have found any problems. Right?"

"Presumably."

"Jimmy died for these papers."

Leandro leaned forward to gaze at the documents on the coffee table. Whatever he thought, he didn't speak. Finally, he said, "Come with me. I need to find Mr. Harris Brighton and talk with him."

"Are you sure you want me along?"

He brushed his fingers along her cheek, a ghost of a touch, so soft she barely felt it. "I want you with me. I can protect you."

As it had from their first meeting, everything inside her rose to meet that touch, to desire more. She stepped back. Distance was the key. It was imperative that she keep her distance. She would give him what he wanted eventually, but it was crucial that she keep control of herself until then. She'd consider her desire for him an illness and she'd fight it as long as she could.

"What about these?" She held up the papers.

He studied them for a moment, then said, "Bring them."

Rose folded the papers and stuck them in her pocket. Leandro walked out the door first and, as she followed him, Rose removed the papers and dropped them behind the couch. No point in carrying something so valuable into danger.

Chapter 24

Ryan staggered toward Lola as soon as the door closed. She cowered there where Deep Voice had left her, standing alone and trembling. She'd cursed and fought while they held her, but gave into fear when released. Ryan caught her as she collapsed, then almost went down with her. He had to sit, too, so he carried her over to the wall where Esteban sat, pale and breathing hard. Lola's body trembled in his arms as he drew her down and cradled her against him.

"Are you okay, Esteban?" he asked.

"I'm not seriously injured, if that's what you mean." Esteban still sounded rough.

"Lola?" Ryan stroked her hair.

"I'm all right." She clung to him.

"Where was Leandro, Esteban?" Ryan asked. "Sam said he arrived with you."

"Following the delicious scent of his newest object of passion, I suppose." His voice had a casual note that sounded odd given the situation. "I see she is not here, either."

"No." Ryan hugged Lola tighter. "Guess that means it's up to the two of them to rescue us." He wanted to demand answers from Esteban. Had someone else known of and coveted whatever Jimmy had?

"Leandro will come for me," Esteban said.

The only light in their block-walled, windowless prison came from a single bulb suspended from a cord in a tiny washroom on the opposite wall.

The washroom had a window; Lola could get out if bars

hadn't covered it. What about the roof? Solid steel. No escape there. The pleasant, seventy-degree March weather outside would soon drop low enough to allow a dangerous chill to seep into the concrete room. Somehow, he had to keep Lola warm.

Esteban carefully raised his arm and picked gently at his jacket sleeve. He drew out an object the size of a small, thin cell phone, then used the wall as a brace to force himself to his feet. He clung to that wall as he slowly shuffled to the bathroom and placed the device in the window. When he turned back, he gave Ryan a smug smile.

"What did Jimmy have on you? He was blackmailing you." Ryan asked as Esteban carefully lowered himself to the floor again. "Is that what these assholes want? Or do they want money?"

"Mr. Beecher and I had discussions recently about a certain object in his possession. As for what these brutes want, it may be, as you said, money. You, yourself, are not a poor man. Perhaps they think to double their return. They are most unwise, however, to underestimate Leandro."

Ryan shifted to ease the ache in his legs.

"You sure Leandro will come for you, Esteban?" Lola asked.

"Absolutely." Esteban smiled.

"And what do you base that certainty on?" Her voice filled with hatred.

"Leandro is quite loyal, though sometimes I wonder why." He sounded so condescending. "And of course, your charming flower is intelligent enough to not give him what he wants, until he finds *you*."

* * * *

Leandro drove to the Rising Sun Marina on the banks of the Intracoastal Waterway. Rows of concrete piers stretched out into the water. Each pier had multiple boats of all sizes attached at their bows like nursing puppies. Such a beautiful day. The sun glinted on the water farther out as a breeze lifted it to a light chop. A few boats made their way back and forth, though it was early for the unruly racket and irritating presence of jet skis.

"Can you imagine living on a boat?" Rose asked.

"Yes. I have a boat and I often live there," Leandro said. He sounded amused.

"Really? Seems to me you would always want a back door to sneak out."

Leandro laughed. It sounded companionable and free; as if she'd touched upon some facet of him he truly wanted her to understand. "Back doors are always advisable, but not always possible. Sometimes, I'm required to fight my way out instead of running."

He turned into the parking lot and drove past the large marina buildings and retail store. Behind them were huge open buildings where more boats were stored out of the water, suspended on top of one another in dry dock.

Leandro parked at the end of one pier, not far from a white Town Car, probably the one Esteban had used the day she met him. The two goons who had accompanied Esteban that day propelled a woman toward the car. Each held an arm, but she struggled and kicked at them with long, lovely legs; legs shown off by incredibly short shorts. Her bathing suit top, two black triangles with strings, barely covered the nipples of perfectly rounded, surgically shaped breasts. Copper hair, redder than Brianna's, danced in the sunlight as she fought. As she reached the car, she spotted the Escalade. She jerked one hand free and gave a provocative, brazen, universal salute with her middle finger. Her lovely face twisted into a sneer.

"Oh, my," Rose said. "What does that mean in Spanish?"

Leandro sighed. "Please wait here."

He opened his door, climbed out, and walked to the woman. The slightest wave and the goons backed away. The redhead crossed her arms, emphasizing her breasts, and glared at him. He brushed a strand of that magnificent hair from her face as he spoke to her. Her body relaxed, suddenly docile, and her head bowed. Leandro lifted her chin with one hand and kissed her. Kissed her and she relaxed and melted against him like sweet oil.

Rose's stomach tightened. Her own reaction to him had been the same. She bit her lip.

"All right, Rose," she said. "Suck it in, girl. No more of his shit."

Leandro killed people. Leandro used people, including the beauty he kissed again and carefully eased into the Town Car. He used that one for sex and told her sweet lies she wanted to believe. Unfortunately, in spite of her resolve, jealousy chewed at Rose like a dog worrying a bone.

Leandro carefully closed the door to the Town Car, and it rolled away. He returned and opened Rose's door. "Come, *mi dulce*."

Rose climbed out. "That's a mighty fancy babe you've got there, buddy."

"Anita?" He shrugged. "A woman of many fine qualities. Unfortunately, intelligence and discretion are not among them. Her curiosity in this matter would be dangerous. For her—and me. It's not safe to know too much."

Leandro laid an arm across her shoulders and drew her close. It tipped her off balance and she had to grab him to steady herself. He laughed again and led her toward the dock. What would happen when the laughter stopped?

"You think I'll show discretion?" Rose asked. "What happens to me if I get to know too much?"

Leandro stopped. He had one hand on her waist and the other gently caught her chin. His thumb brushed across her lips. "Look at me."

Rose met his eyes, dark expressive eyes that could be killer cold or wide and open as they were now. Leandro lied, she reminded herself. He lied with words, and he lied with his eyes.

"I will never hurt you, Rose. I swear that on my life and in the name of my father and mother, whom I truly loved."

He'd used her name, not the lighter *mi dulce*. If he meant to comfort her, to reassure her, he failed. And he knew it.

"Of course." Amusement edged into his voice again. "You now have the sworn word of a psychopath."

He held her hand as they walked out the pier toward a massive yacht. The lean, sleek, hundred and fifty foot vessel floated graceful as a sea bird ready to fly. Smoke-colored windows lined all three decks, making a stark contrast against the blinding white hull.

"That's incredible," Rose said.

"Thank you. This is my Guarida."

Rose frowned. "It's yours?"

"Yes. A gift from Esteban."

"How many lives did it cost?"

"More than I remember." Leandro frowned. "You didn't leave those papers where they would be easily found, did you?"

Rose shook her head. Damn him.

"Good. I'll retrieve them later."

Leandro led her up a carpeted ramp and onto the bottom deck, a simple affair of white with brass fittings, then inside and up finely finished wooden stairs to the second deck. The room they entered would rival a five star hotel she once rewired.

Rose pictured the comfortable cottage she shared with Ryan, her home with its used, lumpy couch and mismatched chairs. They, certainly Ryan, could afford better. Somehow, though, the place suited them. It comforted them, grounded them in the real world where people worked to build something substantial, monuments to their endless labor. She doubted she'd be happier if she lived in a floating palace with gold and white covered furniture and sparkling glass coffee tables.

A U-shaped bar with hanging racks of glassware sat in the middle of the expansive room, and the tinted windows on both sides gave an excellent view of the marina and Intracoastal Waterway. Would sipping champagne out of crystal glasses be as much fun as hoisting a mug at Brody's? Ryan suited her, loved her. So why did her body betray her—and him—at Leandro's touch.

"This is a sophisticated vessel," Leandro said. "With a little extra fuel, we could sail to the Mediterranean. Would you like that? To see the Greek islands. So beautiful, the Mediterranean. On the north, the mountains of Italy come right down to the sea."

"I never thought about it." Rose realized the narrowness of her world. Each year she would vow to do something about it, and each year there was another job site to quell her curiosity.

An older woman met them there, a plain, gray-haired woman in a plain, gray dress. Leandro spoke to her in Spanish, and she nodded, then disappeared toward the front of the ship.

Leandro walked to a polished wood panel wall. He touched it, and it opened to reveal a large computer system complete with three screens and other equipment Rose couldn't identify. He sat in a chair and the screens surged to life.

"Sit, *mi dulce*." He picked up a phone and began speaking Spanish.

Rose didn't know the words, of course, but she heard the command in his voice. She sat in one of the damask chairs.

The woman returned, bearing a tray with a bottle of wine and two glasses. A young man in a white uniform followed, carrying a tray of fruit, cheese, and thin slices of bread. They set the trays on a coffee table in front of Rose. The woman poured two glasses of wine. One she placed in front of Rose, and the other she carried to Leandro. He accepted it, his eyes never leaving the screens.

The man and woman left as silently as they entered.

"Eat," Leandro said. "It may be a while before we have the answers we need."

Yes, Rose was hungry. Nothing but coffee for her since that morning. Fear had kept the hunger at bay until she saw and smelled the food. The fruit she didn't recognize, but it tasted and luscious as the finest desert. The cheese melted on her tongue like cream with a bit of a smoky flavor. Shame filled her as soon as the edge of hunger dulled. She remembered Ryan and Lola. Would their kidnappers feed them? Give them water?

Leandro continued to speak rapid Spanish into the phone while Rose ate. He watched her and occasionally sipped his wine. She barely touched hers. It was good, liquid gold on her tongue, but she wanted to stay alert.

Finally, he hung up the phone.

"I have found Brighton. He lives in a rather large and secure mansion in Avondale. It is unlikely that he would hold prisoners there. He does, however, own certain properties near the shipyards. I have men observing them."

He leaned back in his chair, watching her. His face was

inscrutable, and his eyes held mystery. What was he thinking?

"Do you enjoy living here?" Rose asked. She needed to break the silence, to focus his attention on something besides her.

He shrugged. "I find it comfortable."

"What about Anita? Where does she live?"

Leandro laughed, his face lively and animated. Had he caught a hint of her jealousy? "Anita lives here at times. But I change residences often."

Rose would bet he changed women often, too.

The silent woman in gray removed the tray, then disappeared into the depths of the ship again. Leandro left his chair and knelt in front of Rose. "Will you not rest a while? Whatever we do will happen much later tonight."

"If that's what you want." Rose kept her voice cool and calm. "I know I can't save Ryan and Lola without your help."

"And you are quite willing to pay any price necessary to achieve that end."

"Yes."

"I don't understand you. But your desire burns me. I feel it. Just the touch, the scent of you makes me want you in my arms. Why do you fight it?"

"I told you. I don't take everything I'm offered."

"So, what you won't give freely you will give in payment for a debt?"

She nodded.

"And would it be such a difficult thing to do?" His dark eyes peered deeply into hers.

"No, not difficult. It's simply not my choice." She sounded pretentious, but at that point, didn't care.

Leandro led her up another set of stairs and down a hallway the length of the ship. They passed closed doors on the way. How many rooms did the thing have? At the end of the hallway, he opened a door and drew her in.

"This is my room," he said. "Men are coming who do not speak Spanish, and you should not be there when we talk. Will you wait here and rest? I'll come for you when it's time. You must trust me on this."

Rose nodded. She had no choice but to believe that he was indeed a professional criminal with cool knowledge of life and death matters. She also had to believe that he had the resources to do as he wished. He kissed her lightly on the mouth, stepped out, and closed the door. Rose wondered if he locked it, but didn't check. Instead, she examined the room.

A closet held a few black suits and white shirts. She glanced at the labels. Armani and others she'd never heard of. He had nice silk ties, conservative but colorful, a few books on a bookshelf, all in Spanish. Other items lay around, but nothing personal.

In the bathroom she found a fine leather case with a razor and men's toiletries. It occurred to her that the man might not actually live anywhere, but move from place to place, knowing someone like the woman in gray would appear and provide certain necessities. Nothing in the room spoke to a female presence. Whatever Anita did there, she didn't linger long enough to leave a mark.

Rose opened one cabinet door and found something interesting—a small arsenal of hand guns in a number of different sizes. Boxes of ammo filled the shelf below them.

"Just what your high class criminal needs in his bedroom," she muttered to herself as she searched through them. All too big for her to carry concealed. She could shoot; Daddy taught her as he taught her pool. Years ago. Better not take a chance on a weapon over which she'd have dubious control.

The next cabinet held something more practical. Knives. Most too big, but one had a boot sheath. Thank God she'd taken the time to put on her boots that morning instead of tennis shoes. Another with a four-inch blade she slipped into the waistband of her jeans along her spine. The sheath for that one clipped tight to the material. She closed the cabinet door after moving the other pieces so possibly no one would notice the absence of the smaller ones. She'd give them back to him later. A minor defense, not much in the way of weapons, but she'd managed to make a difference with a nine-pound pipe wrench just hours ago. She shuddered at that memory.

Rose lay across the king sized bed. Damn, how soft. When she had Ryan in her arms again, she'd buy one. She would rest now, but not sleep. It was, after all, only mid-afternoon. She closed her eyes, trying to picture Ryan's face, to remember the feel of his skin and his hands on her.

Rose woke slowly. The light filtered through the tinted windows and made it hard to tell time. So much for her intention not to sleep. Leandro lay beside her, a bit over an arm's length away. He slept, too. She listened to the sound of his steady, rhythmic breathing.

He'd removed his jacket and rolled up the sleeves of his white shirt. He slept on his side, one hand reaching toward her. The masks he wore when awake faded in sleep; how gentle he seemed there, how human.

He woke instantly like a prey animal at the sound of a predator's step. He rose up on one elbow and frowned. "You are a dangerous woman," he said.

"Why? Because you relaxed enough to sleep on the same bed with me?"

He abruptly rose and left the room. "Come. We need to leave."

"Whoa," she said softly to herself. "Guess I nailed that one." Leandro might screw Anita, but he didn't *sleep* with her—or anyone else.

Rose followed him back into the boat's main salon.

"We have found them. You're perceptive, *mi dulce*. Esteban does indeed have a GPS locator and has activated it only moments ago. I thought it damaged or lost. I don't know why he did not do so before now, perhaps waiting to get to a place where he could be better tracked."

"He trusts you, doesn't he?"

"It would seem so."

"And you're loyal to him?"

"It would seem so. Now, go into Anita's room. On the left, just before mine. She is about your size. Find dark colored clothing. I don't suppose you would wait here on the yacht for me."

"No. I won't wait." He wasn't going to leave her behind. She walked toward the hallway, but then turned to speak before she left him. "In case you hadn't noticed, Anita and I are not the same size. My breasts are much smaller. And mine are real."

Rose opened the door to Anita's room and walked into chaos. Clothing in a myriad of colors lay scattered across the floor and furniture in silk rainbows. Among them were unopened bags and boxes from exclusive stores.

How odd to be pawing through another woman's clothing. Anita had expensive tastes and Rose bet Leandro indulged her. The open jewelry box revealed sparkling diamonds, those too tossed in a careless pile. She picked up one blue silky thing. A camisole? God, how soft.

After much digging, she found a pair of new black jeans in a bag. Versace. They probably cost more than Rose made for a week of hard labor. She unlaced her boots and set them aside, careful to keep the boot sheath with its blade in place. Then she unzipped and pulled off her jeans. Versace's designer threads slid on as if she'd greased her legs with fine lotion. Up over her hips right to the V sewn into the waistband where it lay across her spine. She zipped them and ran her hands over her hips to smooth them. Perfect. The knife sheath hooked into that signature V and clipped tight.

Rose removed a black silk button-up shirt from the closet. It covered a thin tank top made of dark silver gray silk. The tag attached to the tank top? Three hundred dollars. She had her back to the door when she removed her flannel work shirt. She hadn't worn a bra that morning because she thought they'd be coming right back to the cottage. The supple gray silk slipped over her head. It drifted down like fine dry powder.

She turned and Leandro stood at the door. She hadn't heard it open. He had another of those unreadable expressions on his face. If he spied the knife at the back of her jeans, he didn't speak of it. He'd changed clothes, too. Black pants and shirt—and the gun, openly displayed this time. He walked to her and laid his hands on her waist. He slid them up and his thumbs stroked her nipples, easily visible through the fine material. A shock ran from them and spread fire all through her body.

Leandro laughed, deep and intimate. The sound caressed her like sweet lotion smoothed down her skin.

Rose twisted away from him and grabbed the black shirt. She shoved her arms in the sleeves.

"Ah, *mi dulce*," he said. "Again I ask you, why do you deny your own desire?" He sounded genuinely curious.

Safely buttoned, Rose faced him. "And again, I'll tell you. The things people *want* aren't always good for them. Personally, I wish you were ancient, ugly, and had offensive body odor."

"Ah, but then I would be Esteban. It is a matter of value. I paid for much of what I have with my body, which Esteban finds quite attractive."

"You paid for it with your soul, which I'm sure the devil will find attractive, too. Which is worse, to fuck him or kill for him?"

Leandro moved close and breathed in her ear. "I fucked him for wealth. I kill for him because, sometimes, I enjoy it."

"And you'll kill me too, because I already know too much."

"Then why did you come with me?"

"You're my only hope of getting Ryan and Lola free. If you need my body—and my life—to do that, fine."

Leandro abruptly released her and walked away.

Chapter 25

Ryan forced himself to his feet when the door opened. Two men swaggered in, but neither was the deep-voiced bastard in charge. One carried a pistol pointed at them. The other had a grocery bag and a couple jugs of water.

"Lucky you," the one with the pistol said. "You get a last meal." He waved his weapon at them. The barbaric smile on his face was more menacing than the gun. "Send the woman over here."

"Come get her," Ryan said. He doubted the man with the pistol would shoot. If they brought food and water, someone wanted them alive a while longer. No sound came through the open door, so maybe the others left. Here was something he might be able to fight.

A third man entered the room. He carried a Taser. The third man rushed straight toward him while the second went for Lola. He'd have one chance.

As the second man grabbed Lola, Ryan charged, caught him around the waist and twisted him around to use as a shield. The one with the Taser pulled the trigger—and hit his own man. Ryan's shield squealed. Ryan shoved him into the man with the pistol and both went down.

Ryan jumped on top of them. If he could get the pistol . . . he grabbed it and twisted . . . he had it. He rolled, trying to get the pistol right in his hand.

The man with the Taser had a back-up weapon. He shot again.

Ryan screamed as pure agony raced through his body like acid in his veins.

Sounds of Lola's desperate struggle suddenly were silenced by the brutal sound of a fist on flesh. He lay on cold concrete, his own movements involuntary spasms. The door slammed shut, leaving him to recover in silence.

* * * *

Night had fallen when Leandro led Rose to a long gray delivery truck painted with the name and logo of Heat-Zone, a company specializing in HVAC repair and service. Even though he'd given up his suit for black pants, shirt and jacket, he appeared no less elegant. He opened the passenger door for her, and she climbed in. As she did, she glanced into the van's darkened interior. Men sat back there, though she barely could see them. She quickly fastened her seat belt, and stared straight ahead.

Leandro climbed into the driver's seat and started the engine.

"This won't take long, *mi dulce.*"

"What if they're already . . . ?" Rose couldn't bring herself to say it. She'd remained calm most of the day, but as night and impending action closed in on her, fear rose.

"It is possible, yes, that they have been killed. Unlikely, but possible," Leandro conceded. "Then it becomes a matter of vengeance."

"I guess you're an expert. I'm new in the vengeance game." Malevolence filled her voice. Scared, she was so scared. She wanted to strike at something. He was the closest target. If he and Esteban hadn't entered her life, she would be with Ryan. Lola had convinced her of the inevitability of their meeting, in spite of Jimmy's obsession.

"Vengeance?" Leandro spoke the word like a caress. "No, Rose. I'm far better at action than reaction. Do you understand?"

"Yes. You're the one who does the bad things people want vengeance for."

"It's much more satisfying."

"Satisfying? As long as you're not the victim. As long as you're not the one who's afraid. Does it work for you? That preemptive strike against fear?"

He didn't answer her questions.

Rose closed her eyes and tried not to hate Jimmy, tried not to condemn him. His message said he was going to make things right. How? What had he planned to do before he accidentally set off the bomb meant for her? Kill Esteban? Not likely he'd get past Leandro, but if Jimmy knew he was dying, he might have tried. Just giving Esteban the papers back probably wouldn't have worked, either. Esteban would not forgive someone who caused him trouble.

There wasn't much traffic, not that time on a Sunday night. Leandro drove into the Arconell Industrial Park, not far from the river and the docks. Large warehouse buildings, monolithic cement boxes with acres of asphalt parking, lined the entrance road. Multiple semi-trailers backed up to open loading docks under aluminum trees carrying clusters of halogen bulbs to create false daylight. As Leandro drove on, they entered the older area of the park where aging metal buildings lined the pot-holed street. No well-lighted 24-hour operations here. Only repair shops and small businesses, and a few mid-sized warehouses waiting on Monday morning to commence a new week. An occasional security bulb cast a pool of light that emphasized the shadows around it.

He spoke in Spanish, and one of the men in the back answered him in the same. Leandro drove onto the next block, into the shadows, and stopped the truck. The back door opened, and the men inside exited as silently as they had ridden to their destination. Leandro drove on, around another street, and parked behind a building. He shut off the engine and removed the keys from the ignition.

When he spoke, his voice sounded desolate as a land left barren by war and pestilence. "There is nothing that will stop fear, Rose. It is a human condition."

"I know. I'm afraid right now. Terrified. But there are things more important than fear. Saving Ryan and Lola for one." Rose sighed. One vital thing remained. "Ryan and Lola don't know about those papers. There's no reason they should. Will Esteban tell them?"

"And admit his folly? Take a chance that they might kill him for what he'd done? That would be out of character for him."

"Then they're both safe from you. I mean if they don't know about the papers. Whatever happens to me, you won't . . ."

"No, I won't hurt them."

"What about Esteban?" she asked. "Is he going to tell you to kill them?"

"I will deal with Esteban." He opened the van door. The interior light did not come on. "You must stay here, *mi dulce*. I beg you. You cannot help us and it might hinder us to protect you, too."

"How long?" Rose asked. That sudden command surprised her. Why have her dress in dark clothing if he hadn't wanted her to accompany him? Had he planned for her to accompany him? Something had changed his mind. Something she said? Maybe he couldn't see the suspicion on her face or hear it in her voice.

"I will come for you, if things go as planned."

"And if they don't?"

"If I don't return in an hour and a half, get out. Go and hide in the shadows. When daylight comes, find a place to call the police. You may tell them whatever you wish. Promise me you will stay here. You're not trained for this."

"All right. I'll stay."

He climbed out and walked away into the darkness.

What should she do? She clenched her fist tight and bounced it on her knee in agitation. Filled with restless energy, her mind kept replaying the day's images. Leandro's casual use of a gun. Her own use of a pipe wrench and the sound it made against human flesh. Esteban and his GPS, Leandro and his army, too easy, too pat, too organized.

Rose glanced at the digital clock on the dash. She hadn't anticipated waiting. Fifteen minutes. He'd been gone fifteen minutes. A movement caught her eye in the shadows, directly in front of the van. Barely a silhouette . . . how far? A hundred feet? She held her breath, anticipating the next movement. Dread filled her. Leandro didn't trust her after all—and there was something he didn't want her to see. The movement came again. Closer this time.

Rose left her seat and crawled through the van. She would not cower there, hoping for the best. When she reached the back door, she twisted the handle. It opened with a soft click and well-oiled hinges made no sound. If only one person observed the front, she could get away. She dropped to the ground and slid on her stomach into a patch of straggly bushes, then crawled behind a building.

* * * *

Ryan's muscles ached and joints throbbed as the cold from the concrete seeped in and the agony settled there. He didn't move because Lola had fallen into a fitful doze, leaning against him. He had no way of telling how much time had passed. She'd not spoken since the goons had brought her back and shoved her into the room. He held her tight, trying to ease her suffering and comfort her, and she remained calm—except for her fingers pulling at him, trying to draw him closer.

Esteban shifted, as if trying to make himself comfortable. How old was he? He appeared ageless, but he moved slowly, like a man with a vise on arthritic joints. To Ryan's surprise, he had given Lola his suit jacket to ward off the chill.

The door opened and brilliant flashes of light played across the room, blinding him. Ryan averted his eyes as he released Lola and forced himself to stand. He anticipated the worst. Maybe he could do a little more damage before they took him down. Through unintended consequences, Jimmy, a man who loved them, had led them to this.

Heavily armed men dressed in black entered the room. They moved quickly, as if they knew they would meet no resistance, not the high alert of a SWAT team.

Leandro followed them.

Leandro went straight to Esteban and knelt beside him. Ryan helped Lola to her feet. She clung to him, trembling.

Without speaking, Leandro stood and motioned the men to Esteban.

"Are you injured?" Leandro asked Ryan.

Ryan shook his head.

"Good. I'll send you home, then take care of business here."

Ryan followed him out of their prison, holding Lola tight against him. As they left the room, he glimpsed a group of men standing like shadows in the darkness across the building, shapes but no faces. No sound of a struggle had made its way into their prison, but Leandro's men moved quickly, silent and professional, the kind who could kill swiftly and walk away without looking back.

Leandro led them outside to where Esteban's white Town Car waited. His men followed, two of them supporting Esteban.

Ryan helped Lola into the Town Car, then fought his pain and went to Leandro, who waited with more of the black-clad men. Ryan counted eight in that bunch.

"Where's Rose?" he asked. He kept his words steady, not wanting to antagonize the man with all the guns. The man who had Rose.

"Safe," Leandro said. "I thought it best that she not be involved in this."

"And how did she react to you telling her what's best for her?" Fury leaked into his voice. What had Leandro done to her? He knew Rose, and he knew she'd want to be there.

"She objected, but I insisted."

"Then let's go get her," Ryan demanded. His chest ached and it seemed like his body might be giving out.

"I'll bring her to you," Leandro said. His tone was condescending. "The driver will take you home, and Esteban to a doctor."

"Esteban has his own army?" Ryan nodded at the troops standing alert around them.

"I have a small cadre of trusted security operatives for some of my enterprises."

"And the men who kidnapped us?"

"You are concerned about their welfare?" Leandro sounded amused.

"No. They raped Lola. Several of them. I want to hurt them." More than hurt. He wanted to torture and maim.

Ryan heard Leandro draw a breath. Surprised?

"I will deal with the situation," he said. No amusement in that voice. The cool polished killer sounded cold as the bodies he'd sent to the earth. "It is best that you know nothing. Tell me, do you plan to call the police? It would not be advisable at this point. I can arrange for a doctor for your Lola, or a private hospital if necessary."

"Does Rose's safety depend on my not calling the police? Is that why you're holding her?" Ryan clenched his fists.

"No. I will not harm her. I merely want to enjoy her company for a few days. Let me tell you why you shouldn't involve the police. The problem in this city is almost resolved. The only unresolved issue is the bomb, and if you are quiet, that will go away in time. You will have a prosperous future. You will build Olivarez Corporation a fine hotel. I will return your lovely Rose and you may marry her. And you will never hear from me again. Go now."

Leandro's face was unreadable in the half-light. He turned and walked away. Two of the black clad men, armed men, blocked Ryan so he couldn't follow.

Useless to argue, Ryan knew. "Dear God," he whispered. "Please let him love her as much as I do." His heart cringed at the thought of Leandro having her, but if the man loved her, he would keep her safe.

* * * *

Rose had returned to Anita's room before they left, and found a thin, black jacket. Not much protection against the chill that now seeped in, but it wouldn't slow her down. Once she was sure no one had followed her from the van, she eased her way along to the next street. She crossed it, then slipped into the shadows of a five-foot alley between metal buildings. The air had the acrid odor of old motor oil and pesticide. She crouched low and carefully picked her way along a wall, desperate to avoid the piles of scrap metal carelessly tossed away. Something shifted under her foot. Her ankle turned. A single piece of steel clashed against another piece. Not loud to her ears, but tension made it reverberate in her mind. She froze and held tight against the building, apprehensive and alert for the sound of footsteps. Long minutes stretched into the night.

No one approached to investigate.

At the corner, she stopped and peered out. Which way did he go? All the buildings appeared the same, square or rectangular metal-clad boxes. She waited and listened. Road sounds, white noise in the distance, then faint voices from her right. She'd have to cross another street. She tried to see through the shadows, then gave up and drew a deep breath. She dashed across the asphalt and back into darkness.

Voices—again from her right. She followed, creeping between two more of the metal buildings, a car repair shop and a used appliance store. Not much trash here, but . . . something squeaked and moved under her boot.

She jumped, tripped, and dropped to one knee. Tremors, panic driven muscle spasms, shot through her legs. Don't scream. Don't run. She'd started down a reckless path and had to see its end. She wrapped her arms around her body and knelt there shivering until calm returned and she could walk again. Sneaking around in the dark might work in the movies, but it sucked in real life.

A fleeting thought of returning to the delivery truck came—and went. She'd committed herself in this. She had to know what was going on.

Light flashed as she neared the corner. Headlights.

Dear God, footsteps on asphalt, someone coming her way. She backed up and cowered down against the metal wall, low on the ground. Closer now. Breathe shallow, she ordered herself, but don't hold your breath. The ambient light silhouetted a man's form. Another six feet and she could touch him. She kept her white face away from him, but did sneak a quick glance. He faced away from her, staring in the other direction. Dressed in black? One of Leandro's men? Gun ready, on patrol, guarding . . . what?

The man strolled away.

Score one for her on evasion. She couldn't cower there, though. Back to the corner and peek around. Thirty feet away, in a shallow pool of light, sat what had to be Esteban's white Town Car. As she watched, it rolled away.

One of the security bulbs gave her enough light to see

Leandro and his men had gathered in front of a building. Odd, none of them seemed to be in a crisis or attack mode. What happened to the big bang rescue mission? They spoke softly—in Spanish, of course.

Rose bit her lip to stifle a moan. Were Ryan, Lola and Esteban not there? But the Town Car . . . Four or five more men joined them, none of them dressed like Leandro's black-clad troops.

Leandro spoke to one and he answered—in the deep rough voice of the man who had called her to tell her the price she'd have to pay to free Ryan, Lola, and Esteban. For a moment, Rose's mind couldn't comprehend what she heard. Leandro was behind the kidnapping. He'd set it up, probably to force her to find what Jimmy had. Set it up to have her, too.

The men withdrew into the warehouse, leaving only a few behind to stand guard. Get away, her mind screamed. Call the police, reason urged. A sharp spike of pain, a cramp from crouching too long, made its way up her leg. She slowly rose and backed away into the alley. Where was her cell phone? Still in her jacket on Leandro's boat. No matter, if she could hide, stay out of the way until she could get help—

"Hey, bitch," said a voice from behind her. "Remember us?"

"Yeah, bitch." Another voice.

She remembered. Cochran and Bedlow.

Chapter 26

Rose didn't hesitate. She leaped forward and made a desperate attempt to flee into the darkness. Across the street to another building, between it and its neighbor and—trapped against a chain link fence. Too tall to climb, but a two-foot hole gapped at the bottom. Rose lunged for it, head first. She scrambled across the ground, using her elbows and knees, almost through . . . hands grabbed her feet and dragged her back.

"Come on, you stupid bitch." Bedlow's voice squeaked in a high breathless pitch. And she thought Cochran was the one out of shape. She twisted. He couldn't hold onto her as she rolled to her feet. She balled up her fist and slammed it into the middle of Bedlow's face. This was her second time on that target, but now she had a better angle. His nose gave way under her knuckles. He staggered backward.

Rose charged him, punching him square in the chest, directly over his heart. All her strength went into that blow. Bedlow reeled backward. He stumbled and fell against a steel railing that blocked off a loading dock in front of the building. His head hit the rail with a hollow crack. He crumpled to the concrete, limp as the silk camisole she'd slipped on only a few hours ago.

Leandro's men had her then, one at each arm. Like an oiled machine, the others fanned out around her. No escape this time.

Cochran was bending over Bedlow. "You killed him," he choked out the words. He straightened. His pudgy hands made fists. He charged toward her.

"Hey, guys," Rose told her captors, "hang on to me."

"We plan to," one of them said.

Just as Cochran reached striking distance, Rose braced herself against the strong men gripping her arms, jerked both feet up, and smashed them into his gut.

Cochran went down. His wheezing reached catastrophic proportions as he struggled to drag air into his lungs. He rolled sideways and puked, gasped it down, and choked again. He hacked and coughed like a dying engine.

"Why don't one of you big boys call him an ambulance?" she said to her captors.

They both chuckled under their breath.

"Damn, girl," the one on her right said. "Ain't never seen anyone do that outside of them TV wrestling shows."

Leandro arrived then. He gazed first at Bedlow, who lay crumpled and unmoving, then at the still-choking Cochran. He approached Rose. "Watch her feet," the man at her right warned.

"*Mi dulce*, why didn't you stay in the van as I asked you to? You promised me." The bastard sounded so disappointed; like she was a kid who'd given her word she wouldn't leave the yard, then ran off to the candy store.

"Yeah, I promised." He changed the situation, not her. She jerked futilely against the hands holding her. "I promised before you set the imbecile twins on me."

Leandro shook his head. "I did not. They must have been following you. Your lover is on his way to safety and I would have taken you to him. Now . . ."

Leandro spoke again in Spanish, and his men dragged her away.

Did he tell the truth? Had he let Ryan and Lola go? She probably would never know.

They led her back to the now lighted warehouse. Inside, two of Leandro's men were hurling bodies in the back of a van. Deep Voice and his cohorts? Probably. All had bloody shirts and eyes open wide in death. Dear God, how many had died this night?

Rose shivered. She'd probably join them in a few minutes.

Leandro the killer wouldn't leave a witness. With no time for regret, and to fight her fear, she focused on what she had left—the memory of Ryan and the loving safety of his arms.

Another of Leandro's troopers approached her. One of those holding her grabbed her jacket and snatched it off her shoulder, then tore her shirtsleeve. Anita's fine silk garment gave way and exposed her arm. Terror raced through her when the needle appeared. She twisted and kicked in panic, heedless of any harm she might do herself. A strong woman, she fought until two more grabbed her legs. It took four of them to wrestle her down.

Leandro appeared. Close enough.

She spit in his face.

His head jerked back. A prick at her arm and the world wobbled, the lights became streaked blurs, then faded into darkness.

Chapter 27

Lola rushed to the bathroom the minute she walked in her house. Ryan heard the water running for a long time. She'd refused to go to a doctor, even when he begged her. She swore she wasn't injured. When she emerged dressed in a long thick robe, she staggered to him again and he held her tight. She trembled so he led her to sit on the couch. "I'll never be clean again," she said.

Ryan choked on his helplessness. "God, I'm so sorry." He rubbed his hands across his face.

"Ryan, you're one man. What could you do? Damn Jimmy to hell! This is this fault!"

The distress in her voice only increased his misery. He hadn't protected her or Rose. Even with too many men and too many guns, he should have fought harder. He should have died fighting. He wished he had died fighting.

Lola gazed up at him. "Did Leandro kill them? Our . . . kidnappers."

"I don't know. Probably. He told me not to get involved. He said he'd bring Rose back in a few days."

"You believe him?" Lola's voice said she did not.

"I want to."

"Do you want to call the police?" Lola asked.

"No. It's too late." He didn't want to think of Rose as a hostage. All he had to go on was the word of a man who filled him with revulsion. "I'm sure he's cleaned up all evidence at the warehouse by now."

"What should we do?" Lola tugged her robe tighter and her

hands twisted in the fabric.

"Wait. It's all we can do. Now." Regrets, so many regrets.

"Go clean up," Lola said. "Then we can talk." She sounded less despondent, more in control.

Ryan walked into Lola's spare bedroom and flipped on the light. It flashed on the envelope he'd taken from Jimmy's trailer what seemed ages ago. Lola had moved his things to Rose's cottage, and he hadn't been back in the room since then. He should look at it, since Jimmy considered it important enough to hide. He opened it, sat on the bed, and drew out the papers to read. When he finished, he sat stunned for minutes, his body rigid and unable to move. When he could, he walked back into the living room. Lola sat on the couch.

"Lola?"

She turned at the sound of his voice.

"Honey, what's wrong. You look . . ." She caught sight of the papers. "Where did you get those?"

"Jimmy's trailer." He sat on the couch beside her and offered them to her. It surprised him to see the hand proffering the pages shaking.

Lola shook her head.

"You owe me an explanation." Ryan hated the anger and despair he heard in his own voice. He forced his hands to relax before he crushed the documents.

"I promised. Jimmy promised, we . . ."

Ryan wasn't going to accept that. He didn't want to batter an emotionally and physically wounded woman with his words, but he had to know. "Please say it and get it over with! Are you my mother?"

Sobbing, Lola hid her face in her hands. When she raised it, she seemed so miserable he wanted to comfort her, tell her things would be better. He didn't. He couldn't. He simply sat there, waiting for the words that would change his life forever.

Finally, she wiped her red, swollen eyes on the sleeve of her robe and spoke. "When Jimmy went to work for your father, I was seventeen and in my last year of high school. Jimmy persuaded Charlie to hire me and pay for me to go to business school at night. Your mother . . . Abby hated the job sites, so Charlie would go home on the weekends. Simple story. I fell in love with the boss. Completely and utterly in love. And he fell in love with me. I was seventeen and he was thirty-four. I guess I thought it would go on forever. Then Abby was pregnant with Carl, and a few month later, I was pregnant with you. You're actually only three months younger than Carl.

"Right after Carl was born, someone told Abby about me, and she had a justifiable reaction. At first, I thought Abby didn't love Charlie, only the money he made. He let me believe that, but it wasn't true." She made a fist and beat it on the couch. "Abby loved him as much as I did. Your father had talent for making money. That's about all he could do. Indecisive, greedy bastard, he couldn't choose. He wanted both of us. And that's what he got." Lola straightened. Her breathing steadied, as if telling the story relieved her of a burden.

"Abby and Charlie made a devil's bargain, and at nineteen, I signed on. After Carl, the doctors told Abby she couldn't have any more children, something she desperately wanted. She demanded you, and I gave you away. In return, I had Charlie on the job sites, and she had him at home to present a family front. He had unencumbered access to me. She preserved her family honor and accepted half a marriage. She was a good mother, wasn't she?"

"Yes, always." Ryan's heart filled with memories. Mothers were more than a name on a birth certificate. But he loved Lola, too.

Lola held her arms tight across her body. "I wanted to see you, watch you grow, too. That's why you spent your summers with Jimmy."

"But not with my father," Ryan said. "Not with you."

"I made a bad bargain, but I kept it. I swore to Charlie and Abby that I would never tell you. Jimmy did the same. I traded my child for time with my lover. You didn't stay with your father because I was with him."

"And you regret it?"

"I hated it." Her voice quavered. "Regret, yes, but not enough to break the promise I made. Besides, if I had, Charlie would have left me and I couldn't bear that. And I'd have lost you completely. I gave up all legal rights to you. Look at him, Ryan." She pointed at his father's picture. "Did you ever see a man so handsome? Did you ever watch him charm women? Leandro is evil, but if the devil is a woman, Leandro is going to be in her bed not long after he arrives in hell. Charlie wasn't evil, but I'd put Charlie up against Leandro in charm any day."

Ryan did not want to think about Leandro's charms. He clenched his hand at the thought of Rose with that demon. Yet was his father any better?

Lola sighed. "Charlie charmed Abby and, like me, she let her love push her into an incredibly immoral situation. I'm sure that one day she woke up and realized she had received the worst end of a bad deal. Her husband was nothing but a selfish bastard who always got what he wanted. She told Jimmy once that Charlie was her drug of choice, but she loved and protected her sons. Abby died in Charlie's arms, asking him why he couldn't love her. Begging him to forgive her for something she didn't do."

Ryan's stomach churned. "You're wrong, Lola. My father *was* evil."

Charles Vernon had been a distant figure until Ryan had grown old enough to interact with him on an adult level. He'd loved him, but of course, it was Jimmy who played daddy most of the time.

Lola reached out as if to touch him, then drew her hand back. "Sometimes, two people are meant to be together. What would have happened if you were married to Tiffany when you met Rose? What if you loved Rose as much as you love her now, but you'd had a wife at home."

"Rose wouldn't touch me. She'd walk away hurt, but knowing she did the right thing. Rose never lied to me."

"I know," Lola said. "Rose is strong. I'm not. Please forgive me my weakness."

"There's nothing to forgive, Lola. I love Rose, and I've deceived her. I don't have a wife, but I was afraid if . . . There are things I should have told her. Now this. God, my whole life is a lie."

Ryan let his mind flow over memories of his mother—the mother of his heart. He loved her. God, how it must have hurt her. What about his own deception, the secret he hadn't told Rose because he feared she'd leave him.

"Lola, did you know that every time Jimmy would arrive to pick me up for the summer, she cried and begged him not to take me? That she told me to hide where he couldn't find me? That my father had to actually come and haul me away a couple of times? I didn't understand."

Horror painted Lola's face. "I deserve the same hell as Jimmy."

Chapter 28

Rose woke to motion and the muffled sound of an engine. She lay on a bed in a tiny room that curved to a V on one end. A boat, but not Leandro's yacht. Way too small for that. The rise and fall of the hull on the water rolled her stomach, but she swallowed and fought for control. She forced her arms and legs to move, and in a few minutes, she could sit up. The nausea eased. Bathroom, she needed . . . there it was, a small door to her left. She barely made it since she had to back into the tiny cubby.

She still wore Anita's borrowed black clothes, but the jacket was missing. The torn sleeve revealed an angry red dot on her arm. Whoever carried her here had removed the knife she'd clipped to her jeans, but . . . yes! The boot knife remained in place.

Rose stretched and worked more life into her limbs. The last traces of mental fog from the drug faded. Was she locked in? No. She slowly opened the door and entered a narrow galley with an equally narrow table and booth. A cardboard box on the table held bottled water. She helped herself.

Why hadn't Leandro killed her? He'd sworn he wouldn't hurt her, but she had little faith in his words. He'd lied to her about so much. She could see the deck from the galley, so she finished the water and headed that way. The boat's engines grumbled under her feet. Nothing in them or the boat's movement suggested they were plowing through the water in a hurry.

Rose stuffed her fear down. It could keep her from taking action. She bent, loosened the knife in her boot, and walked up the narrow set of stairs. The stairs opened onto a carpeted deck about fifteen feet square. A canvas canopy covered it, and a set of steps to her left led up to a deck that would be the pilothouse.

The clear, intense, turquoise water around them stretched to the horizon. A cool March breeze rippled it, but created no major waves, and the boat's slow speed kept the deck solid under her feet. No land in sight. Great way to get rid of bodies.

Leandro leaned against the deck railing, and Esteban sat in a chair close beside him. Both were dressed casually in light colors, as if on a pleasant journey across the water. Esteban smiled up at Leandro and there was no mistaking his expression. Rose had seen it on Ryan's face when he gazed at her. Esteban loved his psychopath, his personal killer. He ignored the danger of a man with an elegant face and body. The danger of his dreadful black soul.

"Ah, there you are," Esteban said. He smiled at *her* like a tiger that had found something to kill.

"Yeah, here I am." Rose acknowledged his greeting. Act casual, no hostile moves until she got close enough to knife him. Could she do it? Maybe. But Leandro needed to be further away. She knew he'd stop her.

Esteban had papers in his hand. She recognized them. The Brighton papers and the deed to the hotel property. Leandro had retrieved them after all.

Esteban held them up. "Amazing. How many men can die for a handful of paper?"

"Amazing," Rose said. "Only one of those men was important to me."

"Mr. Beecher. Your precious Jimmy."

Rose nodded.

"But he was not the one who should have died," Esteban said. "*You* were the target. To convince him that he had a great deal to lose by keeping these papers. I did not wish to begin an all out war with Ryan Vernon by killing his friend. Vernon has become a wealthy and important man over the last five years."

"So you had someone plant a bomb? That big boom caught a lot of attention."

Esteban shook his head. "No. I hired men to kill you. They made bad decisions."

"Cochran and Bedlow? They did the bomb? You don't know idiots when you see them."

"I accepted what was available at the time. A miscalculation on my part. Leandro always warned me about such things. I shall listen to him in the future."

Rose frowned. Nothing here made sense. "You arranged your own kidnapping? Just to get me to find those papers."

"No. Leandro tells me he has dealt with that situation. One of my rivals has become bold. He will regret it. I wouldn't have caused myself such discomfort. Nor would I have permitted your friend Lola to be raped."

Rose placed her hand over her mouth to keep from crying out.

"She will recover, *mi dulce*," Leandro said.

"But . . ." Rose faltered. Leandro had arranged the kidnapping. Had Leandro killed his own men because they raped Lola? "How did Jimmy get those papers?"

Esteban shook his head. "I don't know. I had them in my possession. A safe location, I thought." He tossed the papers over the side of the boat. The wind caught the miniature kites, but eventually settled them on the water. "I should have done that long ago."

Rose didn't think her legs would hold out much longer. She went and sat on a large bench seat bolted to the deck. Leandro smiled at her, his eyes dark and knowing.

"Such a beautiful ocean," Esteban said. "But beauty is deceiving at times. Do you understand?"

"Yes." Rose heard the irony in her own voice. "I've met Leandro, too."

Esteban laughed. "You have indeed. An excellent analogy. Death lies under this lovely tranquil ocean. Sharks will eat almost anything. A drop of blood from a mile away and they come. They are numerous in this area."

Rose kept her face straight, her body calm, and reminded herself the game wasn't over. Leandro could have killed her last night, but for some reason he did not. She wasn't completely shocked when Cochran lumbered down the steps from the pilot's deck above. This, she could deal with.

Rose grinned at him. She slapped her knee in a gesture of joy. "Hey, asshole. One down and one to go."

"Bitch." Cochran sneered. "I get to do you." He nodded at Esteban. "He said his pretty boy wouldn't want to get dirty. I'm gonna hurt you." His fat hands clenched into fists.

Rose glanced at Leandro. The soft ocean wind brushed his dark hair across that angelic face. She doubted he'd interfere. Leandro might kill her, but certainly, he wouldn't care what she did to Cochran. She didn't rise to face Cochran. That kept her hand closer to the knife in her boot.

"Cochran, you need the word imbecile tattooed on your forehead. They're going to kill you, too. You made too many mistakes. Bombs, arson. And you're like me. You know too much."

Cochran started toward her.

"Not yet," Esteban said.

Cochran glanced at him, and as he did, Rose grabbed the knife from her boot. When Cochran shifted his bulk toward her again, she was already on her feet. She had a firm grip on her weapon. One good step, draw back the arm and punch the knife in.

Rose didn't hold back. This man and Bedlow killed Jimmy. Strength, earned by manual labor and regular exercise, carried her forward. The knifepoint pierced his chest, caught briefly on a rib bone and slid in. She missed his heart.

Too short. The blade was too short. She twisted it. Not a quick killing blow she wanted, but incapacitating. He would bleed to death out here on this lovely ocean.

Cochran remained standing. He stared wide-eyed at his shirt where the scarlet stain grew and spread in a sheet down his massive gut. Rose jerked the knife out and drew back to strike again–and changed her mind.

She rammed her shoulder into Cochran's massive frame, planted her feet, and shoved hard. A big man, but one with a hole in his lung. That close, the smell of blood almost overwhelmed her. Cochran staggered, struggled to stay on his feet. Then he toppled over. She aimed him at Esteban and Leandro and shoved again with all her might.

Esteban started to rise, but Cochran's mass hit him straight on. The big man's body knocked him out of the chair and then crashed on top, crushing Esteban under it. Cochran rolled off, his arms flopping. His chronic wheeze turning to a liquid gurgle.

Esteban lay sprawled on the deck. Rose threw herself at him. She landed too low on his body. It didn't matter. She punched the knife up again and the blade slid into his body below the rib cage. As with Cochran, she twisted the knife.

Esteban screamed.

Then Leandro had her. He gripped the wrist of her knife hand and slid his other arm around her waist as he lifted her off Esteban. Leandro held her, her back against his body.

"I'm sorry, *mi dulce*. I understand, but he is not yours to kill." Leandro spoke directly in her ear.

Dear God, he sounded happy, almost joyful.

"No!" Hysterical rage filled her voice as she struggled. "He killed Jimmy. They did it together." She twisted uselessly against him.

Esteban writhed at her feet, his hands cupped over the flow of blood from his side.

Rose kicked him, aiming for the area of the wound.

Leandro anticipated her move and dragged her back. He turned her around to face him, but he kept her knife hand in a savage grip. He smiled. Not the practiced smile of a killer soothing his prey, but a true smile that reached his eyes. A smile that held some sympathy.

"Leandro!" Esteban cried. Rose heard agony and despair in his voice, and a desperate plea for help.

Leandro's smile faded. He spoke to Esteban, but he didn't release her. "You called, Master." He spoke in Spanish then, and Rose only understood one word—*perro*. The dog. She understood. No aid for Esteban would come from Leandro, no mercy and no pity for the man bleeding on the deck.

Cochran lay beside him, gasping for air. He coughed and sprayed blood. A few more seconds of struggle and his body went slack. His eyes remained wide and staring.

Leandro released her and went to Esteban.

Stab him in the back, Rose's rational mind shrieked. Her rage had propelled her action on Cochran and Esteban. Somehow, she couldn't manage to project it onto Leandro.

Leandro knelt by Esteban. He spoke softly, again in Spanish. Esteban gaped at him as if he suddenly realized a vital truth, one he had foolishly ignored.

Leandro stood and faced Rose again. She held the knife ready and prepared to fight. She couldn't stab him in the back, but he wouldn't take her without a struggle.

"*Mi dulce*, do you need my life, too? Will it ease your loss? I was not directly responsible for your friend's death, but I am no innocent."

He stepped closer, easily within striking range.

Innocent? No, he wasn't. So what was he? It didn't matter. She couldn't kill him.

Esteban released his wound and fumbled at his pocket with bloody hands.

Leandro, seeing her expression, turned.

Esteban held a pistol. It wavered, but that close . . .

Leandro shook his head. "Ah, my master, you think me that stupid."

Esteban steadied the gun and pulled the trigger.

Chapter 29

Nothing broke the silence except the gentle sound of the wind across the water.

Leandro went to Esteban, tore the gun away from him, then tossed it over the rail into the water. He knelt beside his mentor, but he watched Rose as he spoke. "I was a good servant, *mi dulce*. Fetch, Leandro, I want this thing. Kill, Leandro, that man troubles me." His attention went back to Esteban. "Alano Mendez, Esteban. Do you remember that name? So long ago. Rose wants to kill you in the name of her friend. But I am going to kill you in the name of my father."

Leandro glanced at Rose again. "Your hatred, your vengeance is pure, Rose. Mine is not. But I will have it. Please go and sit down while I finish." He held out his hand. "Give me the knife."

She gave it up willingly. Then she rushed to the other side of the boat, leaned over, gagged and spit up the water she drank along with bitter burning bile. She heaved and gasped until nothing remained. What had she done in her life that led her to this terrible bloody place? When she finally finished, she turned and staggered back to the bench to sit. She wanted more water, but would not leave to go into the cabin and get it.

Leandro had wrestled Cochran's bulk over the side of the boat, balanced him on the edge, head down. Cochran didn't move. He'd probably bled to death. The way he hung he had to be leaking a dinner call to any sharks in the area.

Leandro rolled him over.

Rose wasn't sick again. She was cold. Cold, as if the quiet, cool breeze had risen to a raging storm blowing from the mountains far to the west. Cold as the icy blood that ran in Leandro's veins. It got worse. Frantic splashing and the sharks feasted. She couldn't move, so she sat there huddled like a small, frightened animal.

Esteban had grown weaker as more blood leaked from his body. Leandro knelt beside him and again spoke in Spanish. Though she didn't understand the language, the tone of his voice . . . Oh, God, he was speaking to a man he was going to kill in a soft, gentle voice, that seemed filled with compassion.

Esteban made a choking sound, and Rose realized he was laughing. Blood drained from his mouth when he spoke.

Whatever Esteban said then had a profound effect on Leandro. For the first time since she'd met him, his face twisted with rage. Gone was the psychopath, the cool emotionless killer who shot a man as easily as tossing a dirty shirt in the laundry. He punched the knife up under Esteban's ear and the blade slid up and into his brain. Esteban jerked, and it was over.

Rose didn't watch as his body went over the side. Whatever fury, whatever desire for vengeance she'd carried in her heart for Jimmy, had faded under the onslaught of such violence.

Leandro approached. He knelt in front of her. He carefully sheathed the now clean knife in her boot. He had known all along that she carried it. And for all his actions, he had no blood on his clothes. The only thing that remained was the drying scarlet pools on the deck.

"You spoke of vengeance, last night," Leandro said. His face held an expression of curiosity. "The men who murdered your friend are dead. You killed them. The men who raped Lola are dead. I had them killed. Are you satisfied? Exultant?"

"No. I wish the whole thing had never happened. Are you satisfied? You said Esteban killed your father."

"Yes. It sounds noble, doesn't it? It is not. I swore vengeance. I was a child. I educated myself as I grew older, trained myself in stealth and weapons, and made myself strong to enter Esteban's service as a guard. I needn't have bothered. While he appreciated my tactical abilities, he preferred other things about me. I could have killed him within months after he hired me. Could have killed him and easily escaped. But I had seen how he lived, the wealth and the power, and it seduced me as vengeance never could."

"You waited? Let him make you rich before you . . .?" That appalling bit of information stunned her. It had to show on her face.

Leandro laid a hand on her cheek. "You are so clean and honest, *mi dulce*. Honorable, as is your stalwart lover. Come."

Since there was little else to do, Rose followed him up the stairs to the pilothouse. She didn't look back to the bloody smears on the deck. There were two white seats, tall chairs, and a panel of multiple instruments.

"This is not my Guarida, *mi dulce*," Leandro said. "But it will do." He climbed in one seat, pushed buttons and the engines grumbled to life. She was still standing when he turned the wheel and the engine's gentle vibrations swelled to a roar. The boat surged forward. Rose had to grab him to keep from falling back down the stairs to the deck. He laughed and slipped an arm around her, drawing her close. He caught the back of her neck and dragged her mouth to his.

Chapter 30

Ryan stayed with Lola on Monday. He couldn't bear to be alone in the cottage without Rose. Lola didn't need to be alone, either. Misery radiated from her like heat from a furnace. She'd stopped crying but didn't talk much.

He called O'Malley and told him the story. Everything from the kidnapping to discovery of his parentage and Leandro telling him he would bring Rose back in a few days—everything except what happened to Lola. That was hers to tell if she chose.

"I am stunned," O'Malley said.

"So am I." Ryan sat back in the chair and propped his feet on the coffee table.

"Where's Lola?" O'Malley asked.

"Asleep."

"What can I do?"

"You could come and be with her. I think she needs that."

"I'll be there tomorrow." O'Malley hesitated. "Or shall I come more quickly?"

"Tomorrow should be fine. Do we have the resources to find Leandro if Rose doesn't make it back? She may call and tell me to forget her. If she does, fine. If she disappears, I'm going after him."

"And I will help you cut him into pieces. I'll begin the search now, just in case."

One other thing Ryan wanted to know. He'd trust O'Malley to tell him the truth. "O'Malley, did you know about me and Lola?"

"No, Ryan, I did not. I'm shocked because I thought I knew

everything about the Vernons. I knew Charlie and Lola were lovers, but not that they had a child. How are you dealing with it? Are you angry at Lola for deceiving you?"

"I have no right to anger when it comes to deception. I think I'm doing better than Lola. She's beating herself up pretty bad." Ryan thought about Lola and his father too much, but it was the one thing that took his mind off Rose. "Lola loves you, O'Malley."

"And I love her. I'll let you know if I find anything on Leandro."

Ryan hung up the phone. Tomorrow, Tuesday, he would have to go back to the hotel site and try to fend off the questions about Rose. In the back of his mind, though, he sketched out his plans. Plans to kill Leandro.

* * * *

Leandro steered the boat west toward the falling sun. Rose leaned forward at the sight of land. The great rolling ocean had no appeal for her in the past, and would never do so in the future. Her world would always be man-made and anchored in the natural earth.

He'd slowed once and gone below to wash the blood off the deck but, other than that, kept a steady speed and course. He followed the channel markers and entered the Intracoastal Waterway about four o'clock. When they passed inside, he steered south.

"Where are we?" Rose asked.

"Fort Matanzas."

"And where are we going?"

"Flagler Beach. Would you go below? I think there is a bottle of wine in the chiller."

When she stepped out of the chair, Leandro reached over and drew her to him. "Give me another kiss. I love your mouth."

Rose gave him what he wanted. She let him draw her to the velvet warmth of his lips. She surrendered to him and relaxed against his body. Only hours ago, that soft mouth on hers had ordered the execution of men. The hands caressing her had taken lives, men of his world, men who engaged in a dangerous game against a master player and lost.

She herself had killed men in the last twenty-four hours. Cochran and Bedlow, stupid, incompetent assassins. She'd helped kill Esteban, too. Guilt would not trouble her, but memory of violence would. Leandro's deadly plans still ruled her life.

Leandro shuddered and released her. "Ah, *mi dulce*, you find the wine and let me see if I can make this boat move faster."

Rose left him there and went to the galley. The refrigerator held a bottle of red wine, imported from Italy, and a six-pack of her favorite bottled beer. She picked up a bottle of the beer. Leandro had made his plans, and it appeared everything was on schedule. He'd been true to his word so far. He hadn't hurt her. He must think her strong enough to deal with any emotional trauma he tossed at her.

She opened the wine, snagged a couple of the beers, and went back up to the pilothouse.

"I guess things are going according to your cunning scheme," she said as she returned.

"Yes, of course. Did they get the right kind of beer?"

"They did." She poured a generous amount of wine into a glass she'd found in a cabinet, where it was safely secured against high seas. "Who are *they*?"

Leandro accepted the glass. "*They* are a few competent people who ask no questions and tell no tales while they earn the exorbitant sum I pay them."

Rose went to the other seat and opened her beer. "Leandro, you're an arrogant ass. But I have to admit that you do the egocentric thing with style."

He lifted his cup of wine in a mock salute. "Rose, you are a willful, stubborn woman. But I have to admit that it suits you. And I love you."

Rose shook her head. She didn't want to hear those words from him.

"You don't think you could love me?" Leandro asked. His

voice sounded light and jovial, but she caught an undercurrent of something else. It sounded almost like a plea for affection she couldn't give.

Rose shrugged. She wouldn't lie. It was too important. "There's too much violence lying between us for love."

Leandro turned his eyes away from her. "You are right. Violence rules me. And yet, for these few days, you will be mine."

"Do you think something will change? I'll fall in love with you?"

"My rational mind tells me you will not, but my heart prays that you will."

"It's your game, Leandro. I'm a pawn, not a queen. You set the price yesterday, and I'll pay it." She took a long swallow of the beer. "Will you tell me the truth, the whole story?"

"I owe you that much, at least."

She thought he owed her more than that, but she let it pass.

He sat silent for a few moments, maybe deciding what words to use. Finally, he spoke. "Esteban was much older than he appeared. He had excellent doctors to keep him looking young, but over the last seven years, his mind frayed like loose woven cloth. I gradually took control of the business, the properties, leaving him a figurehead. He knew it, but he let it be. Perhaps he felt his own mortality. He called me his heir, his successor. This last year, he turned erratic, more unpredictable. I controlled almost everything, but I had to leave him something to do, something to play with."

"The hotel."

"Yes. Such a fiasco. Ryan defied him in Miami once, and won. I told him to let it go, it was too petty to deal with. He became obsessed."

"He bought the hotel property and finagled Ryan into building for him."

"Yes. I have no idea how or where your Jimmy found those papers. We'll probably never know that. Esteban told me there was a problem, but he wouldn't speak of it. He said he had hired men to deal with the situation, and I shouldn't bother."

"That explains hiring stupid one and stupid two, a.k.a. Cochran and Bedlow. So, you orchestrated a kidnapping to force me to find the papers." Rose drained her first beer and opened the second.

"If I had known what they were, those documents, I would have taken different actions. Such an easily corrected matter, that deed." Leandro shook his head.

"What? You planned to let him die of old age?"

"No, *mi dulce*, but less violence would have occurred. I arranged for the security guards to be replaced, made sure the cameras were off. I told the men who kidnapped Esteban and the others to make it realistic, but not to injure them. I am truly sorry for what happened to Lola. I dealt with it the only way I could."

And Leandro's way of dealing with things meant death.

The falling darkness closed in around them, and Rose grew weary. Leandro seemed alert, as usual. "What about the two guys at the hotel yesterday?" she asked. "The ones who tried to kill you."

"And you," he reminded her. "They were, as I told you, enemies from the past. Certainly not a part of my plans. They probably had been following me and found an opportunity. Are you truly concerned about them?"

"I'm concerned with the body count." And concerned about her own part in it. "It's occurred to me that I don't owe you anything. You rescued Ryan, Lola, and Esteban from a kidnapping you staged. What would you have done if I hadn't figured out where Jimmy stashed those papers?"

"I would have bargained with you, carried out the rescue, and have you as I wished. Let me remind you, though. That night, at the pool table, you offered me anything I wanted in order for you to learn who killed your friend. Now you know."

"A wager on a pool game we never played."

"No, that went far above anything laid down before. You named the stakes. You wanted to know who killed your friend. I arranged for you to have that. I have won, and will claim my prize."

He was right. She'd raised the stakes beyond a mere pool

game and lost. Would Ryan understand? She'd have to deal with it later.

Rose understood that Esteban and the other men Leandro slaughtered had probably killed many innocent people before they met their fate. Cochran and Bedlow planted a bomb without a thought of others it might injure. A school bus full of kids passing by, tourists walking down the street, they'd call it collateral damage. Esteban? Countless families had probably wept over loved ones because of him. The men Leandro killed wouldn't hurt anyone again. It still didn't make any of it right.

Night pressed down, and a chill wind cut through her shirt, actually Anita's shirt, but she didn't go below. At nine o'clock, Leandro turned the boat and eased it to a dock. Several men waited for them and secured the boat as it glided in. Again, they spoke Spanish, and again words she couldn't understand whirled around her.

Leandro held her arm as they walked down the dock to dry land. A car and driver waited for them, but the journey didn't last long. Flagler County Airport, the sign proclaimed. They drove around away from the main terminal to a series of hangars.

A sleek airplane, twin engines idling, waited for them.

"You're not afraid to fly, are you?" He gestured grandly at the plane.

"I don't know. I've never been on an airplane. I might puke again."

"Oh, I'll give you a plastic bag." He led her to the steps. He stayed behind her and gently urged her up the stairs.

"Go up front," Leandro said. The door to freedom closed behind her.

The plane had twelve white leather passenger seats and carpet in the center aisle. Elegance, typical of Leandro.

"Who's going to fly this thing?" she asked.

"I am." He stepped up behind her, slid his arms around her, and nuzzled her neck.

"But it's dark outside." Her protest sounded false.

"There is a complete set of instruments."

Rose shivered and pulled away from him. She ducked her head to get into the cockpit. "Which side?"

"The right." He climbed in as she slipped into her seat. He positioned a set of earphones on his head and a microphone at his mouth, then spent a few minutes checking instruments. The engines roared.

Rose fastened her seat belt, leaned back, and closed her eyes. The plane moved, rolling slowly away. Leandro spoke into the microphone and received instructions. She kept her eyes firmly closed and clenched her hands as they started down the runway. She drew a breath as the ground dropped beneath them and the plane rose into the pure onyx sky.

"Why do you close your eyes?" Leandro asked.

"So I won't see the ground coming when you crash."

"*Mi dulce*, you should have more faith in me. I've only gone down once. There was a little mishap in California, but I was already on the runway. Don't worry, we're not going far. Only a couple of hours in the air."

Rose leaned back and kept her eyes closed as the airplane slid through smooth, silky, black sky. Leandro kept his word, and two hours later, he spoke into the microphone again, requesting permission to land.

"Where are we?" She asked.

"Key West."

A car met them when Leandro taxied to a hangar away from the main airport. A limousine, actually, with a driver who opened the back door for them. Leandro sat close to her. Not intimate, but close enough his arm rubbed against hers

"I have a house on Cudjoe Key, twenty minutes from here. Are you tired?"

"Yes."

They rolled through the darkness across the bridges that made up the Overseas Highway until the car slowed and turned, and turned again. It stopped. Leandro waited for the driver to come around and open the door.

"You sure know how to act rich, don't you?" Rose said.

"Certainly. You will learn to enjoy it, too. Ryan Vernon is

not a poor man."

"He's not rich like this." At least she didn't think he was. An unpretentious man, Ryan could have a billion dollars in the bank and it wouldn't show in his words or actions.

The door opened, and Leandro climbed out, offering her his hand.

Rose stepped out, and her eyes widened. She hadn't expected him to live in a tarpaper shack, but the sheer size and luxury of the place, as with the yacht, shocked her. The house was long and low, but it had the look of the Guarida, sleek and ready to fly rather than remain grounded in the earth.

She'd exited the car under a portico. Etched glass panels covered the front of the house and created symmetry around double doors. The tidy jungle between the concrete drive and the glass kept it from feeling hard and cold, and indirect lighting cast a golden glow over everything. They'd left north Florida's light chill for semi-tropical warmth.

Leandro led her through a foyer larger than her cottage in Jacksonville. They crossed white marble floors, passed fine, earth-brown couches and chairs, glass and wood tables. Large colorful paintings hung on the walls, and occasional vases of fresh flowers and deep green potted plants graced tables. Only their footsteps broke the silence.

They walked out across a veranda, past a small lake of a swimming pool, and on a walkway to a smaller building set above the ground on concrete piers. Rose followed him up the stairs. "This is my bedroom," he said.

His *bedroom* was a three-room suite. Expansive glass paneled windows held back the darkness outside. In the sitting room, spare modern furniture equaled the luxury of the front house. No personal effects cut the room's clean lines. It seemed he had no true home. A nomad, he camped from house to yacht to whatever place necessity or fate carried him. The bedroom held nothing but an enormous platform bed.

"Will you rest a while?" Leandro asked. "I must see to more business now."

Rose nodded.

"The bathroom is there. Look in the drawers and you should

find any personal items you need." He walked out and closed the door.

Rose went into the bathroom. Wow! Black tile and glass filled the expansive room. The shower alone was bigger than her whole bathroom at the cottage. The decorator had arranged several padded benches along the wall as if a person would need to rest after crossing from the shower to the marble sink. The toilet? Yes, there it was, tucked in its own roomy closet. She opened one drawer. New, packaged toothbrushes and toothpaste filled it. The next held brushes and combs, soap and lotions. Thick white blankets of towels were neatly rolled and stacked on a rack.

She searched for a phone. If he had one here, he'd hidden it. There was a small kitchen, and a refrigerator. Food. Some cheese, bread, milk; she barely tasted it, but it settled her stomach.

She removed her boots, dimmed the lights, and lay on the platform bed. It molded to her body, not too hard, not too soft. A blanket lay across the foot of the bed and she drew it over her, not because she was cold, but because it felt like a thin, but familiar, layer of protection. She fell asleep wondering what Ryan was doing at that moment. Rose didn't know how long she slept, but she knew when she dreamed. Her eyes popped open at the sound of water churning as the sharks devoured their banquet.

It was dark outside, but the faintest hint of dawn painted the horizon. The glass windows faced a great expanse of the blue water. Rose tossed the blanket aside. She walked over and tried the entry door. Locked. There was nothing to do except wait for him.

In the bathroom, she quickly undressed, showered and washed her hair. She felt incredibly vulnerable in this place—Leandro's place. She dressed and went back to the suite's living area.

The light streaming through the window now had the newness of morning. What would the day bring? No more death, she hoped. She turned at the sound of the door opening.

Leandro entered. He'd shaved and dressed in clean clothes,

khaki pants, and a white polo shirt. He walked to her slowly, languidly, as if a man completely satisfied with his life. He carried a plastic bag, printed with palm trees.

"I brought you clean clothes," he said. "We need to visit someone today."

Rose accepted the bag and dumped the contents out on the bed. He'd brought her a full beige skirt, soft and supple, and a cotton blouse with a delicate floral print that matched the skirt. A pair of leather sandals completed the outfit. He walked to the couch, sat and relaxed, his legs stretched out in front of him. "Dress, please," he said. "There is someone I want you to meet."

Rose went to the bathroom and dressed in the clothes. She'd thought he would return wanting sex, but he hadn't said anything. He might have wanted her to change in front of him, but he hadn't asked that either. The clothes fit well, and they felt expensive. They felt feminine. When she returned to the bedroom, he handed her a cell phone. "Call him. Don't tell him where you are."

Chapter 31

Ryan sat at a desk in the office area of the hotel, listening to the sounds of construction around him. Tuesday morning and forty-eight hours without Rose. Long hours. She'd become a part of his life so quickly.

He'd gone to the cottage that morning. Herman lay on the counter, broken in three pieces. Jimmy had hidden the grand prize, whatever it was, inside. Ryan should have known when he found the picture in Don Quixote. At least Rose figured it out.

In the bedroom he had touched her things. The worn terry-cloth robe she always wore lay draped across the bed. Ryan picked it up and buried his face in it to remember her scent. His rational mind told him it would all work out, that she would come home, but his heart cried.

At least Carl and Brianna had taken their kids to Orlando, and he didn't have to deal with explaining things to them, yet. Sam gave him some odd looks, but said nothing.

Lola sat at a desk across the room. Her former constant working companion, the little television, was on a shelf behind her. She hadn't turned it on. She'd aged over the last few days.

"Lola?"

She raised her head.

"Honey, it's okay," he said. "I love you, as much as I ever did. You need to stop beating yourself up for the past." He'd been trying, without success, to lead her away from guilt.

"I can't stop thinking about it. And worrying about Rose."

Ryan understood.

"O'Malley will be here this afternoon. He loves you. You need to keep him close."

"And I love him." She frowned and rubbed the bridge of her nose. "Did you tell him? About me and you."

"Yes. Just that, though. Nothing else. I think he understands. He's known us for so long. And he rarely judges us."

"Should I tell Carl?" Lola asked. "Do you want to do it?"

"Wait a while, until this is over. Lola, my father sold me sixty percent of Vernon Construction for one million dollars I didn't have. Paper money on a contract. He remained the boss as long as he lived, but the company was mine. You know all that, but can you tell me why he did it?"

"No, I . . ." Lola drew a deep breath.

"No more lies, Lola. No more secrets. I can't bear it."

Lola's face looked gaunt as an old woman near death. "Jimmy blackmailed him. Jimmy and I each owned twenty percent of the company and he was going to divide the rest equally between you and Carl. By that time, we all could see Carl's direction in life. He could destroy the company even if he owned only 30 percent.

"Charlie wasn't a good man. I think you've already figured that out. Jimmy cleaned up after him a lot and knew things. He found something Charlie didn't want exposed. I never knew what."

"That's why Jimmy left Carl the money. To make up for my having the company. One of the reasons. I've already told you the other."

Ryan's cell phone rang, and he opened it automatically. "Vernon."

"Ryan?" Rose's beautiful voice spoke in his ear.

He jerked and leaned forward. "Rose, where are you?"

"Somewhere south. I'm fine. I don't want you to worry."

"Not worry! Rose, I'm out of my mind."

She didn't reply.

Leandro's voice came on. "Be at the Rising Sun Marina tomorrow night at ten, and I will return your love to you."

The phone went silent. Ryan squeezed it as if he could force more words from it.

Lola walked to him. She leaned on the desk, her face lined with worry.

Ryan swallowed, and carefully closed the phone. "She sounded okay. He said he'd would bring her home tomorrow night. I guess that means she wants to come back."

"You're not angry with her, are you? Because she's with him."

He stared at her, surprised at her comment. "No. Why should I be angry at her?"

"I don't know. Men do that at times. Remember, she loves you, but she'll either come to you or stay with him. Her choice."

Ryan's stomach clenched. His whole being recoiled at that thought. "You think she'll choose to stay with him?"

"Not for a minute."

Ryan rubbed the back of his neck, trying to massage away tension. "You're right. I think he loves her, though. He's rich and handsome—"

"And a stone cold killer. He doesn't even deny it. Whatever charm he has, I'll bet our Rose will see through it. Rose doesn't lie. She's a straight line woman in a crooked world."

"What if he won't give her up?" Ryan asked. Panic filled him. He clenched his hands into fists. "What if he decides to destroy her rather than let her go?"

"Then we'll hunt him down and send him to hell."

* * * *

Leandro drove the Mercedes northeast in a smooth ride across the long bridges that made up most of the Overseas Highway. Rose had told herself many times she wanted to see it, mostly because she liked massive structures, stone and steel. Even though the car had tinted windows, the brilliant sun reflecting off the water made her squint. She'd enjoyed the weather, warm with a breeze off the ocean. Leandro pulled over and parked at an open shanty tourist store with a palm frond awning stretched across the front.

"You need sunglasses," he said.

Beach towels, tee shirts, plastic flamingos, dolphin wind chimes, and rows of other official Florida souvenirs lined the shelves inside the shanty. All made in China, of course, but they were selling atmosphere, not reality.

Three young girls entered the store while Rose tried on sunglasses. Twelve or thirteen, awkward, self-conscious, they stood across the room and stared at Leandro. They giggled, blushed, and whispered to each other. Sadness filled her as it always did when she'd see such girls. She'd never had a girlfriend with whom she could share secrets. She moved on too quickly, changing schools as her father changed jobs. Even if she'd stayed in one place, he consumed most of her life, most of her time.

"You have admirers, pretty man," Rose told Leandro.

Leandro raised an eyebrow as he glanced their way. "Sweet children. God protect them from my world."

The giggling girls were still there when they left the store. Leandro stopped and spoke softly to them. They gravitated toward him, captured by his looks and voice. Each was a slim-bodied woman-child, adolescent, only a few years from sexual power and elegance that time would bring. Rose didn't hear what he said, but they watched him with adoring faces as he left. A casual, merciless killer, and yet not a predator in that manner. His concern for innocence seemed genuine. Would the real Leandro please stand up?

Leandro drove to a restaurant where the staff obviously knew and catered to him. They opened the door and locked it behind them. The place opened only for lunch and dinner, but they made an exception. Leandro smiled, gracious and kind as a young god. When the chef stepped out of the kitchen to speak to them, Leandro asked about his family and called them by their names.

Their sterling service extended to Rose, and for the first time, she wondered how it would be to live such a life of pure luxury. Never to have to punch a time clock or strip wire again. Ryan could offer her that, and he might know a chef or two, but she'd bet it would be at Billy Bob's Barbecue or Tommy's Crab Shack. Leandro seemed to revel in the opulent life. He savored it much as he savored the fine food on the table before them. Maybe he'd been born to it, but she thought not. He enjoyed it too much. If he'd been born to wealth, he'd probably take it for granted.

Another short trip, then off the highway onto a side road. Such an interesting place. Palm trees and colorful tourist shops lined the main roadway, and condos and cabins arranged side by side sat near the waterfront. He drove up and stopped at a small marina.

"Another boat?" she asked.

"I understand, but it's the only way."

When she climbed in, Leandro held her tight and kissed her with so much desire it frightened her. *He* didn't frighten her, but his hunger did. Whatever Leandro needed in his life, money couldn't buy it.

The slim twenty-foot craft skimmed along the clear smooth water, propelled by two high-powered engines. Rose gritted her teeth at the speed, suddenly thankful for the sunglasses.

Other boats plied the water with them. Sport fishing boats made their way among the archipelago of islands, and an occasional sailboat slid along, driven by a gentle warm wind.

Leandro slowed and steered toward an island. Rose could see a house there, and a small dock. He carefully maneuvered their vessel to the dock where two other boats floated, carefully secured to the wooden frame. Three dark skinned men hurried to tie off lines and drop steps so they could climb to the dock. Professionals, these men, not dock flunkies working for minimum wage. They spoke in Spanish, and the feeling of separation again made Rose uneasy. She'd become familiar with that over the last two days.

Leandro led her up the dock toward a low sprawling house of deep copper stucco, topped by a red tile roof. A great, long pillared veranda stretched the length of the building, and graceful palm trees rustled in the sea breeze. Deep green hibiscus bushes covered with scarlet flowers lined the edge of the veranda and the path to the boat dock. The lawn itself carved out a semi-circle of civilization on a wilder island filled with native bushes and mangroves.

"I'm impressed," Rose said. "Where does the fresh water come from?" She reached out and touched the velvet petals of a scarlet flower.

"It rains often, and I believe there is a small solar desalination facility somewhere. Drinking water is delivered with supplies."

A woman waited for them on the veranda. Slim, elegant, and fair-skinned, not young, she wouldn't see forty again, as if it mattered in someone so beautiful. She wore her soft fawn colored hair in a tight bun at the nape of her neck, and a string of pearls lay on her flowing mint-green silk dress. Rose wondered if she'd seen them coming and dressed for Leandro. Her calm face carried a half smile, non-committal and much like his.

Leandro nodded at her. "*Mi dulce*, allow me to introduce Consuela, Esteban's wife."

Damn, what was he up to? Rose placed a neutral smile on her face.

Consuela's expression never changed. "Leandro calls you his sweet. What do you call him?"

"Nothing nice, most of the time," Rose told her. "I'll spare you the foul language. My name is Rose Norris. I'm pleased to meet you."

Consuela's soft laughter sounded gentle as the breeze across the water. "Rose. And I am pleased to meet a woman who is obviously not completely enthralled with our lion. Welcome. Come in."

They followed her into a house that matched her grace and sophistication. The terra cotta tile floors covered with patterned rugs, solid wood furniture carved with complex patterns, fine paintings and mirrors created an Architectural Digest perfect room. It was so flawless that, like Leandro's house, it seemed no one actually lived there. Leandro squeezed Rose's hand. "I must speak with Consuela alone. Will you wait for me here?"

"Sure." Unlike the industrial park, there was no place to go.

Leandro and Consuela walked away, and as they did, he slipped his arm around her waist. Her face went soft like Anita's, and she leaned into him.

"Must be something wrong with me," Rose muttered. Her body cried with desire when the man touched her, but the kind of idolization Consuela and Anita offered him wasn't in her.

She wandered around looking at the pictures and fine objects. Consuela liked jade. One glass case held hundreds of pieces, from two inches to a foot tall vase probably worth a fortune. Some had the worn patina of great age. The house invited exploration, but she suspected neither Leandro nor her hostess would welcome that.

It wasn't long before Consuela rejoined her.

"Come with me, Rose," she said. "I will show you my garden."

Consuela led her out a door, away from the open water, and toward the primitive area of the island. She must have come here often, because there was a narrow concrete path.

"The house has ears," Consuela said. "I wanted to talk to you alone. Leandro tells me I am a widow."

Chapter 32

Rose didn't say anything. She hadn't forgotten Monday's disaster, but she wouldn't talk about it. She might tell Ryan someday. Maybe when she could no longer hear and smell the sound of death.

"I understand," Consuela said. "I would not speak of it, either. But please know that I will thank God every day for the circumstances that led you here."

They walked on in silence as the vegetation closed in around them.

"Leandro is in love with you," Consuela said. "This is something new. Many women love him. You are different from the others."

Rose had nothing to say on that subject, either. What should she do? Apologize? Leandro's love wasn't her fault.

Consuela walked faster. Rose matched her pace.

"Leandro is a most attractive man," Consuela said, still apparently trying to draw Rose into conversation.

Rose could agree with that. "It's hard to miss how he looks, but I love someone else. A man I want to marry." A man who might not have her when she returned.

"Many women love Leandro." Consuela sighed.

"Sure. Airhead bimbos, blinded by jewels and expensive clothes. A woman with any intelligence at all, a woman who knew him . . ." Rose stopped. Damn, she seemed intent on planting a foot in her mouth.

"And I know him, and have loved him for many years." Consuela's voice filled with dark, ironic humor.

Static Resistance and Rose

"I doubt you're blinded by material things, Consuela. You understand what he is. You live in his world and accept it. I can't."

"Oh, I do understand. But I doubt that you do. You think he is evil. Like Esteban?"

"I've lived a sheltered life, it seems," Rose said. "I once thought I knew evil. Now I'm not so sure." She wasn't sure she and Consuela understood evil in the same way, either.

The path ended at a short dock next to a narrow channel of water. The channel cut through the tenacious mangroves and away toward the island's far side. A twelve-foot aluminum boat floated there. Not something she would want to take across a large expanse of water, but big enough to get a person out where they might hail a passing yacht.

Consuela climbed in and beckoned Rose to follow her. Rose sat on one of the bench seats and tucked her skirt around her legs. Mosquitoes hummed in the distance. How long before their blood sensors locked on lunch?

"Are we running away?" Rose asked. Alarm tickled in the back of her mind.

Consuela pushed a button and the low-horsepower engine started immediately. She let it run until it smoothed to a quiet hum, then shut it off. "Leandro arranged for me to have this small craft. A precaution. No, we are not running—yet. For now, we must watch. A certain man will come to us. If it is not that man, we will leave this place and try to find safety." She drew a pistol out of a pocket on her dress and laid it beside her. Yes, Esteban's widow definitely belonged in his and Leandro's world.

Rose shifted, trying to be more comfortable. The boat gently rocked in the shallow water. She could see tiny fishes and miniature crabs gliding over the sand bottom and through the mangrove roots.

"If the wrong man comes out," Rose asked, a bitter taste rolling on her tongue, "does that mean more people have died?"

"It means Leandro is dead." Consuela spoke the words gently, as if she'd already prepared to mourn.

Rose drew a sharp breath. She started to rise, to go help

him, but stopped, knowing she would be in the way.

Consuela laughed, not loud, but with real humor. "You lie to yourself, pretty flower. You love him, our lion. Maybe not as he wishes, or not as I do, but it is there."

Rose sighed. "I doubt my definition of love is the same as yours. I can't live his kind of life. I do love Ryan and I do want to marry him. If he'll have me after all of this."

"He will. I know your Ryan by reputation. I met him once, though he wouldn't remember me. I've heard Esteban curse him many times."

"Esteban. You married him. Why?" It sounded rude to ask, but these people had forced their way in and changed her world.

Consuela didn't sound offended. "I married him because my father asked me to do so. I was young and considered quite beautiful. Esteban was older, but rich, charming and very handsome. I quickly agreed. At seventeen, I was inexperienced in the ways of men, the perversions of men."

"Just because Esteban didn't want women . . ." Rose held no prejudices of that kind.

Consuela sighed. "Oh, if it were only that simple, that clean. There are men who care for other men rather than women. I accept that. Esteban's men were not always men, but boys. They were adolescents, too young and naïve to understand how he would corrupt them. He gave them money and gifts. When he was younger, he came to my bed occasionally. He asked me for a son. I refused. I would not trust him."

"Why are you telling me this?"

"I want you to know that with regards to Esteban, *you* need carry no guilt."

Rose hadn't considered guilt. The need for justice overwhelmed that. The violence sickened her, but she would do it again. She thought she liked Consuela. Certainly, she felt pity for her, forced to live a life that had to be the greatest of lies.

Mosquitoes hummed around them, drawing ever closer. The insects and the water that slapped gently against the aluminum hull were the only sounds as they sat waiting. Rose's legs grew cramped and she longed to remove the sandals and wash her feet. As the minutes crawled, Consuela sat with her spine straight and her hands folded gracefully in her lap. She could have been sitting in one of the elegant chairs in the house.

Consuela's chin rose and she studied the house, barely visible through the bushes. A man trotted along the path toward them and she quickly laid her finger on the button that would start the engine. As he came closer, Consuela relaxed. She picked up the pistol and tucked it back into her pocket.

"Now, you see," she said. "Leandro, as usual, has made everything suit his plans. Has he made love to you yet?"

The question surprised Rose. "Ah . . . no."

"He is a powerful man, in all that he does. Perhaps . . ." Consuela left the thought, whatever it was, hanging.

Rose didn't comment on it. She couldn't really think of anything to say. Leandro liked women—apparently a lot of women—beautiful women of all ages. So what did he see in her? A working woman, not a beautiful doll. An electrician who pulled wires but never lived in the magnificent structures she helped create. A challenge, maybe. A woman who admitted desire but fought it? She dropped those thoughts. Speculating on the question of what Leandro wanted and why was as dangerous as assuming she knew the answer to all questions.

They left the boat and went back into the house. No bodies littered the tile floors, no blood spattered the wall, its elegant silence held, just as it had when Rose walked in. Whatever violence occurred, it kept secret.

Consuela spoke quietly in Spanish to the man who had come for them.

"Rose, will you assist me?" she asked as he left the room.

"Sure."

She led Rose into her bedroom where Rose helped her pack some of her clothes. Not all, since she had a closet half as big as Rose's cottage. It would take a much larger boat to get all of her things to the greater island. Esteban's widow shared Anita's expensive tastes, but Consuela had a lot more class—and bigger diamonds. Rose asked no questions. She wanted nothing to delay departure from that house.

Consuela rode in the boat with them back to Pine Key,

where another car and driver waited for her. Leandro and Consuela spoke little. He would touch Consuela occasionally, and the tone of his voice carried reassurance. Rose didn't speak at all. Before she left them, Leandro kissed Esteban's widow and held her tight.

The sun filled the sky with red and gold as they rode back west toward Cudjoe Key and his house.

"Consuela didn't like the island?" Rose asked.

"Her prison?" Leandro shook his head. "No. She's free now. She has her own money and a place in Miami. She might go home to Nicaragua."

"Esteban kept her a prisoner?"

"Five years ago, she tried to leave him. He refused to let her go. She knew far too much about him. I persuaded him that it would not be prudent to kill her. Her father is dead, but she has a powerful and dangerous family. They probably don't care about her as an individual, but murder would be an insult to the family."

"And you would, of course, make sure they knew exactly what happened."

"Of course."

"Consuela loves you," Rose said. "You could do worse. Certainly, she'd be better for you than Anita and her soul sisters in cosmetic surgery and designer clothes."

"But, *mi dulce*, I am doomed to give my attention to Anita and the soul sisters. Unless . . ." He laughed softly. "You could be all of them for me."

"Bullshit."

"But I think you could be happy."

"Happy?" Rose wondered how he could believe that. "Happy knowing someday I'd have to bury you? If you didn't disappear like . . ." She didn't say Esteban's name. She didn't say, *and you wouldn't be faithful or promise never to tell me lies*. She didn't say, *death would hover over my bed, haunting me, while you touched me with bloody hands*.

"You should have more confidence in me. I might live to be a hundred and five."

"What do you *want*, Leandro? To find a nice simple girl, settle down, and have little lion cubs crawling at your feet? Not likely."

"I could ask you the same." He reached over and ruffled her hair.

"I asked first."

"Yes, you did." For a moment, the only sound was the whisper of asphalt under the tires. "When Esteban had my parents killed, my aunt moved us from Miami to California. I wanted to survive. As I grew up, I wanted vengeance. I graduated high school at sixteen and used my cousin's birth certificate to join the army. I wanted to learn. The soldiers gave me an excellent education in the art of killing. When I made it back to Esteban, and took measure of what he had, I wanted it all."

Rose gazed out over the gently rippling water. "Why don't you marry Consuela?"

"What?" Surprise filled his voice.

"That hadn't occurred to you?" Rose could see the suggestion intrigued him.

"No, it had not."

"She loves you, understands you. She has strength and courage. She could be your lioness. If you give her enough time and attention, she won't be unfaithful. She'd probably tolerate a few Anitas if you didn't stay with one too long or throw them in her face. Then you could take everything from Esteban. It wouldn't equal what he took from you, but he still owes you."

Leandro laughed softly. "I think you understand me better than Consuela. Perhaps that is the problem. She would close her eyes and regret my sins. You would cheerfully feed me to the devil's fire." He sighed. "Or maybe you would try harder to save me."

* * * *

Ryan pulled the trigger again. The gun barked and smacked against his palm. Another good hit. Three more and he popped the magazine and reloaded. He'd been at the gun range for over an hour, familiarizing himself with the feel of the weapon. His father's gun, carried but never used for anything but practice, always a *just in case* thing. No such ambiguity existed this time. He was going to kill Leandro.

* * * *

Rose leaned back in her chair. Leandro's servants brought them a lobster dinner and then disappeared. They sipped sweet wine by the tranquil, blue-water pool. The sun had long gone, but a half-moon hung directly over them.

"I'd get fat if I stayed with you," Rose said as she drained a glass of wine. He poured her another. He barely ate, himself, apparently preferring to watch her.

Rose stood and went to the pool. She knelt and ran her fingers through the water. "It's warm."

"Yes. You may swim," Leandro said. "We're alone. I've sent the servants away for the night."

"No." She returned to her seat. "What happens now?"

"I'm going to make love to you tonight, and tomorrow I'll take you to Jacksonville."

Jacksonville. Yes, that's where she wanted to go. To the future, whatever it might be. She wanted to move on, go past the killing, past death. Nothing in her power could stop such things. She couldn't pretend it never happened, but she'd never forget the grim reality and luxury of Leandro's world.

"Go upstairs," he said. "I'll be there in a while."

Rose nodded and walked away. Once in the suite, she undressed and showered, using the fine scented soap she found in the drawers. Leandro had said this was his bedroom, but it seemed far more impersonal than his room on the Guarida. Now that she thought of it, she suspected it was a guesthouse. A guesthouse that kept its residents isolated and easily confined.

She dried her hair, rubbed on perfumed lotion and crawled naked between the sheets of the bed. Part of her waited for him with anticipation and part with dread. She'd desired him from the day she met him. She desired Leandro like some women wanted diamonds and fine clothes. Luxury. It carried a price she couldn't afford. He'd cut a place for himself in her heart and memory. Love? Yes—and no. Her thoughts went to Ryan, wonderful solid Ryan. There was love. Love of the kind she had searched for all her life.

Rose fell asleep, dreaming she was back in her cottage with Ryan, struggling to find room on a bed far too small for her and the big man to share. She woke, not alarmed, but with the knowledge that someone had entered the darkened room.

Leandro? Yes. Silent as ever, he came to the bed and lay down beside her, on top of the blanket that covered her. She waited for him to move, undress, pull the covers from her body, kiss her, but he didn't.

Then he began to speak. He spoke of things she didn't want to know, but she knew he needed her to listen.

"My mother's name was Gracia," he said. "It was July, Miami, hot, wet and choking. I was ten. I came home from school." He shuddered. He draped his arm over her and drew her close. "Late. I was late, so I thought to sneak in through my bedroom window. The house, so quiet, it felt . . . odd. My door was open, and I peeked around the corner. My father lay on his back in the living room. I recognized his clothes. His face was gone. They'd shot him when he opened the door. My mother, she was lying near him. She was naked and they had cut her. But she moved. I ran to her. Her face, her eyes . . . so horrified to see me. Then I heard sounds, laughter coming from the back of the house. 'Run, Leandro,' my mother said. 'Run!' Barely a whisper, but . . . she died. Sometimes I dream about her voice, an angel's voice, urging me to run."

Leandro's grip on her tightened, not in anger, but in desperation, as if she would leave him before he finished crawling through memory.

"I heard them coming," he said. "I couldn't get out. I hid behind a chair. Two men. They dragged my sister's body with them. She was eleven. They had raped her before they strangled her.

"One went outside and brought in a can of gasoline, and they poured it on the bodies. They were wise enough not to light it too close, so the second they were out of sight, I ran for the back. When the gasoline exploded, it threw me out the door. I can still smell it where it burned my hair.

"I ran to my aunt's house, begged her to call the police, I said I could identify the men. She would not. She cried and said, 'My Leandro, my orphan, you are too young.' She grabbed what she could, loaded us in her car, and we left. Her house burned, too, a few hours later."

"What did Esteban say to you before you killed him?" Rose asked. "It's the only thing I've ever seen that made you angry— or at least show anger."

"He said he knew me. He didn't recognize me at first, but then he did. The men he paid to kill my parents were supposed to bring him a pretty young boy, but I escaped. He thought it amusing that he could corrupt me. Turn me from vengeance for so many years. He said, 'You are the heir to my kingdom, a most worthy successor.' I killed him then, because I knew it was true." Derision and self-loathing filled his voice.

"But you would have killed him anyway, wouldn't you? No matter what he said."

"Yes. But I had planned cold clear-eyed vengeance, and he twisted it back upon me. Isn't it amusing, *mi dulce*, the irony, the charade?"

Rose didn't find it amusing at all. "Why did Esteban target your family?"

"My father worked for one of Esteban's rivals. Esteban had a lover, a rather stupid lover, and my father's employer, a man named Duval, cured the lover of his stupidity one night. Esteban knew my father was important to Duval and his organization, so we became the target. My family paid the price, simply by association. It was always Esteban's way never to strike directly at his enemies."

"Esteban had a vile, malevolent nature coupled with a complete lack of morals."

"Careful, *mi dulce*. You have described me, too. The men who killed my parents? I had no qualms, showed no mercy." Leandro kissed her, his gentleness belied the venom of his words.

"Did you kill their families? Those men who slaughtered yours?"

"No. I did not."

To her surprise, he rose from the bed. "Get dressed," he said. "I'll take you home."

Rose heard finality in his voice, the finality of a man who had accepted what fate had given him. He would not make love to her. Disappointed? If she asked, if she threw off the blanket and stood before him . . . she would not. He went to the door, a door that she suspected symbolized something rare in most men's lives—true change. Perhaps for the good, perhaps not. Perhaps Esteban's death had set him free—or chained him forever.

"Leandro?"

"Yes, Rose."

"Esteban left you a kingdom filled with death and destruction. That's on his soul. What you do with that kingdom from now on, from this new day, that's on yours."

Chapter 33

Ryan glanced at his watch—again. Nine-thirty. The hour stretched on. Not long now, and he'd kill a man. Something in the back of his mind, some rational thought, protested. He shut that out and concentrated on what lay before him.

He'd parked at the far end of the Rising Sun Marina parking lot and walked the rest of the way. The gun slid neatly into his jacket pocket. In all his life, he'd only wanted to kill two men. Esteban and Leandro.

Esteban? O'Malley had heard rumors. Esteban had disappeared and was probably already in hell dealing with the devil. Leandro? Somewhere out there in the darkness with the center of Ryan's life, Rose. God, the thought of her made him want to cry.

He felt no apprehension, no dread. His only emotion was his unbending need to kill. It had helped that he'd spent most of the days since their rescue comforting Lola—and coming to grips with her place in his life. Finally, he gave up. Nothing had changed. He loved Lola no more and no less, but the beautiful, sad woman he had called Mother would always come to mind at the word.

He passed the marina building and stepped into the dense shadows. The long, wide concrete piers, marked every twenty feet with security lights, easily provided mooring for a hundred fifty boats. They sat soundless except for the gentle thumping lap of water against hulls. Beyond that, the river stretched into the black night. The yacht at the end of the fourth pier surprised him. He rarely saw one that big away from Miami.

Three lighted decks, at least a hundred fifty feet long, that one could cross the ocean without much trouble.

Ryan stepped back closer to the building. Two men and three women loaded an open fisherman, probably to head out at first light. Another smaller boat arrived and two men climbed out carrying their gear, probably on their way home.

Security guards would be making rounds soon. Cameras on poles covered the area of the docks, but he kept well out of their range. He had to wait, had to keep his restlessness from betraying him. His legs grew tired, aching, mostly from tension. It was cool near the water, and gentle waves of fog rolled off the river as time passed. They carried the scent of the ocean not far away. A security guard did make a half-assed pass-by, but Ryan crouched behind a bush and easily avoided detection. They concentrated on the areas where people might want to break in.

What was he going to do? Would he simply shoot Leandro and let him fall at her feet? What would she do? His mind made a tenacious step back to reason. A deep ache grew inside him and he closed his eyes, remembering her gold streaked hair and green eyes. He remembered her touching him, her mouth against his. He remembered her clean perfumed scent when she crawled into bed after a shower, and the musky, sweet smell of her after sex. Would he ever know that again if he killed Leandro?

A boat approached the marina, its engine so quiet it drifted as little more than a dark shape in the fog. The thirty-foot cruiser slid gently into a slip not far from the ocean yacht at the fourth pier. A man ran from the yacht to help with the docking. He leaped onto the front of the smaller boat carrying a mooring line. Within minutes, he had it secured, and quickly hurried back to the yacht. Ryan remained rigid, alert. Two people stood in the shadows on the back deck of the smaller boat. Only silhouettes. They waited there for long minutes, then embraced.

* * * *

Rose moved close to Leandro. He gathered her in his arms. She realized that death had walked beside her for the last few days as she'd made her way through Leandro's war-damned world. He didn't kill children or non-combatants. Did that make him good? Did it make her safe? Certainly not. Should it suit his needs, he'd leave the innocent grieving for loved ones.

"I can't stay with you, Leandro. I don't belong. It seems you know that better than I do." She laid her cheek against his. "Tell me why you didn't . . ."

"Make love to you? Because I am patient. Maybe I'll see you again some time. A time when things have changed." He ran his hands down her back and drew her tighter against him. The scent of him, now quite familiar, overwhelmed her. She would always remember that.

"But I'll be with Ryan. I do love him, and I'll marry him if he still wants me."

"If he does not, will you come back to me?" He whispered in her ear and kissed her throat.

"No." She knew that. If Ryan didn't want her, she would leave and go somewhere time might ease the pain.

Leandro held her tight, so tight it hurt—and then he let her go.

* * * *

Ryan recognized Leandro the moment he jumped from the boat to the dock. Rose followed him. They strolled slowly, side by side, down the pier toward the marina. They didn't speak; he'd have heard that in the tranquil night air. Instead, the silence between them told him something profound had happened. Would she go with Leandro? If so, why was she coming back to Jacksonville now? Maybe to say good-bye. Retrieve the few personal things she owned. Careful, organized Rose wouldn't leave anything undone. It wasn't in her nature.

The pair left the dock and walked onto the sidewalk, silently crossing the concrete, not touching. Would lovers walk like that? The distance between them seemed much farther than the actual inches he could see.

Ryan's grip tightened on the pistol.

They passed by him. Leandro suddenly turned to face him, hand inside his jacket. The man didn't miss much, but this time he was too late. Ryan stepped out from the shadows, his gun already aimed.

Leandro froze—and slowly brought his empty hand out for Ryan to see.

Ryan stared at him, letting rage and hatred fill him. Leandro couldn't have her. His finger tightened.

"Ryan?" Rose spoke softly.

Ryan swallowed. God, how beautiful she was. He suddenly felt as if he'd wakened from a bad dream. What was he thinking? To kill Leandro made him no better than the man he wanted to kill. Or Esteban for that matter. He lowered the gun. His rage was not for Leandro, but for himself and his failure. He might as well point the gun at his own head.

Rose smiled. She seemed poised to come to him, then stopped. The ache inside him grew to catastrophic proportions. He'd lost her.

Leandro chuckled. "She hesitates because she is unsure. Do you want her?"

"Yes. Oh, yes."

"Then put your gun away and open your arms." Leandro spoke softly.

Ryan let go of the hatred and the pain. Rose was there, holding him, crying. He held her tight and buried his face in her hair. "Oh, God, I missed you. I was afraid. Afraid I'd lost you." He stroked her hair.

"So was I, love." She touched his face and kissed him.

Ryan glanced at Leandro, but Leandro was quickly walking down toward the pier.

"What were you afraid of?" he asked her.

"That you wouldn't want me. That I'd have to go back to a life that didn't fit me anymore." Rose slowly stepped out of his arms. She turned toward Leandro and drew a breath, maybe to call to him, then sighed.

"Rose, if you want him, I won't hold you back." Those words cost Ryan. He knew he had to say them, though, had to give her a choice.

"If I wanted him, I'd be with him now," she said. "I was only going to say goodbye."

He heard truth in her words—and sadness. Before he heard

Lola's story, it might have hurt him or made him angry. Love was a simple path at times, a man, a woman, and a few kids to cherish. Life had carved out a more torturous path for him and Rose. If she had chosen Leandro, could he have left so casually? No, he could not.

The sound of engines rumbled across the water—big engines. Lights flashed on the enormous yacht, and men scurried around the front and lower decks preparing it to get underway.

Rose leaned against him. "I have so much to tell you."

"And I have so much to tell you." He kissed her again.

Ryan unloaded the gun and stuck it in his pocket. What insanity had made him believe he needed such a thing anyway?

Chapter 34

Rose slid her arms around him, needing his warmth. He held her a moment, then said, "Let's get to the truck."

When they reached the parking lot, she glanced back one last time. The Guarida had moved away from the dock and slowly veered toward the river, then on to the ocean. She could be there, lying in Leandro's arms, gliding into a future of luxury. She tried to find regret, but couldn't. That might come later, but not now. The only thing she could find was pity for a man who didn't deserve it, but who needed it so much.

When they climbed in the truck, Ryan didn't start the engine immediately.

"Let me talk first," he said. "Let me tell you about Tiffany."

"Your ex-wife?" He hadn't spoken much about his marriage, only that it was volatile and doomed from the start. Rose hadn't pressed him, preferring to dwell on their future together.

Ryan drew a deep breath, as if preparing to run a race. "I met Tiffany my third year in college. Tall, blond-haired, blue eyed, and the best figure money can buy. Her parents were rich—so was my father—but not in that league. I followed her around like a puppy."

The words tumbled from him, heavy with a need she didn't understand. It frightened her, because he sounded much like Leandro. What would he tell her?

"I did everything from write her theme papers to paint her toenails." He spoke in a rough voice, edged with anguish. "I'm not sure what she wanted from me, other than the fact that I'd be her willing, low maintenance, slave. The man she fucked when no one else better would have her. She wasn't faithful. Not before or after marriage. She'd set herself up in situations where I'd have to fight to get her out. Big man, hot temper, bare knuckles, the more blood I drew, the more men I beat the hell out of, the better she liked it. She called me her warrior. Me, stupid, I obliged. It felt good. I liked the way her eyes glowed when I won." He didn't speak for a moment and Rose allowed him his thoughts.

"After I begged her for a year, she agreed to marry me," he said. "I think her parents pressured her, their wild-child, hoping she would settle down. But then the real stuff started. I had to bail her out of jail once because she got drunk and pissed in the fountain in a high-class hotel lobby. I came home and had to kick two men out of my bed one night. The next night it was a woman. She loved it. I almost killed a man." Ryan's voice deepened. "A married man with kids. He rejected her and she told me he raped her. My father paid a lot of money to buy me out of that."

He rubbed his eyes and his breathing slowed. "One day, Tiffany sat on the bed cursing in pain. She'd been pregnant. Maybe my child, maybe not, but the abortion slowed her down for a few days."

Ryan twisted in his seat. "Rose, I've lied to you. We didn't need condoms. Tiffany told me she'd leave if I didn't get a vasectomy. She didn't want to have kids. Because I was stupid in love, I gave her everything she wanted. I can try to have it reversed, but there's a chance I can't ever give you children. You've always been honest with me. I haven't always been honest with you. I just wanted you so much. I was afraid."

Rose cringed inside, not at the idea of never having children, but at the betrayal of such a lie. Not a single lie, but months of living that lie, of letting her believe something so false. It hurt, that betrayal. "Ryan, I wouldn't marry just to have children, but, oh, I wish you'd told me."

"I'm sorry." He choked on the words. "I'm so sorry. Eventually, I learned what I believe you know about Leandro. What you knew from the minute you met him. Blind desire isn't enough to sustain love. Tiffany cried and begged me to come back when I finally found the courage to leave. I thought it would kill me. Thought a couple of times about killing myself."

Rose fought back tears. His pain beat at her like a brutal wind from the north; added to her own, it became a monstrous storm.

"I love you," she said. "You *don't* have to be perfect for me. You *do* have to tell me the truth, though. If you lie to me again, I think it will destroy me." She considered that it might have already done that.

"If I lie again it will destroy both of us." Ryan's voice pleaded with her. "Will you still marry me? Do you think we can leave this behind us? Walk away from what happened?"

"Yes, I'll marry you. Not tomorrow, but I will." She hoped that was true. Certainly she intended it to be. "No, we can't walk away from what happened. It's going to be there, and we'll live with it. Time may help."

Rose knew she loved him, belonged in his world. No children? How bitter. That ache would stay with her. Would it eventually poison their relationship? She drew a deep breath and released it. She ruled her life. Made her own decisions. Like rejecting a man she desired, but knew was wrong for her. As for no children, a reversal might work. But if not, Ryan was what she wanted. If they remained honest and true to one another, they could build a good solid future. The alternative wasn't Leandro's riches, but an empty life.

Ryan Vernon filled a hollow place in her heart. He had since the day she met him. She wasn't above temptation. Temptation might come again. She would deal with it. Perfection didn't exist, but love and friendship could be enough.

Epilogue

Rose stroked the satin-soft cheek of the miracle that had arrived in their lives. "Look at her, Ryan. She's so beautiful."

"You are both beautiful." Ryan stood by the hospital bed.

Rose could see the weariness in him. He'd gone home for a few hours, but probably hadn't rested. The doctors hadn't given them much hope that the vasectomy reversal surgery would work. Now, eighteen months later, Lillian Abigail Vernon, tiny Lilly, slept in her arms.

She and Ryan were married in late September, months after the momentous events that began in Jacksonville that January. Ryan completed the hotel ahead of schedule and rid himself of Olivarez Corporation, no matter how legitimate it was. Esteban had disappeared, so it really wasn't relevant any more. She told only Ryan and O'Malley how he had died, and only Ryan of the carnage that night had brought after he'd left the warehouse where the kidnappers held them.

Vernon Construction moved its main offices from Miami to Ashville, North Carolina. Rose wanted to be far from the ocean and Ryan didn't want to go back to a place where he'd known such unhappiness. Unspoken was the fact that they'd be more likely to encounter Leandro in Miami. She thought it worried Ryan far more than it worried her. She'd made her decision, committed herself to her husband, and that commitment would stand.

She had a beautiful home in town and another in the cool shadows of the mountains. For the first time in her life, she had a place to anchor herself. She pulled no more wires, except in her own houses, and didn't miss it at all.

Ryan held two envelopes. "These were delivered by personal courier this morning."

"What are they?" She moved and Lilly grumbled softly.

"They're not addressed to me." The tone of his voice told her where *he* thought they came from.

Ryan hadn't asked her about her time with Leandro, but she told him the truth. She hadn't had sex with the man. Leandro's personal confessions, she buried deep in her heart and would not speak of them to anyone. Ryan had accepted it, and he'd seemed willing to love her no matter what had happened.

When she learned of the depth and breadth of the lies his mother, father, Jimmy and Lola had perpetrated on him, she found more compassion than she thought possible. He had lived a lie his whole life. He had told her, "Rose, I love you, but Leandro loves you, too. You had a very personal relationship with him, even if it didn't include actual sex. He's still a part of your life. A memory, I hope. I know you're here with me by your own choice and you won't lie to me. Don't lie to yourself. I also know he's probably waiting for me to screw up. Do something stupid and lose you."

Rose thought that Leandro had held back on sex because he thought it better to remain a mystery, an unfulfilled desire, something she might dwell on in troubled times.

Rose laid a hand on Ryan's arm. "Will you open them for me?"

Ryan drew a card out of the first envelope. He frowned. It wasn't what he expected. "It says, 'a small gift for your daughter. I know you will be excellent parents and raise a beautiful, compassionate child.'" He held the card so she could see it. A single letter, L, signed the note. A tiny thin box was included. Ryan opened it. It held a slender gold chain with a cross. He sighed. "He's still watching you."

He'd kept his voice neutral, but Rose knew it cost him. Leandro had watched her closely enough to know of the birth of her daughter yesterday. He was a man with powerful emotions, driven by a life neither she nor Ryan would ever truly understand.

Ryan opened the second envelope. He frowned, then smiled. Better news, then. "It's a wedding announcement. Leandro and Consuela were married six months ago in Managua, Nicaragua." Two handwritten words flowed across the card. *Gracias,* and in smaller letters it was signed, *Consuela.*

"Consuela is a strong woman," Rose said. "Maybe she can find enough good in Leandro to save him." Since Ryan found that news to be more comforting, she didn't remind him that Consuela was probably twenty years or more older than Leandro. He might have married her out of love or kindness, but it was just as likely the marriage gained him something of value.

Rose brushed a finger across Lilly's forehead. "Do you think we can make life better for this little angel? Better than what we had?"

"Yes." He lifted Lilly's hand. Her tiny fingers curled around one of his. "We can't make it perfect, but we can make it honest. She won't have to live with lies."

Rose started to tell him how much she loved him, but Lola rushed in, followed by O'Malley, Brianna, and Carl. Family, the family she never expected to have. Ryan's presence, their presence, in her life meant more than all the words of love she could speak. It was enough for today.

About the Author

Lee hasn't always been a writer, but has always been a daydreamer. She was particularly talented at rewriting her school day behavior lapses into happy endings when explaining the situation to her mother. She currently lives in Florida with her husband and children.

Contact Lee at lee@leeroland.com and see her other works at www.leeroland.com

Praise for Highland Press Books!

"Ah, the memories that **Operation: L.O.V.E.** brings to mind. As an Air Force nurse who married an Air Force fighter pilot, I relived the days of glory through each and every story. While covering all the military branches, each story holds a special spark of its own that readers will love!
~ Lori Avocato, Best Selling Author

* * * *

In **Fate of Camelot**, Cynthia Breeding develops the Arthur-Lancelot-Gwenhwyfar relationship. In many Arthurian tales, Guinevere is a rather flat character. Cynthia Breeding gives her a depth of character as the reader sees both her love for Lancelot and her devotion to the realm as its queen. The reader feels the pull she experiences between both men. In addition, the reader feels more of the deep friendship between Arthur and Lancelot seen in Malory's Arthurian tales. In this area, Cynthia Breeding is more faithful to the medieval Arthurian tradition than a glamorized Hollywood version. She does not gloss over the difficulties of Gwenhwyfar's role as queen and as woman, but rather develops them to give the reader a vision of a woman who lives her role as queen and lover with all that she is.
~ Merri, Merrimon Books

* * * *

Rape of the Soul - Ms. Thompson's characters are unforgettable. Deep, promising and suspenseful this story was. I did have a little trouble getting into the book at first, but as I pushed on, I found that I couldn't put it down. Around every corner was something that you didn't know was going to happen. If you love a sense of history in a book, then I suggest reading this book!
~ Ruth Schaller, Paranormal Romance Reviews

* * * *

Southern Fried Trouble - Katherine Deauxville is at the top of her form with mayhem, sizzle and murder.
~ Nan Ryan, NY Times bestselling author

* * * *

Madrigal: A Novel of Gaston Leroux's Phantom of the Opera takes place four years after the events of the original novel. Although I have not read Leroux's novel, I can see how **Madrigal** captures the feel of the story very well. The classic novel aside, this book is a wonderful historical tale of life, love, and choices. However, the most impressive aspect that stands out to me is the writing. Ms. Linforth's prose is phenomenally beautiful and hauntingly breathtaking.

~ Bonnie-Lass, Coffee Time Romance

* * * *

Cave of Terror - Highly entertaining and fun, ***Cave of Terror*** was impossible to put down. Though at times dark and evil, Ms. Bell never failed to inject some light-hearted humor into the story. Delightfully funny with a true sense of teenagers, Cheyenne's character will appeal to many girls of that age. She is believable and her emotional struggles are on par with most teens. I found this to be an easy read; the author gave just enough background to understand the workings of her vampires without boring the reader. I truly enjoyed the male characters, Ryan and Constantine. Ryan was adorable and a teenager's dream. Constantine was deliciously dark. I look forward to reading more by this talented author. Ms. Bell has done an admirable job of telling a story suitable for young adults.

~ Dawnie, Fallen Angel Reviews

* * * *

The Sense of Honor - Ashley Kath-Bilsky has written an historical romance of the highest caliber. This reviewer was fesseled to the pages, fell in love with the hero and was cheering for the heroine all the way through. The plot is exciting and moves along at a good pace. The characters are multi-dimensional and the secondary characters bring life to the story. Sexual tension rages through this story and Ms. Kath-Bilsky gives her readers a breath-taking romance. The love scenes are sensual and very romantic. This reviewer was very pleased with how the author handled all the secrets. Sometimes it can be very frustrating for the reader when secrets keep tearing the main characters apart, but in this case, those secrets seem to bring them more together and both characters reacted very maturely when the secrets finally came to light. This reviewer is hoping that this very talented author will have another book out very soon.

~ Valerie, Love Romances and More

* * * *

Highland Wishes by Leanne Burroughs. This reviewer found that this book was a wonderful story set in a time when tension was high between England and Scotland. The storyline is a fast-paced tale with much detail to specific areas of history. The reader can feel this author's love for Scotland and its many wonderful heroes. This reviewer was easily captivated by the story and was enthralled by it until the end. The reader will laugh and cry as you read this wonderful story. The reader feels all the pain, torment and disillusionment felt by both main characters, but also the joy and love they felt. Ms. Burroughs has crafted a well-researched story that gives a glimpse into Scotland during a time when there was upheaval and war for independence. This reviewer is anxiously awaiting her next novel in this series and commends her for a wonderful job done.

~*Dawn Roberto, Love Romances*

* * * *

I adore this Scottish historical romance! **Blood on the Tartan** by Chris Holmes has more history than some historical romances—but never dry history in this book! Readers will find themselves completely immersed in the scene, the history and the characters. Chris Holmes creates a multi-dimensional theme of justice in his depiction of all the nuances and forces at work from the laird down to the land tenants. This intricate historical detail emanates from the story itself, heightening the suspense and the reader's understanding of the history in a vivid manner as if it were current and present. The extra historical detail just makes their life stories more memorable and lasting because the emotions were grounded in events. The ending is quite special and bridges links with Catherine's mother's story as well as opening up this romance to an expansive view of Scottish history and ancestry. **Blood On The Tartan** is a must read for romance and historical fiction lovers of Scottish heritage.

~*Merri, Merrimon Reviews*

* * * *

The Crystal Heart by Katherine Deauxville brims with ribald humor and authentic historical detail. Enjoy!

~ *Virginia Henley, NY Times bestselling author*

* * * *

I can't say enough good things about Ms. Zenk's writing. **Chasing Byron** by Molly Zenk is a page turner of a book not only because of the engaging characters but also by the lovely prose. In fact, I read the entire thing in one day. Reading this book was a jolly fun time all through the eyes of Miss Woodhouse, yet also one that touches the heart. It was an experience I would definitely repeat. I'm almost jealous of Ms. Zenk. She must have had a glorious time penning this story. As this is her debut novel, I hope we will be delighted with more stories from this talented author in the future.

~*Orange Blossom, Long and Short Reviews*

* * * *

Moon of the Falling Leaves is an incredible read. The characters are not only believable but the blending in of how Swift Eagle shows Jessica and her children the acts of survival is remarkably done. The months of travel indeed shows hardships each much endure. Diane Davis White pens a poignant tale that really grabbed this reader. She tells a descriptive story of discipline, trust and love in a time where hatred and prejudice abounded among many. This rich tale offers vivid imagery of the beautiful scenery and landscape, and brings in the tribal customs of each person, as Jessica and Swift Eagle search their heart.

Lee Roland

~Cherokee, Coffee Time Romance

* * * *

Jean Harrington's **The Barefoot Queen** is a superb historical with a lushly painted setting. I adored Grace for her courage and the cleverness with which she sets out to make Owen see her love for him. The bond between Grace and Owen is tenderly portrayed and their love had me rooting for them right up until the last page. Ms. Harrington's **The Barefoot Queen** is a treasure in the historical romance genre you'll want to read for yourself! Five Star Pick of the Week!!!

~ Crave More Romance

* * * *

Almost Taken by Isabel Mere is a very passionate historical romance that takes the reader on an exciting adventure. The compelling characters of Deran Morissey, the Earl of Atherton, and Ava Fychon, a young woman from Wales, find themselves drawn together as they search for her missing siblings. Readers will watch in interest as they fall in love and overcome obstacles. They will thrill in the passion and hope that they find happiness together. This is a very sensual romance that wins the heart of the readers. This is a creative and fast moving storyline that will enthrall readers. The character's personalities will fascinate readers and win their concern. Ava, who is highly spirited and stubborn, will win the respect of the readers for her courage and determination. Deran, who is rumored in the beginning to be an ice king, not caring about anyone, will prove how wrong people's perceptions can be. **Almost Taken** by Isabel Mere is an emotionally moving historical romance that I highly recommend to the readers.

~ Anita, The Romance Studio

* * * *

Leanne Burroughs easily will captivate the reader with intricate details, a mystery that ensnares the reader and characters that will touch their hearts. By the end of the first chapter, this reviewer was enthralled with **Her Highland Rogue** and was rooting for Duncan and Catherine to admit their love. Laughter, tears and love shine through this wonderful novel. This reviewer was amazed at Ms. Burroughs' depth and perception in this storyline. Her wonderful way with words plays itself through each page like a lyrical note and will captivate the reader till the very end. The only drawback was this reviewer wanted to know more of the secondary characters and the back story of other characters. All in all, read **Her Highland Rogue** and be transported to a time that is full of mystery and promise of a future. This reviewer is highly recommending this book for those who enjoy an engrossing Scottish tale full of humor, love and laughter.

~Dawn Roberto, Love Romances

* * * *

Bride of Blackbeard is a compelling tale of sorrow, pain, love, and hate. With a cast of characters, each with their own trait, the story is hard to put down. From the moment I started reading about Constanza and her upbringing, I was torn. Each of the people she encounters on her journey has an experience to share, drawing in the reader more. Ms. Chapman sketches a story that tugs at the heartstrings. Her well-researched tale brings many things into light that this reader was not aware of. I believe many will be touched in some way by this extraordinary book that leaves much thought.

~ *Cherokee, Coffee Time Romance*

* * * *

Almost Guilty - Isabel Mere's skill with words and the turn of a phrase makes **Almost Guilty** a joy to read. Her characters reach out and pull the reader into the trials, tribulations, simple pleasures, and sensual joy that they enjoy. Ms. Mere unravels the tangled web of murder, smuggling, kidnapping, hatred and faithless friends, while weaving a web of caring, sensual love that leaves a special joy and hope in the reader's heart.

~ *Camellia, Long and Short Reviews*

* * * *

Beats A Wild Heart - In the ancient, Celtic land of Cornwall, Emma Hayward searched for a myth and found truth. The legend of the black cat of Bodmin Moor is a well known Cornish legend. Ms. Adams has merged the essence of myth and romance into a fascinating story which catches the imagination. I enjoyed the way the story unfolded at a smooth and steady pace with Emma and Seth appearing as real people who feel an instant attraction for one another. At first the story appears to be straightforward, but as it evolves mystery, love and intrigue intervene to make a vibrant story with hidden depths. **Beats a Wild Heart** is well written and a pleasure to read, but you should only start reading if you have time to indulge yourself. Once you start reading you won't be able to put this book down.

~ *Orchid, Long and Short Reviews*

* * * *

Down Home Ever Lovin' Mule Blues - How can true love fail when everyone and their mule, cat, and skunk know that Brody and Rita belong together, even if Rita is engaged to another man. Needless to say, this is a fabulous roll on the floor while laughing out loud story. I am so thrilled to discover this book, and the author who wrote it. I adore romantic comedy. Rarely do I locate a story with as much humor, joy, and downright lust spread so thickly on the pages that I am surprised that I could turn the pages. **Down Home Ever Lovin' Mule Blues** is a treasure not to be missed. Thank you, Ms. Rogers, for all of the laughter, and joy that you bring to the reader of your fabulous book. Major Kudos to you! Now, when is your next book published? I am ready for more . . .

~*Suziq2, Single Titles.com*

* * * *

Saving Tampa - What if you knew something horrible was going to happen but you could prevent it, would you tell someone? Sure, we all would. What if you saw it in a vision and had no proof? Would you risk your credibility to come forward? These are the questions at the heart of **Saving Tampa**, an on-the-edge-of-your-seat thriller from Jo Webnar, who has written a wonderful suspense that is as timely as it is entertaining.

~ *Mairead Walpole, Reviews by Crystal*

* * * *

When the Vow Breaks by Judith Leigh - This book is about a woman who fights breast cancer. I assumed the book would be extremely emotional and hard to read, but it was not. The storyline dealt more with the commitment between a man and a woman, with a true belief of God. There was some sentiment which became even more passionate when this scared man disappeared without a word just as Jill needed him most.

The intrigue of the storyline was that of finding a rock to lean upon through faith in God. Not only did she learn to lean on her relationship with Him but she also learned how to forgive her husband even before he returned to the States. This is a great look at not only a breast cancer survivor but also a couple whose commitment to each other through their faith grew stronger. It is an easy read and one I highly recommend.

~ *Brenda Talley, The Romance Studio*

* * * *

A Heated Romance by Candace Gold - A fascinating romantic suspense, **A Heated Romance** tells the story of Marcie O'Dwyer, a female firefighter who has had to struggle to prove herself. While the first part of the book seems to focus on the romance and Marcie's daily life, the second part seems to transition into a suspense novel as Marcie witnesses something suspicious at one of the fires. Her life is endangered by what she possibly knows and I found myself anticipating the outcome almost as much as Marcie.

~ *Lilac, Long and Short Reviews*

* * * *

Into the Woods by R.R. Smythe - This Young Adult Fantasy will send chills down your spine. I, as the reader, followed Callum and witnessed everything he and his friends went through as they attempted to decipher the messages. At the same time, I watched Callum's mother, Ellsbeth, as she walked through the Netherwood. Each time Callum deciphered one of the four messages, some villagers awakened. Through the eyes of Ellsbeth, I saw the other sleepers wander, make mistakes, and be released from the Netherwood, leaving Ellsbeth alone. There is one thread left dangling, but do not fret. This IS a stand-alone book. But that thread gives me hope that another book about the Netherwoods may someday come to pass. Excellent reading for any age of fantasy fans!

~ *Detra Fitch, Huntress Reviews*

* * * *

Dark Well of Decision by Anne Kimberly - Like the Lion, the Witch, and the Wardrobe, **Dark Well of Decision** is a grand adventure with a likable girl who is a little like all of us. Zoe's insecurities are realistically drawn and her struggle with both her faith and the new direction her life will take is poignant. The secondary characters are engaging and add extra 'spice' to this story. The references to the Bible and the teachings presented are appropriately captured. Author, Anne Kimberly is an author to watch; her gift for penning a grand childhood adventure is a great one. This one is well worth the time and money spent; I will buy several copies for friends and family.

~Lettetia, Coffee Time Romance

* * * *

In Sunshine or In Shadow by Cynthia Owens - If you adore the stormy heroes of 'Wuthering Heights' and 'Jane Eyre' (and who doesn't?) you'll be entranced by Owens' passionate story of Ireland after the Great Famine, and David Burke - a man from America with a hidden past and a secret name. Only one woman, the fiery, luscious Siobhan, can unlock the bonds that imprison him. Highly recommended for those who love classic romance and an action-packed story.

~ Best Selling Author, Maggie Davis, AKA Katherine Deauxville

* * * *

Rebel Heart by Jannine Corti Petska - Ms. Petska does an excellent job of all aspects of sharing this book with us. Ms. Petska used a myriad of emotions to tell this story and the reader (me) quickly becomes entranced in the ways Courtney's stubborn attitude works to her advantage in surviving this disastrous beginning to her new life. Ms. Petska's writings demand attention; she draws the reader to quickly become involved in this passionate story. This is a wonderful rendition of a different type which is a welcome addition to the historical romance genre. I believe that you will enjoy this story; I know I did!

~ Brenda Talley, The Romance Studio

* * * *

Pretend I'm Yours by Phyllis Campbell is an exceptional masterpiece. This lovely story is so rich in detail and personalities that it just leaps out and grabs hold of the reader. From the moment I started reading about Mercedes and Katherine, I was spellbound. Ms. Campbell carries the reader into a mirage of mystery with deceit, betrayal of the worst kind, and a passionate love revolving around the sisters, that makes this a whirlwind page-turner. Mercedes and William are astonishing characters that ignite the pages and allows the reader to experience all their deepening sensations. There were moments I could share in with their breathtaking romance, almost feeling the butterflies of love they emitted. This extraordinary read had me mesmerized with its ambiance, its characters and its remarkable twists and turns, making it one recommended read in my book.

~ Linda L., Fallen Angel Reviews

* * * *

Cat O' Nine Tales by Deborah MacGillivray. Enchanting tales from the most wicked, award-winning author today. Spellbinding! A treat for all.
~ *Detra Fitch, The Huntress Reviews*

* * * *

Brides of the West by Michèle Ann Young, Kimberly Ivey, and Billie Warren Chai - All three of the stories in this wonderful anthology are based on women who gambled their future in blindly accepting complete strangers for husbands. It was a different era when a woman must have a husband to survive and all three of these phenomenal authors wrote exceptional stories featuring fascinating and gutsy heroines and the men who loved them. For an engrossing read with splendid original stories I highly encourage reader's to pick up a copy of this marvelous anthology.
~ *Marilyn Rondeau, Reviewers International Organization*

* * * *

Faery Special Romances by Jacquie Rogers - Brilliantly magical! Ms. Rogers' special brand of humor and imagination will have you believing in faeries from page one. Absolutely enchanting!
~ *Dawn Thompson, Award Winning Author*

* * * *

Flames of Gold (Anthology) - Within every heart lies a flame of hope, a dream of true love, a glimmering thought that the goodness of life is far, far larger than the challenges and adversities arriving in every life. In **Flames of Gold** lie five short stories wrapping credible characters into that mysterious, poignant mixture of pain and pleasure, sorrow and joy, stony apathy and resurrected hope.Deftly plotted, paced precisely to hold interest and delightfully unfolding, Flames of Gold deserves to be enjoyed in any season, guaranteeing that real holiday spirit endures within the gifts of faith, hope and love personified in these engaging, spirited stories by these obviously terrific writers!
~ *Viviane Crystal, Reviews by Crystal*

* * * *

Romance Upon A Midnight Clear (Anthology) - Each of these stories is well-written and will stand-alone and when grouped together, they pack a powerful punch. Each author shares exceptional characters and a multitude of emotions ranging from grief to elation in their stories. You cannot help being able to relate to these stories that touch your heart and will entertain you at any time of year, not just the holidays. I feel honored to have been able to sample the works of such talented authors.
~*Matilda, Coffee Time Romance*

* * * *

Christmas is a magical time and twelve talented authors answer the question of what happens when **Christmas Wishes** come true in this incredible anthology. **Christmas Wishes** shows just how phenomenal a themed anthology can be. Each of these highly skilled authors brings a slightly different perspective to the Christmas theme to create a book that is sure to leave readers satisfied. What a joy to read such splendid stories! This reviewer looks forward to more anthologies by Highland Press as the quality is simply astonishing.

~ *Debbie, CK2S Kwips and Kritiques*

* * * *

Recipe for Love *(Anthology)* - I don't think the reader will find a better compilation of mouth watering short romantic love stories than in **Recipe for Love**! This is a highly recommended volume–perfect for beaches, doctor's offices, or anywhere you've a few minutes to read.

~ *Marilyn Rondeau, Reviewers International Organization*

* * * *

Holiday in the Heart *(Anthology)* - Twelve stories that would put even Scrooge into the Christmas spirit. It does not matter what *type* of romance genre you prefer. This book has a little bit of everything. The stories are set in the U.S.A. and Europe. Some take place in the past, some in the present, and one story takes place in both! I strongly suggest that you put on something comfortable, brew up something hot (tea, coffee or cocoa will do), light up a fire, settle down somewhere quiet and begin reading this anthology.

~ *Detra Fitch, Huntress Reviews*

* * * *

Blue Moon Magic is an enchanting collection of short stories. Each author wrote with the same theme in mind, but each story has its own uniqueness. You should have no problem finding a tale to suit your mood. **Blue Moon Magic** offers historicals, contemporaries, time travel, paranormal, and futuristic narratives to tempt your heart. Legend says that if you wish with all your heart upon the rare blue moon, your wishes were sure to come true. Each of the heroines discovers this magical fact. True love is out there if you just believe in it. In some of the stories, love happens in the most unusual ways. Angels may help, ancient spells may be broken, anything can happen. Even vampires will find their perfect mate with the power of the blue moon. Not every heroine believes they are wishing for love, some are just looking for answers to their problems or nagging questions. Fate seems to think the solution is finding the one who makes their heart sing. **Blue Moon Magic** is a perfect read for late at night or even during your commute to work. The short yet sweet stories are a wonderful way to spend a few minutes. If you do not have the time to finish a full-length novel, but hate stopping in the middle of a loving tale, I highly recommend grabbing this book.

~ *Kim Swiderski, Writers Unlimited Reviewer*

* * * *

Legend has it that a blue moon is enchanted. What happens when fifteen talented authors utilize this theme to create enthralling stories of love? **Blue**

Moon Enchantment is a wonderful, themed anthology filled with phenomenal stories by fifteen extraordinarily talented authors. Readers will find a wide variety of time periods and styles showcased in this superb anthology. **Blue Moon Enchantment** is sure to offer a little bit of something for everyone!

~ *Debbie, CK²S Kwips and Kritiques*

* * * *

Love Under the Mistletoe *is a fun anthology that infuses the beauty of the season with fun characters and unforgettable situations. This is one of those books that you can read year round and still derive great pleasure from each of the charming stories. A wonderful compilation of holiday stories. Perfect year round!*

~ *Chrissy Dionne, Romance Junkies*

* * * *

Love and Silver Bells - I really enjoyed this heart-warming anthology. The four stories are different enough to keep you interested but all have their happy endings. The characters are heart wrenchingly human and hurting and simply looking for a little bit of peace on earth. Luckily they all eventually find it, although not without some strife. But we always appreciate the gifts we receive when we have to work a little harder to keep them. I recommend these warm holiday tales be read by the light of a well-lit tree, with a lovely fire in the fireplace and a nice cup of hot cocoa. All will warm you through and through.

~ *Angi, Night Owl Romance*

* * * *

Love on a Harley, is an amazing romantic anthology featuring six amazing stories by six very talented ladies. Each story was heart-warming, tear jerking, and so perfect. I got tied to each one wanting them to continue on forever. Lost love, rekindling love, and learning to love are all expressed within these pages beautifully. I couldn't ask for a better romance anthology, each author brings that sensual, longing sort of love that every woman dreams of. Great job ladies!

~ *Crystal, Crystal Book Reviews*

* * * *

No Law Against Love - If you have ever found yourself rolling your eyes at some of the more stupid laws, then you are going to adore this novel. Over twenty-five stories fill up this anthology, each one dealing with at least one stupid or outdated law. Let me give you an example: In Florida, USA, there is a law that states 'If an elephant is left tied to a parking meter, the parking fee has to be paid just as it would for a vehicle.' In Great Britain, 'A license is required to keep a lunatic.' Yes, you read those correctly. No matter how many times you go back and reread them, the words will remain the same. Those two laws are still legal. The tales vary in time and place. Some take place in the present, in the past, in the USA, in England . . . in other words, there is something for everyone! Best yet, profits from the sales of this novel will go to breast cancer prevention.

A stellar anthology that had me laughing, sighing in pleasure, believing in magic, and left me begging for more! Will there be a second anthology someday? I sure hope so! This is one novel that will go directly to my 'Keeper' shelf, to be read over and over again. Very highly recommended!

~ Detra Fitch, Huntress Reviews

* * * *

No Law Against Love 2 - I'm sure you've heard about some of those silly laws, right? Well, this anthology shows us that sometimes those silly laws can bring just the right people together. I can highly recommend this anthology. Each story is a gem and each author has certainly given their readers value for money.

~ Valerie, Love Romances

Static Resistance and Rose

Now Available from Highland Press Publishing:

**Non-Fiction/
Writer's Resource:**
Rebecca Andrews
The Millennium Phrase Book

Historicals:
Cynthia Breeding
Return to Camelot
Isabel Mere
Almost Silenced
Jean Harrington
In the Lion's Mouth
Cynthia Breeding
Prelude to Camelot
Cynthia Breeding
Fate of Camelot
Dawn Thompson
Rape of the Soul
Ashley Kath-Bilsky
The Sense of Honor
Isabel Mere
Almost Taken
Isabel Mere
Almost Guilty
Leanne Burroughs
Highland Wishes
Leanne Burroughs
Her Highland Rogue
Chris Holmes
Blood on the Tartan
Jean Harrington
The Barefoot Queen
Linda Bilodeau
The Wine Seekers
Judith Leigh
When the Vow Breaks
Jennifer Linforth
Madrigal
Brynn Chapman

Lee Roland
Bride of Blackbeard
Diane Davis White
Moon of the Falling Leaves
Molly Zenk
Chasing Byron
Katherine Deauxville
The Crystal Heart
Cynthia Owens
In Sunshine or In Shadow
Jannine Corti Petska
Rebel Heart
Jeanmarie Hamilton
Seduction
Phyllis Campbell
Pretend I'm Yours

Mystery/Comedic:
Katherine Deauxville
Southern Fried Trouble

Action/Suspense:
Chris Holmes
The Mosquito Tapes
Eric Fullilove
The Zero Day Event

Romantic Suspense:
Candace Gold
A Heated Romance
Jo Webnar
Saving Tampa
Lee Roland
Static Resistance and Rose

Contemporary:
Jean Adams
Beats a Wild Heart
Jacquie Rogers
Down Home Ever Lovin' Mule Blues
Teryl Oswald
Luck of the Draw

Young Adult:

Static Resistance and Rose
Amber Dawn Bell
Cave of Terror
R.R. Smythe
Into the Woods
Anne Kimberly
Dark Well of Decision

Anthologies:
*Anne Elizabeth/C.H. Admirand/DC DeVane/
Tara Nina/Lindsay Downs*
Operation: L.O.V.E.
Judith Leigh/Cheryl Norman
Romance On Route 66
*Cynthia Breeding/Kristi Ahlers/Gerri Bowen/
Susan Flanders/Erin E.M. Hatton*
A Dance of Manners
Deborah MacGillivray
Cat O'Nine Tales
*Deborah MacGillivray/Rebecca Andrews/Billie Warren-Chai/Debi Farr/Patricia Frank/
Diane Davis-White*
Love on a Harley
*Zoe Archer/Amber Dawn Bell/Gerri Bowen/
Candace Gold/Patty Howell/Kimberly Ivey/
Lee Roland*
No Law Against Love 2
*Michèle Ann Young/Kimberly Ivey/
Billie Warren Chai*
Brides of the West
Jacquie Rogers
Faery Special Romances
Holiday Romance Anthology
Christmas Wishes
Holiday Romance Anthology
Holiday in the Heart
Romance Anthology
No Law Against Love
Romance Anthology
Blue Moon Magic
Romance Anthology
Blue Moon Enchantment
Romance Anthology
Recipe for Love

Lee Roland

*Deborah MacGillivray/Leanne Burroughs/
Amy Blizzard/Gerri Bowen/Judith Leigh*
Love Under the Mistletoe
*Deborah MacGillivray/Leanne Burroughs/
Rebecca Andrews/Amber Dawn Bell/Erin E.M. Hatton/Patty Howell/Isabel Mere*
Romance Upon A Midnight Clear
*Leanne Burroughs/Amber Dawn Bell/Amy Blizzard/
Patty Howell/Judith Leigh*
Flames of Gold
*Polly McCrillis/Rebecca Andrews/
Billie Warren Chai/Diane Davis White*
Love and Silver Bells

Children's Illustrated:
Lance Martin
The Little Hermit

*Check our website frequently for
future releases.*

www.highlandpress.org

Highland Press

Single Titles

☐ 978-09815573-3-5 **Madrigal** $12.95
☐ 978-09800356-8-1 **Down Home Mule Blues** $ 9.95
☐ 978-09815573-7-3 **The Wine Seekers** $12.95

Highland Press Publishing
PO Box 2292, High Springs, FL 32655
www.highlandpress.org

Please send me the books I have checked above. I am enclosing $_____ (Please add $2.50 per book to cover shipping and handling). Send check or money order—no C.O.D.s please. Or, PayPal – Leanne@leanneburroughs.com and indicate names of book(s) ordered.

Name_____

Address_____

City_____State/Zip_____

Please allow 2 weeks for delivery. Offer good in US only. (Contact The.Highland.Press@gmail.com for shipping charges outside the US.)

Highland Press

Single Titles

- ☐ 978-0-9823615-3-5   **Luck of the Draw** $12.95
- ☐ 978-09815573-0-4   **A Heated Romance** $12.49
- ☐ 978-09815573-6-6   **Saving Tampa** $12.49

Highland Press Publishing
PO Box 2292, High Springs, FL 32655
www.highlandpress.org

Please send me the books I have checked above. I am enclosing $_____ (Please add $2.50 per book to cover shipping and handling). Send check or money order—no C.O.D.s please. Or, PayPal – Leanne@leanneburroughs.com and indicate names of book(s) ordered.

Name_____

Address_____

City_____ State/Zip_____

Please allow 2 weeks for delivery. Offer good in US only. (Contact The.Highland.Press@gmail.com for shipping charges outside the US.)